# UNPLAYABLE

Simon Rae is the award-winning author of 'the best biography of WG [Grace] ever produced' (Christopher Martin-Jenkins). He second cricket book, *It's Not Cricket: A History of Skulduggery, Sharp Practice and Downright Cheating in the Noble Game*, was praised as 'wildly entertaining'. *Unplayable* is his first cricket novel.

by the same author

*W. G. Grace: A Life*

*It's Not Cricket*

# UNPLAYABLE

## SIMON RAE

TOP
EDGE
PRESS

First published in 2009
by Top Edge Press
Lane End, Cheyne Lane, Bampton OX18 2HB

Typeset by CB editions
Cover image by Nigel Stanton
Cover design by Shona Andrew
Printed in England by T. J. International Ltd,
Padstow, Cornwall

website: www.unplayable.co.uk

**FSC**
**Mixed Sources**
Product group from well-managed
forests and other controlled sources
Cert no. SGS-COC-2482
www.fsc.org
© 1996 Forest Stewardship Council

ISBN 978 0 9545495 4 1

for Michael and Naomi
who met Tom first

# Foreword

## by Mike Gatting, OBE

O N 4 June 1993, in the first Test of the new Ashes series, I faced what has come to be known as 'The Ball of the Century'. There would be other contenders – ask Geoff Boycott about facing Michael Holding – but wherever you'd put it in the Top Ten, the ball Shane Warne bowled to me at Old Trafford that day was one of the very best deliveries of all time.

I can remember it as though it were yesterday – and given the number of times I'm reminded of it, it might just as well have been. We'd all heard of Shane Warne, the new kid on the block, but frankly he hadn't done that much in the warm-up matches, so we weren't too worried about him. I was always a pretty confident player of spin bowling so I was looking forward to the challenge.

I'd been in long enough to hit a four, but had hardly got my eye in when Warne came on to bowl his first ball in an Ashes Test. I went through my usual routine, checked the field, then looked down the wicket to show I was ready. Ready, but not for what Shane was about to send down. He had a very laid-back approach to the crease, walking in a few steps before finally gathering pace for the delivery stride.

The ball looped out of his hand, heading originally for around leg stump, I thought. No problem. Get a big front pad down the line with the bat snug in beside it. No way through!

But then the magic happened. The ball dipped and swerved in the air, drifting outside the leg stump. As it pitched in the bowler's footmarks, it's probably an understatement to say 'it did a bit'!

Let Richie Benaud take over: 'He's done it. He's bowled the most beautiful delivery. Gatting has absolutely no idea what has happened to it . . . He still doesn't know.' And Richie was right, I just hadn't got a clue how that ball managed to turn enough to beat both pad and bat and hit the off stump. The famous footage shows me standing my ground for a moment. This wasn't because I was contesting the fact that I was out: I just couldn't work out how it had happened. I had been bowled by a ball as near Unplayable as you're going to get.

Of course, Tom Marlin the character in this book isn't Shane Warne, but he acts out a common childhood dream of waking up one morning a world-beater. Tom can bowl magical deliveries at will, but finding something easy doesn't stop his life becoming difficult. The more successful he is, the more challenging the path ahead becomes.

Whilst the rise of Tom to the top level of cricket is thrilling, it's also a story about a boy in a man's world. About him facing up to the challenges life sometimes can throw at you.

*Unplayable* is a great story that will appeal to anyone of any age, who has ever dreamed of coming to his country's rescue against the old enemy.

I am also extremely happy that Simon has chosen to support the charitable campaign *Chance to shine*, which aims to educate children through cricket. I wish *Unplayable* all the success it deserves!

MIKE GATTING
*Chance to shine* Ambassador

UNPLAYABLE

# Chapter 1

Tom had a freak accident. Except he wasn't sure how much of an accident it was. He got scrunched going for a header by Devlin and Sherwin. They'd been after him all term, and when Mr Giles made him play lone striker with the two of them in midfield on the other side, he feared the worst.

'Good cross! Jump, Tom, jump!' Mr Giles had shouted. Up he went, and that was fine. He even got his head to the ball. It was when he came down that things went wrong. Devlin and Sherwin moved in from either side. There was a sickening crack and Tom was left writhing on the ground, clutching his right shoulder.

'Sorry, Mr Giles, is it bad?'

Even through the intense pain, Tom felt the insincerity in Devlin's voice.

'We didn't mean to.' That was Sherwin. Tom was quite sure it was a lie. But at least he sounded genuinely sorry.

He didn't remember a great deal more. Realising it was bad, really bad, Mr Giles opted to drive him to Accident & Emergency himself rather than wait for an ambulance.

'Nasty rough game,' said Dr Gupta as he looked at the X-ray photographs on a back-lit screen. 'That, my friend, is going to take a lot of work.'

'Will it take a long time?' Tom asked, thinking quite optimistically of the time off school.

'Weeks, I'm afraid,' said Dr Gupta. 'But don't worry, Mr McCulloch is one of the best in the business. He'll get you right. Just in time for the cricket season. Now, there is a civilised game.'

Mr McCulloch was older than Dr Gupta and had sprouty white hair. Tom had been worried that he wasn't a proper doctor because he was a 'Mr', but his father explained that surgeons were always called 'Mr' and that Mr McCulloch would certainly be up to the task of putting his shoulder right.

Tom found his eyes irresistibly drawn to Mr McCulloch's eyebrows, which climbed like a thicket above each eye. You could, he found himself thinking, actually rest a pencil across them.

Mr McCulloch smiled as though he could read Tom's mind.

'Right, laddie,' he said with just a hint of a Scottish accent, 'let's see what you've been doing to yourself, shall we?'

He turned to the bulky brown folder in front of him and pulled out an envelope containing the X-rays.

He walked over to his back-lit screen. Once again Tom looked at the ghostly pictures of his shoulder. You didn't have to be any sort of medical expert to see that the damage was severe and complicated.

'They did a job on you, didn't they, the two of them?' Mr McCulloch looked round at Tom.

'Promise me this, laddie: when I've done the work on this shoulder of yours, take up a sensible game – like cricket. Will you do that for me?'

Tom nodded his head, and Mr McCulloch smiled encouragingly at him.

'Good. We'll have you fixed up – better even than before. But you'll have to be patient. I can't work miracles. At least, not overnight.'

*

4

You could say that again, Tom thought as the next few weeks crawled by. Nothing really bad happened. It's just that everything went on too long. Being in hospital to begin with was quite fun. Everybody made a fuss of him, his friends came in with bags of grapes which they then proceeded to eat while they told him all the gossip. But after a while he pined to go home.

Being at home too was OK to start with. His mum let him watch television in the afternoons. Even the visiting teacher who made an effort at keeping him up with his school work was very patient with him. She understood that he couldn't be expected to write anything with his arm strapped across his shoulder, so there really wasn't much homework apart from reading.

But after a while, even living the life of luxury at home got boring. He found himself wanting to go back to school.

'Right, young man, let's have a look at you.' Dr Gupta smiled at him as the nurse helped him off with his shirt and carefully released his arm from its strapping.

'Tell me when it hurts.' The doctor took hold of Tom's elbow and moved his arm very very gently away from his body.

'Ah!' said Tom. It didn't really hurt, but Tom just wanted to be sure Dr Gupta would stop the second he wanted him to. He did.

'Just relax. Mr McCulloch has done a wonderful job.'

Of course Mr McCulloch wanted to see his wonderful job for himself, and Tom had to go to the hospital a few more times before the final appointment at which the smiling surgeon said, 'Well, laddie, do you feel fit to go back to school?'

Tom nodded his head vigorously.

'All right, then, but you must be extremely careful. I put my best effort into that' – he pointed at Tom's shoulder – 'and I don't want you coming back here with it damaged again.'

He gave Tom a big grin, and his eyebrows appeared to do a miniature Mexican wave. Tom gave him a shy smile back. They both stood up, and Mr McCulloch extended a large hand with a lot of white hairs on the back. Tom put out his and they shook hands.

'Didn't hurt, did it?' Mr McCulloch asked anxiously.

'No,' said Tom.

'Good man,' said Mr McCulloch. 'Now off you go and get on with the rest of your life. Don't forget the exercises the physio has taught you. And you should be fit and raring to go by the start of the cricket season.'


On the morning he went back to school, Tom found he was nervous. Which was ridiculous. He'd been going there for years, he had lots of friends, and he'd been looking forward to going back for weeks, if only to end the boredom of being at home. So why the butterflies in the stomach as he walked in through the gates?

It wasn't till break that he had the answer.

'Hey man!'

A face appeared out of the throng. It was Sherwin's – grinning broadly.

'Well, look who it is,' said another voice, just as familiar. At the same time someone barged him hard from the right.

He gave an involuntary cry, and put his left hand up to his shoulder. This brought him face to face with Devlin.

'Sorry pal,' Devlin sneered, looking meaningfully at Tom's protective hand. 'Still a bit tender, is it? Perhaps you should go on home and do a bit more malingering?' Devlin moved his face a lot closer to Tom's, his upper lip curled, his eyebrows raised in mock interrogation. Tom took a step back, but found his way blocked by Sherwin. Devlin held his stare for an uncomfortable length of time.

'Catch you later, pal,' Devlin snarled, before turning on his

6

heel and barging his way through the throng to his next lesson. Sherwin shouldered his way after him.

'You all right?'

Tom looked down. It was Little Paul.

'I saw what happened,' said Little Paul. 'We could report it if you liked.'

Tom shook his head. It would only makes things worse.

'Don't worry,' he said. 'But thanks. What have we got next? I've forgotten the timetable.'

'Maths,' said Little Paul.

Tom groaned.

'Come and sit next to me. I'll help you catch up.'

'Thanks,' said Tom. Little Paul was the best at maths in their year.


Tom had a lot of catching up to do. He seemed to have missed a lot in all subjects, and also to have lost ground in other ways. He was slower on the uptake than before, as though all that daytime television had somehow made him stupid. But friends helped him out by letting him copy their notes, and Little Paul made it a personal mission to bring his maths up to scratch. It wasn't long before Tom was completely back in the school routine.

As the weeks passed the days grew longer and warmer. The endless winter was drawing to a close.

'Walk home?' Little Paul said to Tom one Thursday afternoon.

'Sure,' said Tom. 'I've just got to go to the library.'

'Let's go the back way. I'll meet you by the pavilion.'

'See you there,' said Tom and went off to get his books.

By the time he got outside, the crowds had thinned out. But as he walked down the asphalt path, he heard the clacking of studs behind him. Suddenly he was reeling from a blow to the back of his head.

'Skiving again, Tommo?'

Tom turned. It was Devlin in his football gear, spinning the ball that he had bounced on the back of Tom's head on the tip of his finger. There were a number of other boys standing around, including Sherwin. They were all grinning.

'What did you do that for?' Tom asked, still rubbing his head.

'Oh, so you've got the use of your arm back then,' Devlin observed. He then slipped the football under his left arm and made a feint with his right. Tom backed away.

'Scaredy cat. If you ever fancy seeing whether that arm of yours is fit for purpose, you know what you can do.'

'Come on you boys, what's the hold up?' Mr Giles trotted up in his tracksuit.

'Oh, it's you, Thomas. How's that shoulder of yours?'

'Fine,' said Tom.

'Glad to hear it,' said Mr Giles. 'Thinking about your option for the summer term? Track and field perhaps. You'd be just right for the high jump with those long legs of yours.'

'Yeah,' sneered Devlin, 'something nice and cushy like jumping into a sand-pit.'

'At least he'd be able to get off the ground,' Mr Giles said, with a glance at Devlin's large stomach. There was dutiful laughter from the group and Devlin went slightly red and scowled.

'I'm going to play cricket.'

It was a simple sentence, but it hung in the air like a challenge. It was a moment before Tom realised he had said it. He was as surprised as everybody else. Devlin gave him a sharp look.

'Cricket – you? You hear that, Sherwin? The beanstalk's going to play cricket. Bring it on!'

And with that, Devlin turned and resumed his steady jog, followed by the other footballers.

Mr Giles paused to say, 'Cricket? Well, why not? I'll put you down for it. Well done, Tom.'

And then he sped off to catch up with the boys, his whistle swinging around his neck.

'What's up?' Little Paul asked as soon as he saw Tom's face.

'I've said I'm going to play cricket next term.'

'That's great!' exclaimed Little Paul, who was the school's scorer.

'Is it?' said Tom. 'I'm not sure. I'm really not sure at all. But I can't do anything about it now. I've told Mr Giles.'

# CHAPTER 2

'WHAT *are* you wearing? Sherwin, look at what the bean-pole's got on.'

Mr Giles walked into the changing room.

'What's the matter, Devlin?' he asked.

'He can't play cricket in those, can he, sir?' Devlin said, pointing to Tom.

Tom had known this would happen. A glance round the changing room at all the cream trousers with little flashy darts at the pockets showed that his tacky old white jeans were clearly not going to cut it. He'd tried to make this point to his mum, but she said she wasn't spending money on something he'd never shown any interest in and would probably give up in a week. So there he stood, in his tacky old white jeans with a slightly holey teeshirt, while everyone else looked as though they could walk onto a cricket pitch with the England team.

'They'll do for a practice game,' said Mr Giles. 'Then if he sticks at it he can buy the proper kit.'

'He hasn't got any boots,' Devlin said darkly.

Tom looked down at his horrible black trainers. Everyone else was lacing up expensive-looking footwear with gleaming spikes.

'Tell you what, I've got an old pair in the car. You can borrow those, Tom. The rest of you – outside doing your warm-ups. I want to get a good two hours in this afternoon.'

'A good two hours!' thought Tom. He could honestly say he couldn't remember a more miserable experience in his entire life. Standing out in the field managed to combine boredom and humiliation in equal measure, spiced with occasional spasms of sheer terror.

For a start nothing seemed to happen at all. Sherwin and another boy ran up to the stumps off their long runs and bowled the ball at what looked like a terrifying speed, while Devlin and the other opening batsman either blocked or let deliveries sail through to the wicket keeper. Every six balls Mr Giles would shout 'Over!' and everyone moved round the ground.

Except for Tom, who hadn't a clue where mid-wicket was.

'To your right, Tom. And a little bit deeper. Walk in with the bowler,' Mr Giles sang out. 'Walk in with the bowler' – what was that all about?

'Yours, Tom, yours,' came a cry as Devlin did no more than pat the ball and called for a run. Tom was still on his heels and saw that it was his ball far too late to do anything about it.

'Easy, easy,' Devlin said to his partner as they crossed. 'Always one to the beanpole.'

Tom trotted in awkwardly and bent down to pick up the ball.

'Over,' said Mr Giles. He walked down the wicket to Tom.

'That's why you walk in with the bowler, so you're on your toes and can run in to stop the quick single,' he explained. 'How are the boots?'

'Fine thanks,' said Tom, looking around for someone to throw the ball to and wondering where to go next.

Mr Giles put his hand out for the ball, shouting out at the same time, 'Thank you Sherwin. Well bowled. Rikesh – come and weave your spell, lad.' Turning back to Tom, he said, 'Stay in to begin with, but we may have to push you back if Devlin gets going.'

While Rikesh marked out a short run and stood spinning the ball from hand to hand, Devlin whirled his arms around in a menacing way. Then he looked around the field taking in the new positions and gave Tom a long hard stare, before settling over his bat.

'Play,' called Mr Giles, and with a strange little flurry of steps, Rikesh approached the wicket and lobbed the ball high in the air.

You must be joking, thought Tom. Devlin will hit that into the Science Block.

That certainly seemed to be Devlin's intention. He put a meaty left leg down the pitch and swung his bat with all his might. But to Tom's astonishment, the ball was not launched into the stratosphere, but instead bounced past the swishing blade and into the wicket-keeper's gloves. There was a general '*Oooh!*' to indicate how close it had come to hitting the stumps.

'Well bowled, Rikesh,' said Mr Giles, adding, 'Have a look, Devlin, have a look.' And then, as Rikesh made his way back to the start of his run, he called over to Tom, 'Walking in, Tom, walking in.'

Rikesh hopped up to deliver another high, looping ball. Against his better judgment, Tom took a tentative step forward, hoping that Devlin wouldn't whack the ball straight at him. Devlin raised his bat with obvious aggressive intent, but then changed his mind and lunged forward, playing it back down the pitch to the bowler. The next ball he also played defensively, but slightly to leg. Tom thought it might be his, so ran in, only to find that the wicket-keeper had popped round from behind the stumps, scooped up the ball and lobbed it back to Rikesh. He could see Devlin's sneer through the grille of his helmet, but was pleased when Mr Giles said, 'Well in, Tom. That's better.'

Next ball Devlin turned more forcefully to leg and started to run. But Tom was on it quickly and Devlin's partner sent him back with a high-pitched 'No!' Of course, Tom had then

12

fumbled the ball, and had to go back to retrieve it. 'Come on!' he heard Devlin cry, but his partner said 'No' again, and Mr Giles said, 'Quite right, never risk a run on a misfield.'

Tom could see that Devlin was angry. Someone would have to pay, and sure enough, on the last ball of the over, he went back instead of forward and with all the strength of his meaty biceps smacked the ball as hard as he could at Tom.

As though in a nightmare, Tom was momentarily transfixed by the vicious red missile hurtling towards him. He was dimly aware of a cry of 'Catch!' before he regained control of his body and leapt out of the way. It was a long trot to fetch the ball, which not only cleared the white boundary mark but made it most of the way over the next-door hockey pitch. When he finally reached it, he picked it up with distaste, and started the long jog back. This was a bad, bad, bad idea.

As he approached the field again, he heard a ragged cry of 'Throw the ball back, beanpole.' He rolled it in underarm, glad to be shot of it.

'Stay on,' shouted Mr Giles. 'There, where you are. Stay on the boundary.'

Well, at least that gets me out of harm's way, Tom thought, scuffing at the white line with Mr Giles's studs. But he was wrong about that.

Just how wrong, he found out very soon. There'd been another bowling change while he'd been retrieving the ball. The new bowler bowled if anything even slower than Rikesh, but he clearly lacked some secret element of the bowling skill, as first Devlin's partner, then Devlin himself, started whacking him all round the ground.

One or two shots rocketed past Tom, but not close enough for anyone to expect him to catch them. One of Devlin's bigger hits went straight back over the bowler's head for six, which was worrying. Tom wasn't bothered about the score ticking along – Devlin could hit sixes all day long as far as he was concerned. What Tom did not want was Devlin hitting the ball really hard at him.

But of course, Devlin wanted nothing more. He took another meaty swipe and the ball raced towards the boundary. Tom thought he'd show willing by sprinting off to his right to try to cut it off. He made it just in time, but when he put his boot in the way to stop it, it somehow bounced and carried on over the boundary for four.

'Well tried, Tom. But use your hands next time,' he could hear Mr Giles calling, as he set off once more over the hockey pitch. By the time he'd reached the ball, he felt as though he'd been travelling across a desert for days. He looked up at the clock on the pavilion. They had only been out there for 39 minutes. There were hours to go before he could slink off home.

'How's it going?'

Little Paul had said he'd come along to show support.

'I don't know how you stick it,' Tom said. 'I wouldn't watch this game if you paid me.'

'Better watch it now,' said Little Paul. 'Devlin's trying to hit it down your throat.'

Tom let his eye reluctantly return to the distant centre of activity.

'He'll put one up in a minute. I'll give you a bit of space,' said Little Paul, walking on round the boundary. 'Good luck. And concentrate. Oh,' he added, after he'd walked a few yards off, 'I love the jeans!'

Tom was still working on some sort of killer retort when a hubbub centred on the pitch alerted him to some momentous development. He noticed Little Paul freeze and heard him say, 'Tom . . .'; and at the same time the cry of 'Caaaaaatch!' came winging over on the breeze. Could they be shouting at him? He scanned the sky in panic, and suddenly he felt his knees losing their solidity. Because there, high, high above

14

him was the ball. It seemed scarcely possible that anyone could hit it so high. It looked about the size of a golf ball, as it towered into the sky. And then it started coming down – at an impossible velocity.

'Keep your eye on it,' he heard Little Paul squeak.

Then, like a bird of prey swooping on its victim, the ball thumped into Tom's chest. The breath was punched from his body and he collapsed on the ground.

Tom lay there for a moment wondering whether he had in fact been killed. He was dimly aware of the shouts from far away, but would have been quite content lying on his back looking up at the few whispy clouds indefinitely. Little Paul had other ideas.

'Throw it back. They're running five. The ball. GET THE BALL!'

The ball, the hateful ball. There it was lying a couple of feet away. Tom lurched to his feet, picked it up and flung it from him with all the pent-up fury at his disposal, and turned away in disgust. Surely this torment would be over soon?

Little Paul trotted up with a look of concern. 'Are you all right?' he started to say and then stopped. He was looking past Tom. 'Blimey!' he said. As Tom turned, Little Paul added, 'Golly' and started laughing.

Tom looked where Little Paul was staring. All he could see was a huddle of fielders thronging around a crouching figure.

'Looks like you nailed him,' said Little Paul with a smirk of undisguised pleasure. 'Better go and see.'

Tom did. As he approached, he could see Mr Giles inspecting the back of Devlin's head, as though looking for lice. Devlin suddenly shook himself free, and Tom heard him say, 'I'm fine. Fine. Leave me alone.' Then, seeing Tom coming up, he pushed through the crowd of fielders and said very deliberately, 'You did that on purpose.'

Tom still didn't know what he was supposed to have done,

but it was clear from the fact that Devlin held his hand to the back of his head that he had suffered some sort of blow. It couldn't have been his throw, could it? All he'd done was pick up the ball and hurl it in the general direction of the wickets. He hadn't bothered to look at where it landed. But he began to sense from the grins sprouting around him on all sides, that it must in some way have bounced so as to hit Devlin.

'I'm sorry, Devlin. I didn't mean –'

But Devlin cut him short.

'I'll get you back, don't you worry about that.' Then he grabbed his bat which one of the fielders was holding for him, and stumped off back to the crease.

'Over!' called Mr Giles, and then, coming up to Tom, said: 'That's some arm you've got there. Perhaps aim at the wicket-keeper in future, not the batsman, eh?'

Tom started to explain that he hadn't intended to hit anyone, but there was something about the set of Mr Giles's mouth which suggested that he was not really cross with Tom at all.

'You know, young man, I think we'll have another look at that arm of yours. You've been stuck out on the boundary long enough. Come and have a bowl, next over.'

Bowl? Me? Tom's jaw dropped.

'Next over, all right?' Mr Giles said. 'Now, back to the boundary for Rikesh.'

Tom made his way back to Little Paul on the boundary. After all the stress and humiliation he'd suffered, the last thing he wanted was to be exposed as a failure in yet another department of this awful game.

'Bull's eye!' said Little Paul. 'What's the matter?' he asked, seeing Tom's expression. 'It couldn't have happened to a more deserving target.'

'It's not that,' said Tom. ' Mr Giles wants me to bowl.'

'Wow,' said Little Paul. 'With an arm like that you could be devastating. Brilliant.'

'It's not brilliant. I don't know how to. And Devlin'll hit me into the middle of next week.'

'He'll try,' agreed Little Paul, 'but he won't necessarily succeed. Now, listen up.'

'Over. Come on, Tom!' Mr Giles held up the ball and waved him in. Tom set off like a condemned man walking to the scaffold. His head was buzzing with words like 'line' and 'length' and 'give it a good rip'.

The sight of Devlin pacing at the crease as he approached was enough to drive most of Little Paul's advice out of his head.

'Right,' said Mr Giles, 'same field, I think.'

'New bowler,' he added, and Devlin thumped the end of his bat menacingly on the crease. He looked poised for destruction, like a bull stamping its hooves impatiently.

Tom really had no idea what to do, so he thought he would copy Rikesh. He ran up to the crease, passing Mr Giles, and swung his arm over. This, he found, made him duck down, so his head was pointing at the pitch in front of him. It took him a moment to regain an upright position and see where the ball had got to. There it was bumping over the grass to the boundary with Jamie the wicket-keeper hot in pursuit.

Mr Giles was holding out both his arms as though about to fly. He then waved his right arm rapidly to and fro across his chest and called out to the boy with the scorebook, 'Four wides!' Tom heard Devlin's snort of contempt. 'Bowl me something I can hit, Beanpole,' he called down the pitch. Then he raised his bat and slammed it down again, eager for the carnage to begin.

The ball had made its way back from the boundary and, via a succession of underarm lobs, into Tom's hands once more.

He felt his hand slippery with sweat and wiped it on his jeans. He remembered something Little Paul had said about the seam. Put your fingers across it and give it a rip, something like that. Carefully he fitted the ball into his hand, splaying the fingers so that the seam cut across diagonally. He had quite large hands, and the ball seemed to fit snugly between the fingers. He gave his wrist an experimental twist, as though trying a doorknob.

'Are you ever going to bowl, Beanpole?' Devlin leered at him down the wicket. 'And try to bowl straight. That last one was unplayable.'

Right, thought Tom, might as well get it over with. And he ran up to the crease past Mr Giles again. He swung his arm rapidly past his right ear and as he let go of the ball, gave a sharp flick with his wrist. It felt better than the first time, but again he lost sight of the ball. There was a sharp cry from Jamie behind the stumps and then Tom saw it streaking away over the grass to the boundary. He'd done it again. He waited for Mr Giles to put his arms out and call wide. But he didn't. He put his left arm up and, while waving his right across his chest, called out 'Four byes.' And then, with a perceptible lightness of tone in his voice, said to Devlin, '*That* was unplayable. I don't know how it missed. Well bowled, Tom, it must have turned two feet.'

'Hit a stone,' Devlin muttered ungraciously, settling into his stance again.

'Come on, Tom. Another one there and you'll have him,' Jamie cried out from behind the stumps.

Tom didn't put the next one there, but he had him all the same. This time he experimented by moving his wrist in the other direction. The ball rose into the air, and then, just as Devlin planted his foot down the pitch, it dipped. On hitting the pitch, the seam gripped and the ball deviated sharply, thus avoiding Devlin's scything blade, which carried on in a fine, straight arc, connecting with nothing but empty air, while the ball clipped the top of the exposed wicket and sent the bails flying.

There was a moment of shocked silence, and then a great clamour of congratulations and celebrations. Boys Tom hardly knew came up and slapped him on the back, Jamie came out from behind the stumps pursing his lips in admiration. 'Where did you pull that one from?' he said as he held up his gloves for a high-five.

Of course the one person who wasn't happy was Devlin. He looked back from his position stranded down the pitch at the broken wicket, as though he simply could not believe it. 'You jammy –' , he was saying when Mr Giles cut in with: 'Well bowled, Tom. Sensational. And well batted, Devlin. Good start to the season.'

Devlin left the wicket with his shoulders hunched in anger, swishing his bat crossly across the grass. While his back was turned Sherwin came up and offered Tom a quick high-five. 'Respect man, respect,' he said before getting back into position by the time Devlin next looked out over the field.

Mr Giles said, 'Well, Tom, that was a remarkable delivery. How did you do it?'

The trouble was, Tom didn't have a clue. He showed Mr Giles how he had gripped the ball, and twisted his wrist a bit. But he didn't feel that explained it. Probably Devlin was right. It was a lucky fluke, and the rest of the over would turn out to be as useless as the first ball. But even if that were the case, he'd still got one over on Devlin.

The new batsman arrived at the crease and held his bat up in front of the stumps. 'That's middle and leg,' Mr Giles said, and the boy made a mark with his studs and looked around the field. 'I think we might have a slip in, don't you?' Mr Giles said to Tom. 'Sherwin, come to first slip please.' Sherwin loped across and went and stood behind and to the right of

Jamie. He spat on his palms and rubbed his hands together. 'Go Bro,' he called out to Tom.

'Right arm over, batsman. Four to come.'

Tom ran up to the crease again and, inspired by the thought that he should probably try to aim for his new fielder, propelled the ball towards Sherwin. As before, he gave his wrist a wrench as he released the ball, and as before the ball soared, dipped and then turned. It then passed effortlessly through the gap between bat and pad, and once again the bails flew up and jubilation broke out all over again.

'Oh well bowled, Thomas,' exclaimed Mr Giles. 'That was a beauty. Bad luck, Mason. You won't get many better first balls than that in your life.'

That seemed scant consolation to Mason, who stood his ground as though expecting some sort of reprieve.

'Quite exceptional,' Mr Giles said, as much to himself as to anyone else. 'Hat-trick ball,' he called out as the next batsman presented himself. 'Let's have you all in. Come on, Tom, see if you can get your hat-trick.'

Whether it was nerves, or a touch of complacency, or because of the pressure of so many fielders crouched round the new batsman, Tom failed, producing a wild, fast full toss that sailed past Jamie's left shoulder and made its uninterrupted way to the boundary. Mr Giles signalled another four byes and motioned the fielders back to their original positions. This made Tom feel more relaxed, and he finished the over with two fizzing deliveries which fairly smacked into Jamie's gloves, while the batsman groped hopelessly at them as they passed.

'Over,' called Mr Giles. 'And a truly remarkable one too. Well bowled, Tom. Well bowled indeed.'

'Well bowled, indeed,' Jamie repeated forty minutes later, gently taking off Mr Giles's very slight Welsh accent. '8 for 14,' he went on, in his own voice. 'Not a bad debut! Mind you, without me, we'd be facing a huge total. I must have saved forty runs in byes. Look at that.' He pulled up his shirt and displayed an array of bruises dotted all over his chest.

'Sorry,' said Tom. 'Does it hurt?'

'Not as much as letting through byes.' Jamie dropped his shirt and laughed. 'Wicket-keepers don't feel pain.'

Sherwin snorted in derision and Jamie took a phantom swing at him.

The three of them were sitting in the changing room. Sherwin had taken off his boots and was lying full length on the lockers. Tom was nervous at being in the same space as him, but there was no trace of his previous hostility. When they'd come off the field after Tom had taken the last of his eight wickets, Sherwin had pushed him ahead so that he led the rest of the team off. Everyone clapped – everyone except Devlin, who stood glowering at him from the top of the pavilion steps.

'Let's see the book,' Little Paul demanded, pushing through the crowd. The scorebook was lying open on a little table, and there, in a column marked 'Bowler' was Tom's name, Marlin, eight times. Marlin, Marlin, Marlin, Marlin, Marlin, Marlin, Marlin, Marlin. There were only three other entries in the column: Run Out, Rekish, and Not Out.

Little Paul sucked in his teeth and said 'Terrible', but he didn't mean Tom's performance. Picking up a pencil he made a few quick-fire corrections to the page, muttering 'Who did this? Muppets' to himself as he went through the thickets of numbers – numbers in rows, numbers in columns, numbers and dots arranged in little boxes.

'There you go,' he said to Tom, pointing to the four little boxes crammed with dots and crosses and a lot of little *w*s. Those were his wickets. He stared at them in bewilderment. Eight little *w*s. That was obviously very good, but to be honest, it hadn't seemed that hard.

'Don't know how you got the ball to lift so much on that –'

Jamie jerked his head in the direction of the square, where their side's innings was getting underway. He had taken off his little wicket-keeping pads and was putting on his larger batting ones. 'Even Sherwin could barely get it above stump high.'

'Wasn't just the bounce. You were turning it, man,' Sherwin said admiringly. 'Where'd you learn to do that?'

Before Tom could try to cobble together a reply to this unanswerable question, there was a distant cry of 'Owzat!!' that sent Jamie to the window. 'Just Devlin letting off steam,' he said. 'Mr Giles didn't give it.'

Tom looked out and saw the unmistakable figure of Devlin marching back to the end of his run, turn, and come steaming in to bowl. He looked terrifyingly quick, and just as Tom was thinking that he really didn't want to have to bat against him, he saw the batsman grope half forwards and in the same moment, the wicket explode as the ball struck the stumps.

'Wish me luck,' said Jamie, hurriedly fixing the last of his pad straps. He reached for his helmet which he put on like a motorcyclist, picked up his gloves and collected his bat. Tom was amazed: he looked as though he were positively relishing the chance to go out and face Devlin. Perhaps he was right, wicket-keepers really didn't feel pain – or fear.

Tom wished *he* didn't feel fear. He was walking home from the game with Little Paul, who was bubbling with excitement about everything – Tom's bowling, and the fact that Tom's side had wiped the floor with Devlin's team. They'd won comfortably, with Jamie scoring 50 and Sherwin weighing in with a few cracking boundaries at the end – when they heard an all-too-familiar voice.

'Well, look what we have here.' It was Devlin, who just stepped out from behind a hedge along the footpath from the school playing fields. Tom saw his enormous cricket bag parked on the grass. He'd obviously been waiting for them.

'So you think you're clever, do you? – turning up looking like a tramp and trying to make everyone look stupid.'

Tom just heard Little Paul's half-whispered '*trying*' and gave him a discreet nudge to stop him making what was clearly a bad situation very much worse.

'Beginner's luck,' said Tom, with what was meant to be a disarming shrug.

It seemed to have the opposite effect. Devlin took a step closer and with his face uncomfortably close to Tom's, snarled, 'Don't get smart with me, Marlin, or I'll break every bone in your body.'

Tom was almost sure Little Paul started to say something along the lines of 'You and whose army?' but Devlin dealt him a heavy clip to the top of the head. 'Fortunately I don't do dwarves, because if I did I'd have you on a spit for a barbeque. Now scram. Me and wonder boy have a few things to talk about.'

Devlin shoved Little Paul hard, propelling him further on down the path. Tom saw the hurt and anger in his face, and for a moment thought he meant to throw himself into a suicide mission against their tormentor. He raised his hand and gave his head a quick shake, indicating that he would deal with the situation, that it would be fine.

Little Paul hunched his shoulders to express his dissent, and as soon as Devlin's back was turned on him raised his hand in an unambiguously rude gesture. A flicker of amusement must have shown for a nano-second on Tom's face, because the next thing he knew Devlin had grasped him by the collar. Tom dropped his bag and put his hand to his neck, but Devlin just gripped harder.

'Listen to me, Marlin, and listen good.' Here he shook Tom's collar, just to make sure he had his full attention. 'I don't know what prompted that stunt today, and I don't care. But you are not a cricketer – never have been, never will be, and I will not tolerate you coming along and making a mockery of my sport. First you throw the ball in and nearly kill me.' Tom tried to splutter a combination of apologies and explanations, but Devlin wasn't interested. Instead he tightened his grip on Tom's collar and continued: 'Then you come on to bowl and spray it around like someone with a machine gun. OK, so I'd had a decent knock, but there were kids there who waited the whole afternoon to have a bat and suddenly you start skittling them out with this spinner's freakshow. It's not fair, and I won't have it. Do you read me?'

Tom found it difficult either to agree or disagree with his teeth being rattled together by Devlin's fist.

'So, what you do is tomorrow you go and see Mr Giles and you say thank you for the game but you realise it's not for you and you want to join the other cissies jumping into the sandpit. And you give him his boots back.'

As a measure of how pleased he'd been with Tom's performance, Mr Giles had told him he could keep the boots. Tom had noticed at the time a dark cloud flitting across Devlin's features.

'In fact,' Devlin said, 'I'll have them now.'

Mercifully he released Tom, who took a step back and massaged his throat. Devlin unceremoniously rifled through Tom's bag and ripped the cricket boots out of it.

'Seeing if you're big enough for his boots, man?'

It was Sherwin. Where had he come from, Tom thought, wondering which side he might be on.

'Hello, Sherwin. Just relieving this joker of his little trophy. We've just agreed that as he won't be playing any more cricket, he won't be needing Mr Giles's boots. Isn't that right, Tom?'

Tom opened his mouth. But he didn't get to say anything. Instead it was Sherwin who spoke. In an amiable, level tone, he said, 'Well, that's not the way I understand things. The way I understand things is that Tom here is going to come over to

24

the nets at the club tomorrow night and put in a little practice before the trial match on Friday, so he got a chance of making it into the team for the first match next Saturday. Ain't that right, Tom?'

As he said this, he took the boots from Devlin and thrust them emphatically back into Tom's sports bag, which he picked up. He then put his arm around Tom's shoulder and guided him along the path, leaving Devlin standing slack-jawed in amazement.

# CHAPTER 3

'MARLIN? Jack?'

Devlin looked up from the table where Little Paul was writing the batting order in the 1st XI scorebook.

'Jack?' Tom asked.

'Eleven,' Devlin and Little Paul said in unison, Devlin adding, 'You really don't know anything, do you?'

With that he rumpled Little Paul's hair, and called out, 'Come on, Sherwin, chuck me a few.' Sherwin pulled himself to his feet and picked up a practice ball, then trotted down the pavilion slope after his captain.

Little Paul tried to unmuss his hair. 'Nine, ten, Jack – number 11, last man in. Cards. Nine, ten, Jack of Hearts, yeah? At least you'll be safe down there. You won't have to bat – not on that shirt front.'

He nodded out towards the wicket where Mr Giles and the opposing team's cricket master were putting the bails on the stumps, while the opposition captain was sending his men to their fielding positions.

'Come and sit here next to me.' Little Paul indicated the space on the bench next to him. 'They'd normally have a scorer too, but he cried off sick. I might have asked you to score in their book – if you knew the first thing about cricket. But you don't. Sit there and you might learn. Bowler's name!' he suddenly shouted out in a surprisingly loud voice.

There was a ragged shout back from half a dozen fielders.

'Mexon? Did it sound like Mexon to you?'

Tom shrugged. Why couldn't they have said the bowler's

name before they went out, he wondered as he watched Little Paul inscribing 'Mexon' in the scorebook.

'It's Nixon, you divvy, not Mexon.' Jamie was looking over Little Paul's shoulder. 'Left arm, quite quick. Remember him from last year. Skiddy.'

Little Paul swore quietly and rubbed out 'Mexon' and replaced it with 'Nixon'. Jamie called over to Devlin: 'Let's go, skip.' The two openers punched gloved fists together and then, to a smattering of applause, set off for the wicket together.

Watching them go – Devlin, huge, bear-like, swinging his bat aggressively from his giant shoulders, Jamie, neat, small, but with an air of quiet confidence about him – Tom felt a surge of pride. He was slightly surprised at this, this surge of team spirit he supposed you could call it. But he wanted them to do well – even Devlin, who he knew still hated him, and only tolerated him in the side because he had no choice.

Mr Giles had been quite straightforward about it. 'Tom's playing, Devlin,' he had said. 'The only question is whether you want to remain captain or stand down and let Jamie do it.'

Devlin opted to stay captain. And to be fair, his attitude did seem to have changed as the days went by.

And what days they had been. Sherwin had been absolutely serious about taking him to his club's practice session. He'd passed the ground many times, either in the car when his mum drove out of town for the big weekly shop, or on his bicycle. Occasionally he'd stopped to watch the white-clad figures moving around in their mysterious slightly military formations. He thrilled briefly when one of the batsmen hit the ball, but why some balls were hit, some blocked or some left, he had no idea, and after a while would pedal on his way, none the wiser.

When he arrived with Sherwin it was a very different scene. There were dozens of men and boys milling around, and the action took place not out in the square but in a series of pitches sectioned off by high netting. At one end of these batsmen stood in front of metal wickets while from the other a succession of bowlers took turns to bowl.

As they passed by the side of the end net, Tom heard a terrific crack and shied away as the ball punched the netting a few feet away from him.

Sherwin laughed. 'Don't worry, man. You're safe here. It's at the other end you want to watch out. Rule number one: watch the ball, man, 'cos otherwise you're dead.'

The two boys stood and watched for a moment as a tall man ran in from some distance and bowled. After loping in for several yards, he suddenly went into a spasm of whirling arms and splayed feet, out of which the ball flew so fast you could hardly follow it. The batsman underwent a similar convulsion, jabbing his bat forward and knocking the ball back down the wicket.

'That's Keith,' Sherwin said. 'He's quick. Opens the bowling for the first team.' Tom looked on in awe as Keith jabbed his arm down, retrieved the ball and turned on his heel. Then he looked at the batsman, preparing to face the next delivery. How could he stand there so calmly?

'Rob White,' Sherwin said with a nod. 'First-team captain.'

And one of the bravest people on the planet, Tom added to himself as the next bowler tore in to the crease and delivered another potentially lethal missile. As far as Tom could see, this ball was nearly as fast as the previous one, but it seemed to cause Rob no difficulty at all. With a sudden backward step, he flailed his bat at the ball, and again Tom flinched as the ball powered into the netting.

'Length, man. That's the secret. Line and length. The oldest commandment in the book. That's what my Uncle Winston always says.'

'The one that played for West Indies?'

'Who told you that? Little Paul?' Sherwin shook his head. 'Nah, coupla games for the island, but that's all. Not committed enough. Too many other . . . interests, let's just say that. But he played against the best, that's for sure.'

'Oy! You two going to stand there all evening, or are you going to change and do some work?'

It was Rob White, who'd come up to the netting. He took his helmet off and wiped away some sweat from his forehead.

'Who's your friend, Sherwin?' he asked.

'Tom,' said Sherwin.

'What's he do?'

'He bowls, man. Spins it a mile.'

'What are you waiting for? Get him in a net. Pleased to meet you, Tom. I'll catch you later.'

Rob White was true to his word. But by that time pretty much all the cricketers at the practice session were grouped around the net where Tom was bowling. It hadn't taken long for the adult in charge of the Juniors net to move him on to the third-team net, and from there his progress to the first-team net had been swift. The clang of the metal stumps being hit time after time drew the attention of those in the next door nets. Bowlers stopped in their tracks to watch as Tom ran in and delivered yet another killer ball.

'How does he do it?'

'Search me,' said a burly man in his forties who had just had his stumps clattered nine times out of ten.

'Here, Rob, take a look at this.'

Rob did, and then said, 'Come into my net, Tom.'

A few minutes later, having watched his best middle-order

29

batsman completely bamboozled, he took Tom aside and asked, 'Where did you learn to do that?'

Tom was at a loss, and mumbled something about only just starting to play.

'You're good, kid. Very good. Do you want to play here? With Sherwin?'

'I've got school,' Tom said. 'Mr Giles said I might get in the school team.'

'That's OK. They play their matches on Saturday mornings. You can play for us in the afternoon – like Sherwin. Here, Ed,' Rob called to a balding man who wasn't wearing cricket whites. He came over and Rob introduced him. 'Ed's the club secretary. Ed, Tom – ?'

'Marlin,' Tom said.

'Tom Marlin, our latest recruit. Sign him up, will you? And register him for the league.' Then, in a quick aside, Tom heard him say, 'Don't worry about a sub. Sort that out later.'

And now, here he was picked for the school 1st XI and turning out for his new club later that same day.

'Two pairs of whites?' his mum had said. 'Can we afford it, Rick?'

'Oh come on, Suzie,' said his dad. 'He's found something he's really good at.'

'Well,' his mum said, 'he's not having one of those jerseys. I couldn't believe my eyes when I saw the price.'

'He'll need something. He might get cold.'

'Cold? It's a summer sport, isn't it?'

'A summer sport played in England. It can be freezing at this time of year.'

'If you want him to have a jersey, Rick, fine. But it's not coming out of the house-keeping.'

That was Mum's final word, but Tom knew she was secretly pleased for him. She just didn't want Dad to get carried away.

'Shot, Dev!' someone shouted, and Tom looked out at what

was happening in the middle. Everything had stopped while a lone fielder took pretty much the same path he'd taken that first practice game, trotting over the boundary and half way across the hockey pitch to retrieve the ball. Beside him Little Paul raised his hand to acknowledge Mr Giles's signal. Devlin and Jamie stood in the middle of the pitch watching the progress of the fielder together.

Tom thought about the book he'd brought to catch up on some English homework, but then thought better of it. No, he'd sit there in the sun watching the game, trying to understand the finer points.

'Put the score up,' Little Paul said. '15. Three overs.' He jerked his head towards the scoreboard behind them. Tom fumbled through the heavy tin numbers, each with a round hole at the top.

'Not there,' Little Paul said testily. 'Three *overs*.' He pushed back his chair and marched across to where Tom stood and took the 3 off the board and put it on another hook. 'There, *overs*. Not wickets. We haven't had any wickets yet.'

But they were to come. And when they came they came in startlingly quick succession. In fact, the match was over so quickly that when Rob White turned up to see Tom in action, it was all over.

'What happened?' he asked as he climbed up the pavilion steps. Little Paul swung the scorebook round on the table. 'Bowled them out for 41,' he said proudly. It only took one glance to see what had happened. After a perfectly respectable opening stand, the batting had simply collapsed. The bowler's column read: 'Marlin, Marlin, Marlin, Marlin . . .'

Rob whistled through his teeth. '9 for –'

'12,' said Little Paul. 'And he would have got all ten if it hadn't been for the run out.' He took the book back to do the final bits and pieces.

'Well, well, well, here's the man of the match,' said Rob, as

Tom emerged from the changing room. 'Congratulations. I hope you haven't tired yourself out too much for this afternoon's game.'

Tom smiled: 'I only had four overs. I'll be fine.'

'I'm sorry I missed you,' said Rob White. 'Good luck this afternoon. I brought this for you,' he added, handing over a club jersey. 'It's an old one of mine – keep it.'

And before Tom could thank him, he was away down the pavilion mound and off across the hockey pitch to the car park. Tom let the jersey unfold. It had a green and yellow stripe marking the V of the neck, and a fierce looking creature to the left above the letters KCC.

'Wow,' said Little Paul admiringly. 'Who was that?'

'Oh, Rob White. He's captain of Kumble. I told you I'm playing for them this afternoon. I'm in the thirds – with Sherwin. Why don't you come over and watch?'

'OK,' said Little Paul, 'I will.'

Tom felt a weighty arm descend on his shoulder. It was Devlin.

'So, signed up with Kumble? You should have asked me. I'd have got you a game with Thurston.' Then, seemingly as an afterthought, he said, 'Mr Giles thought I should award you this.'

He thrust something into Tom's hand and said, 'I just hope your head's not too big for it.' Then he picked up his coffin and clattered down the pavilion steps.

'Charming,' said Little Paul. 'But well done, Tom. Your lst XI cap. Try it on.'

Tom wore his new cap and Rob White's club jersey that afternoon. He felt more at home on a cricket field now, and took pride in looking the part. Not that he or anyone else was out on the park for very long. The Kumble 3rd XI captain had no hesitation in fielding first when he won the toss, and after giving Sherwin and his other opening bowler half an hour with the new ball, called Tom into the attack.

'Just bowl like you've been bowling in the nets, Tom, and we'll all be home for tea.'

Later in the bar at the clubhouse he told Rob White what happened.

'Honestly Rob, if I hadn't seen it with my own eyes I wouldn't have believed it. They couldn't lay a bat on him. Apart from one bunny who got a top edge over slip, they didn't score a run off him. Mind you, Smithy couldn't cope. I had to tell him to stand back otherwise I could see us losing on byes.'

Rob gave a sympathetic laugh. Smithy was more a stopper than a wicket-keeper.

'And he just kept hitting the stumps. He was on a hat-trick three times! It was truly amazing.' He took a deep pull at his beer.

'Mind you, made a proper mess of the game. Their skipper wasn't happy at all. And to be honest with you, Rob, although they lapped it up today, I can't see our lads enjoying it if it happens every week. He'll have to go up.'

'You're probably right,' Rob White said. 'I just don't want to do things too quickly. He's only a kid. He hasn't got any experience. What was his fielding like?'

'Not brilliant, but he tries, I'll give him that. And boy, can he throw! Like an Exocet. But I wouldn't say he was a safe pair of hands. He dropped nearly every catch in the warm-up.'

'H'm. That's the problem, isn't it? I mean the odd dropped catch isn't going to matter, not if he's taking hatfuls of wickets – but it might damage his confidence. Still, as problems go, it's a nice one to have.'


Rob White put Tom in the 2nd XI for the next match. It was a disaster. The captain was a lean, balding man called James Jarvis – 'JJ' to everyone in the club. JJ had been away on a late spring holiday and so hadn't seen Tom's bowling at first hand.

'So, you're the genius spinner everyone's talking about, are you?' he said, looking down at Tom. 'Well my boy, I'm not easily impressed, I'll tell you now.'

JJ fancied himself as a tactician. He was also a bowler. On most occasions his tactics were simply to bowl himself for lengthy spells. On this occasion, he opened the bowling with another accurate medium pacer and wickets fell at regular intervals.

But even though wickets were falling, runs were mounting. Most of the team had seen and indeed faced Tom in the nets, and so knew the potential devastation waiting to be unleashed. When the score passed 120 there were audible murmurings about bringing Tom on to bowl.

Unfortunately it was then that one of the batsmen, who was well set and beginning to hit the ball sweetly all round the ground, mis-timed a drive off JJ and sent the ball skimming about a yard above the ground straight at Tom. He'd hit it hard and it was spinning viciously. In the split second that Tom had to react, he knew perfectly well what he should do and also in the same frozen second of decision-making, that he wasn't going to do it.

As JJ told Rob White that evening, 'He just funked it. Didn't make any attempt at catching. I'm sorry, Rob, but the lad's not for me. No one minds if you drop a catch, but not even to try . . .' Jarvis didn't finish the sentence but looked meaningfully at Rob.

Rob White looked back at him. 'So that's why you didn't give him a bowl?'

'Partly. But also because, well, the seamers did a pretty good job.'

'How many did they score – 240? And we gave up the chase around 200?'

'240 for 9 – and the last pair slogged 50 of those.'

'And you didn't think of giving Tom a go?'

'Not against those two, no. You said to look out for him. Putting him on against two guys hitting fours and sixes all over the place didn't seem sensible.'

'Tom got 8 for 4 last week. The point of putting him in the 2nds was to see how he'd do against better batsmen.'

'I thought cricket was a team game,' said Jarvis. 'I did what I thought best. If you want to see if he can hack it against better batsmen, I suggest you pick him for the firsts.' He put his empty glass down on the bar and left.

'I might just do that,' Rob White said to no one in particular.

# CHAPTER 4

'RUBBISH,' said Little Paul. 'Absolute rubbish performance.'
Tom and Paul were walking towards the language lab
for double French on Monday morning. Tom hated French
and felt bad enough about his game on Saturday without Little Paul weighing into him.

'We're never going to win the Ashes if that's the best we can
do. I can't remember when England batted like that. And as
for the bowling . . .'

Tom realised with relief that Little Paul was not talking
about his exploits on Saturday. He also realised that this was a
conversation in which he was required to take little or no part.
If only, he thought, the same was true of the French lesson.

'Bonjour, Messieurs,' Ms Eclestone said as they trooped
in and unloaded their rucksacks on their desks. Tom joined
in the half-hearted chorus of 'Bonjour, Mademoiselle' and
opened his text book at an unamusing cartoon of a large dog
confronting a timid postman. It was going to be a long hour.

'Had a quiet one on Saturday, then?'

Devlin turned to Tom as they waited in the canteen queue
at lunch.

'They didn't bowl him,' said Little Paul. 'Skipper must be
mad.'

'Maybe. Or maybe he's got the best interests of the game
at heart.'

'What d'you mean by that?' Little Paul asked.

'Oh, nothing', Devlin said. 'People are talking. That's all.'

'Saying what?' said Little Paul fiercely.

'Nothing much. Yes, thank you – mash and chips.' Devlin pushed his tray forward to take his plate. 'Got anything with growth hormones in for the midget?' he added as he turned away.

Little Paul was still scowling with anger as they found a table. 'Growth hormones!' he spluttered. 'He'd know about those. Look at the size of him!'

Tom took the trays away and saw Sherwin looking for a place to sit. He joined them.

'Sherwin,' said Little Paul, 'what's this about people talking about Tom?'

'Man, everybody's talking about Tom.'

'Devlin said something about people talking about him – and not in a good way.'

'Devlin,' Sherwin sighed. 'He's jealous, man, jealous as hell. He's just trying to stir things up.'

'But how?'

'Oh, saying stuff. Look, I wouldn't worry about it. It's nothing.'

'But what stuff?' Say what you liked about Little Paul, he was persistent. Tom kept his head down and concentrated on his baked potato. It had been microwaved, so it wasn't very nice. And he'd run out of grated cheese.

'OK,' Sherwin said, realising that Little Paul wasn't going to let it go. 'Take Saturday. We didn't play, right? St Leonard's cancelled.'

'So?' said Little Paul. 'Half the team were down with a bug. Mr Giles said.'

'Sure, but that's not what Devlin said.' Sherwin leaned in and dropped his voice, though with a clatter of cutlery on all sides there was little danger of his being overheard. 'Devlin said their cricket master withdrew because –'

'Because . . .?'

'Because he'd heard about Tom. And he'd heard he was a cheat.'

Little Paul exploded. 'A cheat? How could he possibly be a cheat.'

'Shhh,' Sherwin hissed. 'His action. Throwing. How else could he do what he does with the ball without chucking it?'

'That's ridiculous!'

'I know, man. I agree.'

'I've watched Tom ever since he started. I even looked at him through binoculars. His arm's completely straight, straighter than Devlin's – straighter than yours.'

'What you saying, man – I'm a chucker?'

'No, Sherwin, you've got a great action. You know you have. You were coached by a Test player.'

'How many times do I have to tell you? Uncle Winston played against Test players – all the time. But he had two games for the island, that's all.'

Little Paul brushed that aside. 'You've got a great action. Better than Tom's – far better. But Tom's arm is straighter when he delivers the ball. I can't believe Devlin said that. Does anyone believe him?'

'Shouldn't think so. Jamie said it was rubbish. One or two of the others might swallow it. But don't worry about it. We know it isn't true. We've got a game this Saturday, against the Grammar, and they're not going to pull out. Gotta go!'

Sherwin pushed back his chair and picked up his plate.

'What was all that about?' asked Tom, who hadn't understood a word, but knew it wasn't good. 'Why are they worried about my throwing?'

Little Paul sighed and stirred his custard over his peach halves.

'It's nothing to do with your throwing. It's about your bowling. I'll explain later.'

*

Later, Little Paul said, 'Look, you know when you throw the ball – from the boundary. You've got an amazing arm – it just goes for miles.'

Tom nodded. He hoped Little Paul wasn't going to ask him how he did it. But he didn't. Instead he went on, 'Right – have you any idea what speed the ball travels when you do that?'

Tom shook his head.

'Neither have I – but it's fast. Very fast. That's why it hits the wicket-keeper – or, on a good day, Devlin – so quickly. Now imagine when you came up to bowl, instead of bowling, you threw the ball.'

'But I wouldn't do that,' said Tom.

'No, of course you wouldn't. But what if you did? It would get down the wicket in a flash, wouldn't it? It would be so fast that the batsman wouldn't have a chance, right. And that would be unfair – and dangerous. You could kill someone.'

Tom opened his mouth to protest once more, but Little Paul pushed on. 'Which is why the laws of cricket have always made an important distinction between a legal bowling action and throwing. Over the years the laws change.' He looked up and saw that Tom was not up for a history lesson on the laws of cricket.

'Never mind that, the important point is that the laws say what a legitimate bowling action is and what counts as throwing, and by no stretch of the imagination do you throw. You may look like someone who's been punched in the stomach when you deliver the ball, but your arm is completely straight. In fact, it couldn't be otherwise, as you bowl out of the back of the hand.'

Little Paul saw the blank expression on Tom's face and sighed. 'Boy, you've got a lot to learn. But take it from me – you don't throw.'

*

Rob White made his decision. He would play Tom in the first team. He was clearly too good for the thirds; JJ didn't want him in the seconds, so lst XI cricket it would be. Didn't they say, If you're good enough, you're old enough? The trouble was, the match was away and they'd have to set off before the school match finished.

'Tom? Can you give me a minute?'

Mr Giles was looking sporty in his tracksuit. Tom went over to him.

'I've just had a call from Rob White.'

Tom's heart sank. Word had got back about his awful fielding and he was going to be told not to bother turning up on Saturday.

'He wants you to play for Kumble firsts this Saturday.'

'The firsts?'

'I know, it's a bit of a step up.'

'But I didn't do anything last week – except – are you sure?'

'Absolutely. We had quite a chat about it. He thinks you've really got something, and I agree. Of course you're not the finished article in other aspects of the game.'

You could say that again. Tom felt a slight flush warming the back of his neck as he replayed the moment he opted out of the catch.

'But we can work on that – both here at the school and at the club. Even if you're not a very good fielder at the moment, you can run and you've got a great arm. They did a terrific job on you at the hospital, didn't they? Anyway, like I said, we can work on your basic skills – and even look at your batting. Though frankly, provided you keep taking wickets no one's going to expect you to score many runs. The thing is, it's an away match, so you'd have to miss the school game here. I've said that's OK by me, but obviously the final decision rests with you – and your parents.'

Tom's mind went into overdrive. He felt excited but also

extremely nervous. He remembered the way the net bulged with the power of Rob White's shot the first time he went to practice. He'd be playing against really good cricketers, who could really hit the ball. He might fail, be shown up, humiliated. Possibly hurt. But then, he had by now bowled to every 1st XI player in the nets and they'd barely laid a bat on him. And it would be nice to prove JJ wrong. But what made up his mind was the thought of missing the school game and getting away from Devlin.

'I'll play,' he said. 'If I'm not letting anyone down.'

'You won't be.' said Mr Giles. 'You'll do fine. Just try your best – no one can ask more of you than that.'

'Thanks,' Tom said. 'Mr Giles?'

'Yes?'

He had been going to ask whether people were 'talking about him', but then thought it might be sneaking on Devlin. Instead he said, 'You know my bowling action?'

Mr Giles smiled. Of course he knew Tom's bowling action. It was the most distinctive he'd ever seen.

'Is it all right?' Tom felt he rather blurted the question. He was making himself nervy bringing the subject up.

'If you mean, is it a classic, side-on delivery with an easy approach to the crease and a graceful follow-through, then the answer's no.' He smiled. 'But it's the way you do it and the results are spectacular. I don't think anyone in their right mind would try to change it.' He looked at Tom and then said, 'But that's not what you meant, was it?'

'No.' Tom felt himself getting hot again. How could he put it into words? 'I just wanted to – people are saying – I mean: is it fair? My action – it's not – against the rules?'

'It's fine, Tom. Completely legit. That was one of the first things that crossed my mind when I first saw you turning the ball square. But I've watched you very carefully since – I was standing at square leg when I was umpiring in the match the

41

other Saturday if you remember, and your arm was straight as a ruler. You see, you bowl out of the back of the hand.'

Mr Giles extended his arm and went into a slow-motion delivery, rotating his arm anti-clockwise as he did so.

'It's physically impossible to throw if you bowl like that. Can't be done. It's finger spinners you have to watch.'

He did a slow-mo demonstration and Tom could see the bend in his arm as he delivered an imaginary ball.

'Of course I'm exaggerating, but there have been spinners who would have been better off as darts players. And of course if you get the quick men doing it, well, it can be downright dangerous. But you're fine, Tom. And don't just take my word for it. Rob White wouldn't be putting you in his first team if there were any doubts about your action. OK?'

'Yes. Thanks.'

'So who's been suggesting there might be a problem?'

'Oh, no one. It was just something someone said they'd heard someone else say. You know –'

'Sure. Don't worry about it. You're fine.'

He watched Tom's tall, gawky figure heading across to the main school block. Perhaps he should talk to the team on Saturday when he was away. Or simply take Devlin aside and give him both barrels.

'Look out for him, Rick. He's only –'

A kid? Go on, say it, Tom thought, as he flinched away from his mum's attempt at a kiss.

'Too much the man to be kissed by his mum now – Mr First Teamer.'

'Mum,' said Tom. 'Come on, Dad, we've got to go.'

'All right,' said his dad, picking out the car keys from the key-plate in the hall.

'Well, have fun, you two. I'll be thinking of you.'

There was still an anxious note in her voice.

42

'He'll be fine, love, I'm sure of it. They wouldn't have picked him if they didn't think he could do it.'

'I know.' She waved them away and Tom's dad opened the door. Tom was suddenly overwhelmed with panic. It felt like the first morning of school. Primary school. Instinctively he took a step back towards his mum and hugged her awkwardly. Then he lunged for his cricket bag and walked through the door without looking back.

The Croton ground was far bigger than Kumble's. There seemed an endless succession of cricket pitches, and already there was a huge amount of activity. The car park was busy as they drew in behind Rob White's car, and Tom's dad had to drive some way to find a space.

'Well, Tom, here we are,' he said as he pulled up the hand-brake and turned off the engine. 'I'm proud of you. I can't say I'm not astonished. I am. But I'm proud of you – we both are. And I just want you to know that whatever happens today, your mum and me, we'll still be proud of you.'

Thanks Dad, can we get into the pavilion now please, Tom didn't say. His dad sat for a moment longer, and Tom thought he was going to have to leave him there staring out over the acres of grass. Then, with a shock, he realised something. Dad's nervous, he thought. Dad's really really nervous.

'Come on, Dad, I'll be all right.'

His dad turned and faced him. 'Sure, Son,' he said, and smiled. Tom recognised it as what people called 'a brave smile'.

By the time they'd got Tom's bag out of the boot, the rest of the Kumble team had disappeared into the clubhouse. Tom quickened his pace across the car park.

'They won't start without you,' his dad said.

'I know, Dad, but –'

'It's all right. You go ahead and change. I'll find a nice bench in the sun.'

Inside the clubhouse there was a long corridor with lots of numbered doors off it. Tom didn't have a clue where to go.

Suddenly a small man with greying hair wearing track-suit bottoms and a cricket jersey came out of a side door and looked him up and down. 'Changing Room 9 – right down the bottom,' he said, and then disappeared.

Tom walked down the corridor. There was a lot of noise coming from behind one or two of the numbered doors, but when he walked into number 9, there wasn't a sound. It was completely empty. Where had the Kumble team gone? They must be back in one of the rowdy changing rooms. But which one? He daren't go into the wrong one, that would be terrible. But perhaps he was meant to change in this room by himself because he was so young? The small wiry man was obviously one of the people in charge and must therefore know what was what. Tom put his bag down and slowly changed into his cricket things.


'There you are!'

Tom blinked as he walked out into the sunshine.

Rob White clapped him on the shoulder. 'What happened to you? I thought we'd lost you.'

As Tom explained, the wiry little man appeared.

'Bruce!'

'Rob!'

The two men shook hands warmly.

'What's this I hear about you sending my star player to the Colts Changing Room? Bruce, meet Tom.'

The wiry man looked at Tom. 'I thought he was a bit early for the Colts. My apologies, young man.' Then, to Rob White, he said, 'What's he do?'

'Stick around and you'll see.'

'I will,' and with a nod he was off.

'Bruce Cranley. County stalwart for twenty years. Left-hand bat. Brilliant close fielder. Some say he was unlucky never to get an England cap. Oh look, there's Damien. Better go and toss.'

Tom watched as he strode off to shake hands with the Croton captain, a giant of a man. After a few pleasantries they walked out to the wicket and Tom saw them both look up briefly as the coin glinted in the sun, then look down to see who had won. As the two men approached their waiting teams, Rob White made a gesture with his left hand.

'That means we're batting, Dad,' Tom said.

'And that means you can get that folder out the back of the car and do some homework.'

'Dad!'

But it was all right, the slow grin made it clear he was only pulling Tom's leg.

The Kumble innings did not go according to plan. It was no surprise when the Croton captain opened the bowling. What shocked Tom was how fast he bowled. When he got one through Rob White's opening partner's defence, the stump flew out of the ground.

'He's a yard quicker than last year,' the returning batsman said, and Tom noticed that all the cheerful banter had gone. Two people hurriedly went inside to put their pads on and the rest of the team watched in silence as Rob White battled for survival.

'They're not sending you in against that stuff. You're mum'd kill me if I let them do that.'

'Dad,' Tom said out of the side of his mouth.

Another wicket fell, this time to a brilliantly taken catch in the slips. That was real cricket out there, and Tom suddenly wished that Changing Room 9 had been the right place for him and that he was down to play for the Juniors.

*

'Well batted, Rob.'

'Good knock, mate.'

Rob White arrived back from the crease to warm and rather relieved congratulations. He had batted for nearly two hours, scored 71, and ensured that Kumble had something like a reasonable total. But when he was out there were only three more wickets standing. With the two men to go in before him padded up, Tom wondered whether he should get ready as well. Sherwin had lent him some old pads but when he'd tried them in the nets they made him feel like a deep-sea diver. Not only could he hardly walk, but when he tried hitting the ball with the bat someone else had found for him, he was hopeless. But he could see that in the position they were in, Kumble needed every run they could get, so perhaps Rob would ask him to bat after all.

'Well batted. Great knock.' It was Dad, who stood up as Rob approached.

'Thanks. Phew, that was tough. Shouldn't have tried to pull that one.' He twisted the bat in his hands, replaying the shot. 'Still, got you something to bowl at, young man.' Tom looked at the scoreboard: 138 for 7.

'Don't worry about padding up,' Rob said, as he made his way into the clubhouse. Tom felt relieved.

There was a horrifying yell from the pitch. Tom looked up to see the entire Croton team doing a sort of war-dance at the umpire. After a moment the umpire raised his right arm. After an even longer pause, the Kumble batsman started the slow walk back.

It was Keith, the tall fast bowler.

'I never touched it,' he said when he crossed the boundary line. 'Not even close.' He threw his bat on the grass.

Rob White came back out with a towel round his neck. The next wicket fell, and there was a moment when the Croton team stood and looked to see who was coming out last. Rob

White gave a wave to his not-out batsman, who didn't seem to see it, so he waved his towel to attract his attention.

'Bit early to be throwing the towel in, Rob,' said Bruce Cranley who happened to be passing. 'Doesn't your prodigy bat?'

'We haven't got that far in the coaching manual yet, have we, Tom? Besides, that's plenty.'

'143? I don't think so, lad.'

'Come back after tea, you'll see.'

Tom usually enjoyed tea. But he didn't enjoy it today. His mouth was dry and the sandwiches seemed to turn to cardboard. The atmosphere was subdued at the Kumble end of the table. He sensed that some members of the team were beginning to have doubts about including a boy in the eleven who couldn't even be trusted to bat. He slipped away early.

At least he was now in the right changing room. The door kept banging open as the players came in from their tea. Their faces were serious, and one or two of them growled encouragement to each other. 'Come on, Keith, get fired up!'

Keith pulled his long bootlaces tight and tied them in an elaborate knot, and then stamped them on the changing room tiles. He looked fierce and determined.

'Right, lads,' said Rob White, and the hubbub died down. 'Not our finest performance. But we've got a total, and we've got the bowling. Haven't we, Keith? Haven't we, Tom? So come on, let's go out there and do a job.'

There was a tremendous clatter as the team marched out of the changing room. Tom felt a thump on his shoulder. It was Finn, the wicket-keeper, who said: 'OK, kid, this is it. You'll terrify the living daylights out of them.' He gave Tom a big grin, and then ran ahead so that people could throw the ball to him.

Finn threw catches to the team, but when it came to Tom,

he rolled him one to field along the ground instead. Tom ran to it gratefully, picked it up and threw it back. It smacked into the wicket-keeping gloves.

'Attaboy!' shouted Finn.

And then suddenly they were all trooping off towards the pitch and Rob White was setting his field.

'Tom – fine leg.'

Tom trotted off to the far boundary. He liked fine leg. You got a good view of the game, and the ball never came too hard, even though it could race towards you pretty quickly. Especially with someone like Keith bowling.

Keith was marking out his run. It looked as though he'd forgotten something and was walking back to the clubhouse. But no, he just needed a long run.

By now the batsmen had arrived, the man taking first ball had been given his guard by the umpire, who called 'Play!' and Keith started to run, then sprint towards the crease. Tom hardly saw the ball. He saw the batsman lunge forward, and then Finn rising to take the ball in his gloves.

'Good wheels, Keith,' someone shouted and the fast bowler plodded back to his mark.

Three more balls went past the outside of the bat. Tom would have been happy if this had gone on forever. But the fifth ball was different. Keith changed his line slightly, and with an imperceptible turn of his wrists, the batsman glanced it off his body.

Please don't let me misfield, Tom prayed. Please. The ball sped over the grass to Tom's left. He ran towards it.

'Save two!' someone shouted. Tom wasn't sure he'd manage to cut it off before it crossed the boundary, but he did.

There was a lot of shouting. Tom clearly heard Finn yelling: 'Get it in!' He had the ball in his hand, turned, and saw Finn holding up both his gloves as a target. He threw. It was only after he'd released the ball that he made sense of the other bits of shouting that were still going on. One of the batsmen was shouting: 'No, go back.' But it was too late. The ball smacked into Finn's gloves and he whipped the bails off, leaving the batsman stranded halfway down the wicket.

The noise level rose considerably, as the whole Kumble team broke out into ragged cheers and whoops and started running down towards Tom with their arms outstretched. There were high-fives, and slaps on the shoulder. Keith came up and tousled his hair. 'Never two to Tom. Well done, mate. Well done.'

The excitement died down eventually and Tom went back to patrolling the fine leg boundary. He kept telling himself to concentrate, to watch every ball every inch of the way. But he couldn't stop the excitement bubbling up and almost over-whelming him. Not only to be a part of a team – of really good cricketers – but actually to do something special and have them flocking round him. He couldn't remember having been so happy in his life before.

'Well done, Tom.' It was his dad, who'd walked round. 'Don't look at me – keep concentrating. But I just wanted to say, that was pretty special. The batsman was mad as hell. I won't tell you what he called you –'

'Thanks, Dad. I've got to go. It's the end of the over.'

Rob White had Tom field at fine leg at both ends. It was the best position for him, and he certainly didn't mind the jog across the outfield at the end of each over. Whenever he passed the wicket team mates gave him a thumbs up, or a friendly grin. Tom felt so good he could almost have been flying.

Another wicket fell. Keith got one of the batsmen to edge a catch to Rob White at slip, and Tom felt brave enough to run in and join the throng around the tall fast bowler. He even put up his right hand for a quick high-five. 'Well bowled,' he said rather breathlessly, and was seriously thrilled when Keith looked down at him and said: 'Got to try and get one or two before he brings you on.'

'All in good time,' said Rob White. 'Man in.'

It was the Croton captain. He ran to the crease, kicking his heels up, and then swung his bat around aggressively before he took his guard. Tom went back to his position, glad to be withdrawing from the firing line. The score was 21 for 2.

In what seemed a very short time, it doubled. It wasn't that the Croton captain was slogging, just hitting the ball all over the place like Devlin. A lot of his shots looked like defensive pushes, until you saw the ball race past the fielders. He tucked one shot off his legs and Tom set off to field it, only to find that it streaked over the boundary yards ahead of him. 40-odd for 2, and less than a hundred runs needed.

'Tom.' Rob White held up the ball at the end of an over, and Tom trotted up to him. 'Come and have a bowl.'

A bowl. Yes, of course. He'd almost forgotten that's what he was here to do. And suddenly he felt nervous. Horribly nervous. It didn't help that the Croton captain was going to be facing. He took the ball and let his fingers play over it. It was still very new and shiny. He felt his palms getting sweaty.

Rob White set the field, and then jogged down to slip.

'Fire it up then, Tommie,' Finn shouted encouragingly. The Croton captain adopted his stance, his bat tapping patiently behind his boots. He looked huge. Tom wanted to give the ball to someone else and slink back to fine leg.

Instead he marked out his run, turned and ran up to release the ball. The moment he let it go he knew. It came out wrong. There was a tiny pause when nothing happened, time seemed suspended, there was no sound and everyone was frozen to the spot. Then, with a huge crack, the bat made explosive contact with the ball, which simply soared away, up and up and over the boundary, well over.

There were raucous cheers from the home team, cheers

which sounded horribly like jeers to Tom, and then an agonisingly long time while someone traipsed halfway over the car park to get the ball.

'Don't worry,' Finn sang out as he returned the ball to Tom. 'Let's go again.'

Unfortunately that's exactly what happened. If anything, the ball went further this time, and at a slightly different angle, so it bounced against the clubhouse wall. Tom wished the ground would open. He wished he could be teleported into another century. He wished he'd never got up in the morning. All those high-fives and back-slaps. No one was telling him he was a star now. The scoreboard showed 63 runs, and if he kept getting hit for six the match would be over in about ten minutes.

'Come on, Tommo, use the facilities.' At last Finn had the ball again, but Tom didn't want it. Back it came all the same. Up he ran again, and this time it felt all right. This time he knew it was OK. The Croton captain took a stride down the wicket with his bat raised, obviously eager to help himself to more easy runs. But having left his crease, he suddenly found the ball wasn't as full as he'd expected. It dipped in its flight and, on pitching, it turned sharply away from the flailing bat.

Finn caught in one hand and, almost quicker than you could see, whipped off the bails with a blood-curdling appeal. As the umpire's finger went up, he threw the ball in the air and sprinted down the wicket to Tom.

'You beauty. What a jaffer.'

In no time at all, Tom was mobbed by the rest of the team.

'Great ball, great ball,' someone said; and 'he was looking dangerous' said another.

And Rob White said, 'That was a very good wicket Tom, a very good wicket.'

'We just need seven more, if you wouldn't mind,' some one

else said and the players dispersed with a ripple of laughter as the new batsman took guard.

It was hardly worth his while. Tom's first ball to him pitched well outside his off stump. He lifted his bat to let it go through to Finn, only for it to dart back in and hit the top of his leg stump. The Kumble team gave a pretty good impression of a lottery syndicate whose number has come up, while the batsman looked darkly down the wicket at Tom in disbelief.

'Hat-trick, come on Tom, you can do it.' The whole team clustered round the new batsman, who looked distinctly nervous. He came perilously close to being bowled first ball, but it fizzed over the off stump, and then he managed to get a pad in the way of the next one. 6, 6, wicket, wicket, dot, dot. Everybody seemed to be pretty pleased with that, as Tom took his cap from the umpire.

Tom's next over was similar, but without the sixes. The batsmen pushed forward tentatively as though the ball were an unexploded hand grenade. One got an edge which carried fast to Rob White at slip, another played all round a ball that span in from the leg and hit off. Another tried to fight his way out of trouble but only managed to top-edge a skier into the safe hands of Keith at mid-wicket.

'See what I mean about getting wickets before you come on,' he laughed as he brought the ball back to Tom. 'Only three more and we're done,' Keith added as he went back to his position. The scoreboard read 68 for 6. Tom's next ball kept low and kept on going straight. Finn leapt into the air with a howl of triumph the minute it hit the new batsman's pad. 'Come on, Tom, you can't let me do all the shouting,' he said, as they watched the defeated batsman shaking his head as he walked back to the clubhouse. He gave Tom a pat with his glove and marched smartly back to his place behind the stumps.

As Tom walked back to his place at fine leg at the end of the over he saw a figure waiting for him on the boundary. It was Bruce Cranley.

'Very impressive, young man. I can see what Rob meant. Have you been playing cricket long?'

'About a month,' said Tom.

'Yes. You'd certainly have come up on my radar if you'd been doing that sort of thing any longer than that. And where did that action come from, if you don't mind my asking?'

Tom didn't mind at all. But he didn't have an answer.

'Oh, you know, I just . . .' He shrugged. 'Is it wrong?'

The wiry man laughed. 'What are you on – 6 for 12? I don't think anyone would call it wrong. Unorthodox, certainly, but who's going to try tinkering with something that works that well? That's yours.'

Tom looked up and saw the ball coming. He ran in and threw it into Finn's gloves.

'You've got a pretty good arm too.'

Tom smiled. He liked all the adult attention he was getting, but he wasn't used to it. 'I can't bat,' he blurted out, as though to deflect the wiry man's interest. He kept quiet about the other side of his fielding, the dropped catch side.

'Don't worry about the batting. We can teach you the basics.'

*We?* Who's *we*, Tom wondered.

'It's over. Off you go and get those last three wickets. Nice talking to you. And well bowled, son, well bowled.'

Tom did get the last three wickets. He even tried an appeal, though it came out a bit squeaky and was turned down by the umpire ('Going over the top, lad'). The last man took a despairing heave and was clean bowled, and suddenly Croton were all out for 78. Once again the entire team gathered round him, pummelling him on the back and mussing his hair until he felt as though he'd been through a tumble drier. Then Rob White said, 'Here, you have the ball. Off you go.'

53

It took Tom a moment to realise he was expected to lead the team off the field. It made him feel very self-conscious, but also proud. He could see his dad waving to him on the boundary and clapping his hands above his head. Still, as long as he didn't run onto the field and hug him . . .

The Croton captain was waiting on the boundary, and he came up and shook Tom's hand warmly. It was a strong handshake, but a friendly one. 'That was an exceptional bit of bowling, out of this world. Well done.' Then turning to Rob White and shaking his hand, he said, 'Where did you find him?'

'Don't even think about it, Damien. He's signed up with us and he's staying with us. Aren't you, Tom?'

Tom nodded happily.

# CHAPTER 5

THE phone was ringing. 'Tom, it's for you,' his mother called up the stairs.

'Tom Marlin? Hi, I'm Ned Cope. From the *Echo*. Sports desk. I wondered if I could have a word.'

It wasn't just a word that he wanted. A photographer came round and Tom had to change into his cricket things and go down to the Kumble club to pose with the match ball. The photographer seemed to want an awful lot of photos. 'You never know,' he said to Tom as he drove him home, 'better to have too many than too few. Talking of which . . .' Tom could see he'd had an idea. A picture of him holding the cat?

It was worse than that. 'Proud parents. Come on. Just out in the front garden. It won't take a minute, and then I'll leave you in peace.'

Of course, Mum had to go off and attend to her hair, and then she fussed around Tom, pulling his cricket jersey into shape. 'And Rick,' she said, 'do go and change that shirt.'

Finally they were ready.

'Come on,' said the photographer. 'Smile. It's not a funeral.'

When the paper came out Tom turned to the sports pages at the back. There was the photo of him, holding up the match ball and grinning shyly at the camera. Beside the photo was the match report under the headline: WHIZZ KID SPINNER WINS MATCH FOR KUMBLE; and at the bottom of that there was the match scorecard with the names of all the players with his name appearing more than anybody's: b. Marlin, it said, b. Marlin, b. Marlin, b. Marlin.

'Somebody ought to start a scrapbook. There could be a lot more like that.'

'Well, as long as they don't print those awful ones of us in the garden,' his mum said.

Somebody was keeping a scrapbook of his achievements, well, more a complete record.

'You're averaging 3.756 per wicket. That's amazing!'

Little Paul tapped a brand new ring-binder. 'All in here,' he said.

'Liked your mugshot in the paper, did you?'

Devlin had come up behind them, and gave Tom a far-from friendly nudge in the back with his elbow. 'Aren't you just the the pin-up boy then? Don't suppose you looked any further than your own write-up, did you? But if you had, you might have noticed you weren't the only one to have a good week-end. Perhaps we'll meet on the field of battle next Saturday. I can't wait.'

'What's he talking about?' Tom asked as he watched Devlin pushing through a shoal of Juniors.

'He got a ton – 101 – for the seconds. He might get picked for the first team against Kumble.'

'So I'd be playing against him?'

'Could be. But what's the worry? You tied him in knots last time you bowled to him. He's good, but not half as good as he thinks he is; and not half as good as half the batsmen you bowled on Saturday. Damien Cowper's on the verge of a County contract.'

Tom had a flashback of the two awful blows unleashed by the Croton captain. The thought of being similarly slaughtered by Devlin made his heart sink.

Devlin stopped Tom in the corridor one morning. 'Just heard. I've been promoted to the firsts, so I'll be coming over to Kumble on Saturday to face the Mystery Whizz Kid of Spin. Aren't you going to congratulate me?'

'Well done,' Tom said, without much enthusiasm.

'Yeah, thanks,' sneered Devlin. 'Nice short boundaries at your place. I'm going to hit you all round the ground. Game on, Freak.'

Somehow wind of the weekend's confrontation got out. There's nothing people like better than a bit of healthy rivalry. The trouble was, Tom didn't feel this particular rivalry was that healthy.

Not that he did anything to stoke the fires. Devlin made all the running, constantly telling anyone who would listen what he was going to do to Tom's bowling on Saturday.

Tom didn't like to admit it, but it got to him. At the nets on club night he bowled a lot more bad balls than he usually did. He still managed to bamboozle all the batsmen in the first-team net, but there was enough that wasn't right for Rob White to take him to one side and ask him if there was anything the matter.

'No, not really,' said Tom.

'Not really? Look at me, Tom. This is your captain speaking.'

Tom looked up and saw an encouraging smile. He liked and trusted Rob White, and only wanted to do the best for him.

'I need to know, Tom. What is it?'

So Tom told him. Not the full story. Not about Devlin stopping him on the path home and trying to bully him into giving up the game. But enough for Rob White to get the picture.

'So, he fancies himself, this Devlin lad, does he? Tom, you

don't need to fear anybody. If you can keep bowling like you have been, you're going to give far better batsmen than Devlin serious headaches. I won't tell you what Damian Cowper said to me after last week's match, but he was very, very impressed. And he's going to be pushing for a place in the County side before the season's out. Just do what you do, and the wickets will follow. But thanks for telling me. It's good that I know. Now, I think it's time we introduced you to the art of batting. Go and get your pads on. And no, we won't want you in the first-team net for batting. You go down to the Juniors and see how you get on.'

'Hear you've been practising your batting.'

It was Devlin, standing behind him in the lunch queue on Friday.

'I have my spies everywhere, Marlin, and my spies tell me you were the most rubbish batsman in history.' He laughed his unpleasant laugh, and then, closing his eyes and shaking his head, he said, 'What wouldn't I give for an over against you on Saturday. Just an over.' He snapped out of it and elbowed Tom to get him to move up the queue. 'What you having – a salad? That won't put hairs on your chest. Come on, you can squeeze a few more chips on there,' he said with what he obviously thought was an engaging grin to the dinner lady, and then he was away to his table where Sherwin was already tipping vinegar over his chips.

So that's where the story of his batting came from, Tom thought, as he drifted down the canteen looking for Little Paul.

'Hey,' said Jamie, 'Sit.'

Tom sat down beside him.

'Long time no see. Too busy being a star?'

Tom could see he didn't mean it.

'Listen,' Jamie dropped his voice. 'I really hope you sort

him out tomorrow.' He didn't have to say who he was talking about. 'I am sick and tired of hearing what he's going to do to you.' Tom nodded his head in agreement and ate his salad. 'But you know,' Jamie went on, 'it's a sign of weakness.' Tom shot him a 'you could have fooled me' glance. 'He's talking himself up, pumping himself up. Of course he's trying to do a number on you. But you've just taken I don't know how many wickets in a month –'

'38 at 3.437.'

'Oh, hello, Little Paul. Sit down. I was just saying to Tom, he's got nothing to prove tomorrow. Whereas Devlin has got it all to do. And I'll tell you another thing. There's more at stake than just who's going to come out top on the day. Devlin's in line for a County Fast Track place.'

'What's that?' asked Tom.

'More or less what it says on the tin. The county are always on the lookout for local talent, young cricketers who might go all the way. And there's a scheme called Fast Track to – well, fast-track them up the ladder. Special coaching sessions, a guaranteed game or two in the Club & Ground side, even a possibility of a run-out with the 2nd XI. Bruce Canley runs it.'

'I've met him,' said Tom.

'Yeah, of course. He's coach at Croton. Well, he'll be there tomorrow, I'll bet you. And he'll be making his choice for the Fast Track place pretty soon. And Devlin wants it badly. Very badly indeed.'

'Plotting my downfall?' Devlin looked above their table with his hands on his hips. He was the only pupil in the school who never took his tray back. 'See ya tamorrer, cowboy,' he said to Tom in an appalling Western accent, and he pulled an imaginary gun on him and went 'Pow, Pow, Pow' before strolling down the canteen to the exit.

'In your dreams, fat boy,' said Little Paul, only just quietly enough for Devlin not to hear.

They finished their lunch and took their dirty plates back to the counter and clattered their plastic trays on the pile. 'Good luck tomorrow,' Jamie said. 'And remember, he's under more pressure than you. A lot more.'

That Saturday morning Tom woke with a feeling of dread. For a moment he struggled to work out what was bothering him. Then he remembered. The match against Thurston. He groaned and buried his head in his pillow. After a while he became aware of a familiar sound, but it took him a moment to place it. Then he did. It was rain, rain against his bedroom window; rain that would, with a bit of luck, save him from having to confront Devlin on the cricket field.

'Breakfast's ready!' he heard his mum call up the stairs. There was an enticing smell of bacon. Saturday was fry-up day.

'You're in the paper again, son,' said his dad as he sat down at the kitchen table. 'SPIN KING THE DIFFERENCE IN DERBY LEAGUE OPENER,' he read out. 'Kumble skipper, Rob White, said he believed he had a match winner in new star Tom Marlin. *Star* – I like that!'

'Come on, put that away. No reading at the table.' And Tom's mum whisked the paper out of his dad's hands and replaced it with a plate of full English breakfast.

'Anyway,' she said, as she put Tom's in front of him, ' it doesn't look as though anyone will be playing cricket today.'

Suits me, thought Tom, as he eased his knife into the yolk of his perfectly cooked egg and let it run onto the baked beans. His mum cooked the best fried breakfast ever, and if the match was cancelled, he'd be happy to while away the rest of a lazy Saturday listening to music, playing with his Play-Station and watching an old movie on the telly.

'Said it would clear up. On the forecast. Scattered showers.'

'Ever the optimist, Rick. That's rain, that is. Hard, steady rain.'

'I suppose they'll ring if it's off.'

But the phone didn't ring. And didn't ring. And still didn't ring. And, just as his dad said, the rain petered out and it began to get brighter.

At a quarter to twelve, Tom reluctantly threw his stuff into his bag. He really, really, really didn't want to play. But there was no getting out of it. He couldn't possibly let Rob White, Keith, Finn and the rest of the team down.

'Come on, Tom!' his dad called up the stairs.

'I'm coming.'

The car splashed through a puddle as it turned off the road into the lane that led to the ground. Perhaps, Tom thought with a little rush of hope, it might be off after all, and they'd just forgotten to tell him. But no. As they turned in to the car park there was quite a crowd and out on the square players were pushing the covers away. Rob White and the Thurston captain were inspecting the pitch with the umpires. They looked down at the grass, then up at the sky, and then at their watches before breaking up and walking towards the club house.

'Looks like it's on,' Tom's dad said as he pulled up. 'D'you mind if I don't stop? Mum's got some things she wants me to do around the house. I'll come back later, if that's OK.'

'Fine, Dad. Enjoy your DIY.'

It was better walking towards the clubhouse on his own rather than with his dad. He was well enough known now not to feel a stranger and completely out of place.

The first person he saw was Mr Giles.

'Hello, Tom,' he said. 'Don't look so surprised. We had to call our match off, so I thought I'd come down for the start of yours. I gave one or two of the lads a lift over. They seemed very keen to be here. It should be quite a tussle. Oh, there's Devlin.'

Devlin swaggered up and dropped his coffin at their feet. 'Hello, Mr Giles,' he said jauntily. 'Bit late for last-minute coaching now, Marlin,' he said to Tom. 'See you out there,' he added ominously before picking up his coffin and heading on to the clubhouse.

'Good luck,' said Mr Giles. 'Just do what you do, and it'll go fine.'

Tom returned his smile and, keeping a safe distance from Devlin, went to join his team-mates in the Home changing room.

'Fielding,' Rob White said as he came into the changing room half an hour later. 'It's wet out there, so let's keep the ball off the ground. Try and keep it dry for the bowlers.'

Finn clapped his gloves together. 'Come on, lads. Let's get stuck in.' And out they all clattered, running onto the field to a smattering of applause from the small crowd.

'Opening from the pavilion end,' Rob White called out after the warm-up and the fielding practice. 'Fine leg?' he said to Tom.

Tom took his place near the sightscreen. The Thurston opening batsman took guard and looked round the field, the umpire called 'Play!' and Keith began his long, rhythmical run to the crease. And Tom took a few steps in. These days he knew what 'walking in with the bowler' meant, and why it was important. He found he was excited and pleased to be playing after all.

He couldn't quite see what Keith's first ball did, but judging from the noise the slip fielders made, and the way the batsman walked down the wicket to prod the pitch, it had been pretty good. The next ball flew through to Finn as well, and the next. The fourth did something different. It plucked the middle stump out of the ground. Tom ran in excitedly to join the celebrations, and went back to his point on the boundary with the heady feel of triumph buzzing in his head. As he approached his spot, he noticed a figure walking round the white line. It was Bruce Cranley. Had he seen him? Should he wave, or say hello. He was just too far away for it to seem natural. He was always finding himself in situations like that. Should he speak, should he put himself forward? Almost every time he opted for safety and did nothing. And then felt bad about it afterwards.

It was over, and he set off on his long trot down the field. The only trouble with fielding at fine leg at the clubhouse end was that it left him standing virtually in front of the Thurston team watching the game from the benches drawn up outside the boundary. And of course that meant he was within easy earshot of Devlin.

'All right, Tommo? Found a nice safe spot for you, have they – out of danger? Obviously heard about your fielding, Tommo. Had to hide you, did they?'

Tom felt the tips of his ears begin to burn. But he knew if he turned round, it would be a point to Devlin. Fortunately Mr Giles chose that moment to sit himself down on the bench beside Devlin. 'When are you in, Devlin?' Tom heard him ask.

'Seven,' came the surly reply. 'Just in time to show Tommo a thing or two.'

'If he's needed,' Mr Giles said. 'That's a seamer's wicket if ever I saw one. Look at that!'

Alan Pargett, the other opening bowler, had just got the ball to rear up and the batsman had only just managed to jerk his head back out of the way.

'It's a step up, Devlin, and no mistake. If you get runs out there today you'll have done well.'

It was over and Tom loped off to the other end of the

ground. Keith bowled a maiden, another maiden; because apart from one leg bye, Thurston hadn't scored a single run.

This was obviously beginning to nag at the opening batsman's mind. When Alan dropped another ball slightly short, he swivelled on his hips and tried to pull over midwicket's head. He missed, but it was clear what he had in mind. Two balls later, the same thing happened, except this time the batsman made contact.

It took Tom a nano-second to see what had happened. Instead of hitting the ball in the middle of the bat and thus sending it scudding over the grass to the boundary, the batsman had got a top edge. The ball had gone miles up in the air, but it had also travelled quite some distance – in the direction of fine leg. It was a catch – his catch!

Oh no, it was miles up, and now coming down. Tom took a few uncertain paces forward. Where was it going to land? What if it hit him? What if he didn't even get a hand to it. He heard a noise behind him, but tried to ignore it. And then, with a sickening dead thump, the ball crashed into the sodden grass about six feet in front of him.

'Yee-ha!' He heard a peel of unmitigated delight from the boundary. It could only be Devlin. He stooped to pick the ball up and hurled it underarm towards Finn, who shouted in response, 'Head up, lad, head up. Don't worry, it was a difficult one.'

'Difficult one,' Tom heard Devlin sneer, as he turned back to his position, his head down with the shame of it.

'Dropped catch – and they ran two. Still, at least you didn't kick it over the boundary for four.' Devlin said this quite quietly but Tom heard all right, and Devlin knew that Tom heard. 'I wonder what Mr Cranley made of that. I wonder what he made of that totally pathetic attempt at fielding.'

'I think even you might have found that quite challenging,'

Mr Giles intervened. 'Bad luck, Tom. Keep focused for the next one.'

At the end of the over Tom started to run up the field again, but this time there was no spring in his step. He hated himself, hated the way he had failed, let the team down, let Alan down. Alan, he thought. At least he could apologise. He looked up and saw the fast bowler walking into the covers pulling his sweater on. As Tom reached him his head popped through.

'I'm sorry, Alan. I'm really sorry.'

Alan looked slightly surprised.

'Don't worry,' he said. 'It was really difficult. At least you didn't let it hit you on the head.' He laughed, and straightened out his sweater. 'Off you get. Keith's ready to go.'

Tom looked round. Everybody was waiting for him. He put his head down and put on a turn of speed, swinging round as he approached the boundary so he was facing the action, even though he was still running away from it.

The batsman glanced the ball off his legs towards Tom. It wasn't going particularly fast, and anyway, the wet grass slowed it down. Tom ran in and bent to pick it up. There was a moment's hesitation, but then a stern cry of 'No!' settled the question: one run or two? Perhaps Devlin had warned his team-mates about Tom's arm.

The single brought the batsman Tom had dropped onto strike. Keith started his run, accelerating smoothly as he approached the crease. The batsman moved forward into a drive. Tom instinctively looked into the covers where the batsman intended hitting the ball. Out of the corner of his eye he saw a flurry of activity in the slip cordon, confirmed by a rousing cheer. Rob White was stretched out on the ground, and gradually got up, holding the ball in his hand.

'Bowling, Keith. A beauty.'

As usual, everyone ran into a huddle to congratulate the

heroes of the minute. Tom felt he didn't deserve to join the huddle, but Finn waved a glove at him, and he shyly trotted up.

'There, how good does that make you feel?' Finn said to him. 'No harm done – except to Alan's bowling figures, that is.' There was warm laughter. With a start of pure pleasure, he knew that he hadn't lost the support of his team-mates.

'Man in,' said Rob White.

'Got you out of jail there, cowboy,' said Devlin when he moved down the ground at the end of the over. 'You lucky little –'

But Tom was off, haring round the boundary to cut off what looked like a certain four. He would have tried anyway, but he really wanted to do his best for Alan after the catch. He just got a hand down to the ball inches before the white line. Then he rocked back and threw it in to Finn with all the power at his command.

The batsman, who thought he had plenty of time, suddenly realised he hadn't, and as the ball reached Finn's gloves he was sprawled out at full stretch trying to make his ground. Finn whipped the bails off and let out a furious appeal. One or two of the fielders made a funny square in front of them with their fingers, which Tom didn't understand. It had no effect on the umpire who, after a brief, but agonising pause, shook his head and said: 'Not out!'

'Not even close,' jeered Devlin as Tom resumed his position on the boundary. 'When are they going to put you on anyway?' he followed up.

Tom didn't respond.

'Well,' went on Devlin regardless, 'I'm not worried. Ball must be sopping wet by now. Like a bar of soap. And those nice short boundaries look soooo inviting.'

How long was this going to go on? Knowing Devlin, all

afternoon. But then Sherwin came up and said, 'Fancy a few throw-downs in the nets, Dev?'

'Better get my eye in for the slaughter I suppose. See ya later, cowboy. Don't drop any more catches and disgrace the school,' he said as a parting shot.

'How's it going?'

'Hello, Paul. Much better now Devlin's pushed off.'

'Yeah,' said Little Paul. 'What is his problem?' Then, after a pause, he said, 'Bad luck about the catch.'

'Oh well,' said Tom. 'At least we got him out pretty much straight away.'

'Yeah, that makes it feel better doesn't it?'

It certainly did. And as Keith and Alan continued to tighten the screws on the Thurston batsmen, Tom felt less and less bad about it.

The visitors clearly decided to consolidate. The two batsmen played with extra care and took no risks. They didn't score many runs, but no more wickets fell. Keith and Alan still got the ball past the bat from time to time, but there were fewer *Ooohs* and *Aaahs* from Flinn behind the stumps. Gradually Rob White pulled his slip fielders out until he alone stood there waiting for an edge.

'One more,' Tom overheard Rob White say to Keith as he crossed over, signalling that there would soon be a bowling change. One or two of the team cranked their arms and grinned at Tom. Soon, he could see they were thinking, they'd be sitting back enjoying the clatter of wickets as he produced another spectacular spell.

But it didn't happen. When Keith finished bowling, Rob White himself took over at the clubhouse end. He bowled less fast than Keith, but still got the ball down at a bustling pace. And he definitely troubled the batsmen, who were suddenly back to playing and missing, having become more or less acclimatised to Keith.

And at the other end, he replaced Alan with Lumpy George, a big man, who could hit the ball miles when he was batting, and who generated a surprising amount of pace off a very short run-up. He too troubled the batsmen, and on the last ball of his first over got one of them to snick an easy catch to Finn.

'Bowling, Lumpy – caught, Finn' – the congratulations came thick and fast as the team gathered together. 'Nice bowling change, Skip,' someone said, and Rob White just gave a tilt of his head meaning something like 'I'm not just a pretty face, you know.'

With the fall of that wicket, the score was 48 for 3. Tom was pleased when he walked down to the clubhouse boundary that there was no sign of Devlin. Padding up, he assumed.

He was right. It wasn't long before Devlin strode out looking a bit like a Michelin man with his extra large pads and his helmet.

'Saving you for me, are they Marlin? How thoughtful.' He spread himself out on the bench nearest to Tom, so that he was just there at the edge of vision, a constant irritant.

Don't let him get to you, Tom told himself. But he did. And when the ball snaked past Finn off a thick inside edge and raced towards the boundary Tom was late to spot it and fumbled it badly when he got to it. With the memory of his earlier throw, the batsmen decided against a second run.

'Got lucky again, cowboy,' said Devlin. 'Easy two there.'

Tom had to agree with him, but it didn't make him any more relaxed. The next time the ball came his way, he concentrated as hard as he could, scooped it up with both hands and threw it accurately to Flinn's gloves at the top of the stumps. Finn passed on the ball and then raised his gloves above his head in a silent clap to say well done.

'Friend of yours, is he?'

Tom looked up and met Keith's eyes. There was a brief break

in play while one of the batsmen waited for a replacement glove.

'Who?'

'Bloke down there giving you an earful.'

A friend? Who are you kidding?

'He's our school captain.'

'Is he now?' Keith said and nodded. The batsman had his new glove and the game could continue. The score was 97. Lumpy George got a wicket, and there at last was Devlin, gathering up his bat and batting gloves and swaggering to the wicket.

Rob White made an arm-cranking gesture towards Tom, which meant 'Warm up.' Tom was never quite sure what he was meant to do, but began swinging his arms around as though preparing to bowl. Devlin, he saw, had noticed this, and he too started wheeling his arms about in anticipation.

However, at the end of the over, Rob White put his hand up to stop Tom coming to take the ball from him. Instead he called out, 'Keith!' and Keith wheeled round and, seeing that he was being recalled to the attack, strode up to his captain.

Tom felt both disappointed and relieved. There was no mistaking how Devlin felt. You could see that the prospect of facing Keith was a lot less attractive than having the chance to belt Tom to all parts of the ground.

'Sorry, Tom.' Rob White trotted up to him. 'Changed my mind – captain's instinct. And I think it's time to bring you out of the cold. You come over here – yes, wide mid-on, I think. Thank you.' And then he called out 'Alan – fine leg, please – and next over that end.'

Tom was much closer to the action at mid-on. He was also, of course, a lot nearer the bat and the ball would come to him quickly if struck hard enough. But he didn't feel too worried about that. Devlin had asked for his guard and was now making a deep mark on the crease with his studs. He then looked around the field and when he saw Tom made as though it were a surprise. But for all his show of confidence, Tom suspected that he wasn't feeling confident at all. It even crossed his mind that he had been placed at mid-on as a distraction. But then he looked at Keith pacing out his run-up with ominously deliberate strides. Devlin would have quite enough on his plate without thinking about Tom.

Keith came in off his long run and bowled a ferociously quick ball that beat Devlin all ends up. In fact it nearly cut him in half. Keith's follow-through took him more than halfway down the wicket, and he stayed there for a moment, looking meaningfully at Devlin until someone threw the ball back to him and he started on the long journey back to his mark.

Keith's next ball hit the pitch at more or less the same spot on the wicket. It then hit Devlin in the ribs. There were two distinct sounds: the dull thud of impact followed immediately by Devlin's cry of pain. He threw his bat down and started massaging the bruise with his right hand.

'Take your time, lad.' Rob White had trotted up from slip. 'Nasty one, but you'll be all right.'

Devlin moved around the crease in obvious pain. Tom felt awful. He knew if he went up to offer sympathy Devlin would assume, rightly, that he was not sincere. On the other hand, to stand his ground and look on from a distance seemed unacceptable. He walked in to join the loose ring of fielders standing around as Devlin walked up and down with his hand clamped to his chest. He stopped to take off his helmet. His face had developed an unhealthy pallor and Tom could see that in addition to the pain, he was feeling panic.

'You all right, Dev?' Tom found himself asking.

Devlin swivelled round to face him. Tom could now see cold hatred in his eyes. Devlin opened his mouth, clearly with the intention of making some sarcastic rejoinder. But he didn't, and Tom quickly realised why. Keith, having stayed where his follow-through had left him, now stepped into the circle around Devlin. He was standing next to Tom.

'I'm fine,' he said, through tightly clenched teeth.

'Good,' said Keith. 'I thought I might have hurt you there, but if you're fine, we're ready when you are.'

And with that the fast bowler turned on his heel and marched off back to his mark. Tom and the other fielders went back to their positions, and Devlin gingerly adopted his stance once more.

Keith's next ball didn't hit Devlin; it hit his middle stump. But the celebrations were short-lived. Devlin was reprieved by the umpire who was standing with his arm out, having uttered a cry that sounded something like 'Noaaaaawll'. He then came out from behind the stumps at the bowler's end and showed Keith a point on the pitch beyond the crease.

'Six inches over. At least.'

Keith appeared to take it in bad grace. He looked angrily at the point on the wicket and then shook his head. Meanwhile Finn inserted the stump back in its hole and replaced the bails – under the watchful eye of the other umpire who had come in from square leg.

When everything was to the umpires' satisfaction, Keith ran in again. This delivery thumped into Devlin's pad.

'Howzaaaaat!' bellowed Keith.

'Painful, by the looks of it,' replied the umpire, nodding his head at Devlin, who was hopping about on one leg. His verdict, though, was Not Out. It took Devlin a while to get ready, and Tom could see that all the strutting confidence had leaked out of him.

The next ball was reared up at Devlin's head. He just got out of the way in time but stumbled and nearly fell over.

'Good wheels,' Finn shouted after he'd taken the ball above his shoulder.

Devlin was clearly shaken. His batting partner decided to

71

go down the wicket to give him a bit of moral support, and Tom could see Devlin looking around him miserably and nodding his head.

Tom noticed Keith having a word with the umpire, who called out: 'Going round, batsman.' Tom didn't know what was going on. Keith was marking out his run again, and the non-striker, when he got back to the bowler's end, stood on the other side of the wicket.

There were also subtle adjustments to the field, with people moving two or three yards from their original positions. 'Tom, to your right, and in five,' Rob White called from slip. Tom did as he was told, and Rob White raised a hand to indicate he was in the right place.

Tom was quite a lot closer to Devlin, and could sense his nerves.

'Come on, Keith – all yours, mate,' sang out Finn as he dropped into his keeper's crouch. Tom focused on Devlin and on walking in.

He didn't really see where the ball pitched this time, but he had a very good view of how Devlin reacted to it. It was a bit like a kid when a wasp flies up out of a glass of Coke. But Tom didn't have much time to think about Devlin, because of the cries of 'Catch – catch it, Tom!'

The ball had lobbed up off Devlin's gloves and was now looping up into the air towards him. As he was already walking in, it was easy to break into a run to meet it. It was barely ten yards and when he got there the ball just dropped into his hands.

'Whoa – nice one, buddy. Bowled, Keith.' The congratulations came thick and fast, and best of all was Keith coming up and putting an arm round his shoulder. As they watched Devlin making his way back to the clubhouse trying to shake the pain out of the hand the ball had struck, Keith said, 'Doesn't seem so chatty now, does he?' and gave Tom a wink.

Over on the boundary there was a little outburst of applause, and Tom gave Little Paul and one or two others a wave. He also noticed the figure of Bruce Cranley. He had his hands deep in his pockets and was heading off to the car park.

In just six balls, Devlin's whole world had collapsed.

# CHAPTER 6

THE pitch was still damp and unpredictable when Kumble batted and the Thurston seamers exploited it just as well as Keith, Alan, Rob White and Lumpy George had. Although they only needed 121 to win, wickets kept falling. Rob White alone kept them in the game.

There was one passage of play when the balance tilted in Kumble's favour. Devlin was called into the attack and was clearly determined to make amends for his batting failure. Unfortunately for him, he was up against Kumble's in-form batsman. His first ball pitched a little short and Rob White hit it effortlessly to the mid-wicket boundary. The next was wide outside the off-stump, and that was dispatched to the cover boundary. The third was pitched up and disappeared back over Devlin's head.

'Oh boy, I wish I had a camcorder,' Little Paul said, as he squirmed excitedly on the bench next to Tom.

'Who needs a camera?' said Jamie, who was sitting with them. 'I'm going to remember this for as long as I live.'

Rob White let the next ball go through to the keeper, but steered the fifth ball imperiously to the boundary past a diving mid-on. The last ball he blocked. It came to rest at his feet and Devlin had to walk down the wicket to retrieve it. And that was it. The Thurston captain told him to 'take a blow', and Devlin snatched his sweater from the umpire and marched gloomily into the outfield.

The 16 he'd conceded helped Kumble to 87 for 4, but the next over saw another wicket fall.

'You might have to bat, lad.' Keith leant over the back of the bench as they watched Finn walking out to join his captain. 'He can't declare like last week. If we go nine down, you'll have to get out there with your pads on.'

This was not an attractive prospect, and Tom felt his palms go slippery with sweat while his mouth suddenly went dry.

'Tell you what,' Keith said, 'if you pad up you could have a quick net. What do you say?'

It was the last thing Tom wanted, but he could see the point. Out at the wicket, Finn played and missed at a ball outside his off stump. The Thurston bowlers looked quick and mean, but if he absolutely had to go out there, it would be better to have had some practice.

The changing room was eerily quiet. He felt rather lonely as he strapped Sherwin's hand-me-down pads on and then fitted the funny elongated plastic box down his pants. It felt horribly cold, but he'd seen enough of fast-moving cricket balls to know how important it was. He was just bending down to dig his gloves out of his bag when there was a clatter of studs down the corridor. Then the door bashed open and a bat came sailing through the air, hitting the wall not very far from Tom's head. The flying bat was followed by Finn, who had launched his batting gloves as well before he noticed Tom.

'God, I could have killed you. Sorry. But that was the worst decision, the very worst decision I have ever had in my life. I hit it, practically middled it, but they all went up, and the old fool gave me out. I don't even think it would have hit – going down the leg side.'

He sat down and picked up his gloves.

'And I really thought Rob and I could have done it. The bowling's nothing special. You just have to concentrate. There's bags of time. We've still got a chance. If Lumpy gets going. Alan can bat. And Keith too when he puts his mind to it. You going to have a net? Good idea. I'll come and dob a few down at you.'

Just then the door banged open again. 'Forget the net,' Keith said. 'Looks like you'll be doing the real thing. Rob's out.'

'How?' asked Finn.

'Caught behind.'

'Sugar,' said Finn. 'Score?'

'90-something.'

The big fast bowler sat down heavily and started getting ready to bat. A moment later Rob White came in. Although he didn't throw his bat, Tom could see he was furious with himself.

'Sorry, lads,' he said. 'I should have seen it out.'

'Don't worry, Skip, me an' Tom will knock 'em off, won't we, Tom?' Keith gave his boot laces a terrific tug.

Tom found he could barely speak. Rob White looked at him. 'I'm sorry, but you'll have to go out. I can't declare like last week.'

He sighed. 'Maybe I should have bowled you. I just thought with a wet ball you might struggle. And damn it, we ought to be able to get 121.'

There were footsteps down the corridor, and a head appeared round the door. 'Alan's out. You ready, Keith?'

Keith stood up and reached his helmet down from his peg. 'Ready as I'll ever be,' he said and gave a grim smile to Tom before clomping off down the corridor.

Tom followed in his wake. He felt weak, almost too weak to put one foot in front of the other, and it wasn't any better when he got outside.

The sun had come out, which should have been cheering. In fact, it meant you could see with horrible clarity what was going on out in the middle: the Thurston bowlers whizzing the ball down at an alarming speed. Keith played and missed three balls in a row, and at the other end Lumpy George didn't seem much more comfortable.

For what seemed like an age the score remained becalmed on 97 for 9, but then, for no apparent reason, Lumpy put his foot down and hoisted the ball hard, high and straight, for four. 101. Twenty to win, and a little shiver of optimism in the Kumble ranks. There were quite a lot of people gathered to watch the finale, Tom noticed. Another pressure. Oh, and there was Dad's car nosing into the car park looking for a space. Tom's heart sank further when not only his dad, but his mum got out and started walking to the clubhouse. They'd arrived just in time to see him horribly humiliated – and quite possibly badly hurt. What was it about parents?

The first thing he heard his mum say was: 'They're not sending him out there against that bowling!' Then his father had to try and calm her down and reassure her. Which meant that Tom had to put a brave face on it too.

'Mum, for goodness sake. I'll be fine. Anyway, I might not have to bat.'

As he said that Keith went for an extravagant drive, got an edge and snicked the ball just wide of third slip. They ran three and the score crept up.

Rob White had taken his pads off and come out of the changing room by now. He had met Tom's dad before, but made a big fuss of his mum, charming her with a stream of positives about her son, and treating his coming ordeal with disarming lightness.

'If ten grown men can't get 121 then we really don't deserve to win. All we want of Tom is that he does his best, but if he's bowled first ball so be it!'

Then, turning to Tom, he said, 'Come and have a little stroll – stretch those legs a bit.'

When they were out of earshot he said, 'Mothers! Whenever mine came along to watch me, I'd get a low score, drop a catch or hurt myself. Still, it's nice that they care. But you mustn't let it distract you. Your job, when you get in, is to support Keith or Lumpy, whichever it is. They'll get the runs and all we want of you is that you run when they say and don't run them out. What they'll do is try to "farm" the bowling – which means they'll try to face nearly all of it. Now Thurston will want the opposite. They'll want you on strike and will push the fielders back to allow a single early in the over. But you don't want that, because you don't want to be exposed to their bowler for a whole over. Got that?'

Tom nodded. He was beyond speech.

'Steady on, Keith, plenty of time,' Rob White called out as Keith made another aggressive lunge at a ball outside his off-stump.

'They're batting quite sensibly, but one of them will do something stupid sooner or later. Now, when you're on strike, it's going to be hard, but you might as well give it your best shot. And your best shot is almost certainly going to be the forward defensive that Matt was showing you in the nets. Stretch forward with your front foot and try to get the bat as close to it as possible. If they've any sense, they'll pitch it up to you – it's the best way to get a tail-ender out. But they may decide to mix it up a little, especially after the going-over Keith gave your friend Devlin. If they do –'

He broke off because Lumpy George had just thumped another boundary. There was cheering and clapping from the crowd in front of the clubhouse.

'Under ten to go. It would be a great win. But I meant it – what I said to your folks. If the ten of us can't get the runs, we can hardly expect you to. Oh no!'

Lumpy George had attempted another lofted drive, but this time the ball had eluded his bat and knocked back the middle stump.

'Off you go, Tom,' said Rob White. 'Do your best, and do what Keith tells you.'

Because of their walk, Tom came onto the field from a dif-

78

ferent direction from the clubhouse. There was a cheer as the Kumble crowd noticed him, and in the mix of horrible emotions, mainly different ways of feeling frightened, Tom did feel a little spark of pride.

Unfortunately, his route to the wicket took him past Devlin, who seized the opportunity to tell him what the Thurston fast bowlers were going to do to him. 'What goes around, comes around, Marlin. And there's your mum to see you carried off in the ambulance.'

Keith strode forward to meet him. 'Just ignore him. Right, there's only two balls of this over, so all you have to do is survive. We only need nine, and if I can get the strike I can probably pick them off with a couple of boundaries. I'd take middle for your guard. And then basically get forward. Unless they stick it in short, but that would be stupid bowling.'

'But what if they do?' Tom forced his parched tongue to ask.

'Get out the way.' Keith grinned down at him. 'Good luck.'

Tom wished Keith could accompany him to the striker's end, but of course he had to go alone. The Thurston captain was waving for his fielders to come in to take up close catching positions, so Tom found himself practically ringed.

'Don't be nervous, sonny. You probably won't even see it,' the man closest to him said and the others around him laughed.

'Hold your bat up straight,' the umpire said as Tom stood on the crease with Sherwin's old bat and tried to copy the other batsmen. 'To you,' said the umpire, with a little wave of his hand. Tom moved the bat half an inch. 'That's middle,' said the umpire. 'Right arm over, two to come. Play!'

The close fielders crouched down. Tom lifted his bat and then put it down again. The Thurston bowler charged in like Keith, and when he reached the crease suddenly exploded into a whirlwind of arms and legs, out of which Tom caught the merest glimpse of the ball hurtling towards him. The next thing he knew was that all the fielders were doubled up in a pantomime of disbelief at his having survived. The Thurston wicket-keeper was shouting, 'A coat of varnish, Stan. Same again, mate, same again.'

Tom looked up and saw Keith beckoning him to a mid-wicket conference.

'Are you trying to give me kittens? I don't know how that didn't bowl you. You've got to move your feet. Just try and take a step forward. Go on, you can do it.'

But the fact was that Tom couldn't. The next ball jagged in between his bat and his body and went straight over the top of the middle stump, triggering a chorus of commiseration for the unlucky bowler.

Keith came down the wicket, shaking his head. 'Well done, you're still there. Which means I've got a chance of getting the runs. But they're not going to make it easy. Look, they're giving us a single, but that's only to get you back on strike. Which is exactly what we don't want.'

Tom saw that, just as Rob White had predicted, the fielders had been pushed back.

It was frustrating watching Keith hit the ball firmly into the wide open spaces but not being able to run.

'The thing is,' the big fast bowler said when he came down the wicket after the second ball, 'we can't be sure of running two and getting me back on strike. I'm going to try and hit a boundary.'

Tom stood at the non-striker's end and watched the Thurston bowler bounding in. As soon as he had released the ball, Keith put in a giant stride down the wicket and heaved. He made contact, but not quite as he'd intended. The ball soared up into the air, and it took a moment or two to see where it was going.

'Yeeeesss!' shouted Keith, when he had located it, and Tom hared down the pitch with his pads flapping.

'Look for two,' said Keith as they crossed, but then, when he got to the bowler's end, he put his hand up and said: 'Stay there.'

'Sorry,' he said, coming down to talk to Tom. 'Didn't get hold of it properly. Thought we might make two.' He shrugged. 'Just three balls to go. Remember, move your feet.'

Tom could see the fielders marching towards him, among them Devlin, who waited until Keith was out of earshot before saying out of the corner of his mouth, 'Made a fine mess of that, didn't you, Marlin?'

'Come on, Kubrick,' the wicket-keeper said, clapping his gloves enthusiastically, and the Thurston bowler galloped in. As with his two previous attempts at getting the bat on the ball, Tom wasn't even close, and the *Ooohs* and *Aaahs* flared up again as the delivery whizzed past.

'Mix it up then, Cube,' the keeper shouted and in he came again. This time the ball was short and reared up viciously. Tom was too surprised to get out of the way and it hit him a thumping blow on his chest. The pain tore across his upper body. He flung his bat down and reeled around in the crease.

'You all right, lad?' the Thurston captain asked, coming up to him.

Tom didn't feel all right at all. He wanted to sit down. He wanted to lie down. He wanted to die.

'Oh look, his mummy's coming on.' It was Devlin, of course. But he was right, Tom could see his mum breaking free of his dad's restraining arm. And that decided him.

'I'm fine,' he said.

'Are you sure?' It was Keith looking concerned.

'Sure,' said Tom, and picked up his bat.

'Good lad,' said Keith. 'Last ball.' And he held his gloved fist up for Tom to punch his glove against.

81

'Doesn't want his mummy after all,' said Devlin.

Tom found his hands tightening on the bat handle. The temptation to walk over to Devlin and belt him with the bat was almost irresistible.

He glanced quickly in the direction of the clubhouse. To his huge relief he saw that Rob White had escorted his mum back to the bench, though she still looked poised to come on again at the hint of danger.

'Your skipper fancy her, does he?' Devlin said, just as the bowler was coming up to bowl.

Tom finally snapped. He swung the bat as hard as he could, hoping against all the odds to smash the ball at Devlin. He didn't succeed, but he did manage to make contact, sending it looping over the fielders' heads and off to the long-on boundary.

There were cheers and whoops from the clubhouse, and Keith ran down the pitch and put a huge arm around Tom's shoulders.

'You beauty,' he said, shaking his head in wonder. 'Now just pray I don't stuff up.'

They separated and Tom went back to the non-striker's end.

'Where did that come from?' asked the umpire with an admiring smile. 'You got it right in the middle.'

'Just luck,' said Tom. He was buzzing, but he couldn't really enjoy his big hit until they'd won the match, and he watched nervously as the Thurston bowler ran in to bowl to Keith.

Keith left the first ball. He pushed his big front pad out at it and lifted his bat high above his shoulder. The wicket-keeper clapped. 'Keep it there, Stanley,' he called out.

The second ball was a little shorter and Keith played an attacking stroke, sending it out into the covers. The fielders were still back tempting them to take a single, but Keith raised his hand and told Tom to stay put. Four balls to go, four runs needed to win.

There was something different about the third ball. Tom couldn't quite put his finger on it, but he thought it might have been slightly slower. It was certainly more pitched up, and Keith took a swing at it. Had he connected the game would have been over, but he missed. For a sickening moment, Tom thought it had bowled him. Judging by the wicket-keeper's response, it was very very close.

Keith gave him a nod, and they met for a conference in the middle of the wicket.

'He's bowling well,' admitted Keith. 'That last one was a jaffer. Just held it back. Mind you, it was going if I'd hit it. One bounce into the clubhouse bar. Which is where I'd like to be right now. OK, Tom. Just be ready and do what I say if I call you.'

They punched gloves. Tom realised that for all the nervyness of the situation, he was enjoying himself intensely.

The next delivery was short, too short. Keith had room to hit it hard. Unfortunately, in his eagerness to do just that, he didn't keep it down. The ball went like a rocket, but, Tom realised with a plummeting heart, it was going straight to a fielder. But before he could see whether it was going to be caught, Keith bellowed: 'Come on, Tom, run!'

He set off like a sprinter. There was a noise, a cry, a shout, but he just concentrated on running to the other crease As soon as he got there, he heard Keith shout, 'And back, two, two.'

Tom turned and set off back up the pitch. 'He dropped it,' Keith told him as they passed each other. When Tom regained the safety of the non-striker's end he could get his breath back and look around. It was Devlin, he realised, who had dropped the catch. He was now scuffing the grass with his studs and glaring at the ground.

'Head up, Dev!' the Thurston captain called out to him. He made some adjustments to the field, and Keith strolled down the wicket.

'Not having the best of days is he, your chum?' he said, nodding towards Devlin. 'Right,' he said, 'they've brought a man in to stop the single, but they're still stopping my boundary shots. Just be on your toes, and do what I say.'

Two balls to go, two runs to win. There was quite a lot of noise as the Thurston bowler ran in, and then dead silence as he bowled. Tom thought it was another slower ball. Keith looked at first as though he intended hitting it out of the ground, but then changed his mind and pushed forward defensively. The ball hit him on the pad. There was an explosion of appeals, but making more noise than anybody was Keith shouting, 'Run, run, Tom!'

Tom put his head down and ran as though his life depended on it. The ball was lying on the wicket and Tom passed it just before the Thurston fielder dashed in to retrieve it. He had just made his ground when the wickets were shattered by the underarm throw. Although it was obvious Tom was in, the Thurston team appealed to the square leg umpire. He shook his head, and the umpire at the bowler's end had turned down the lbw shout as well.

Keith came down the wicket. 'Sorry about that. I panicked. Still, it's only one ball. Try to get something on it and we should be home and dry.'

They both looked over to the scoreboard. It showed 120 for 9, and the first innings also read 120.

'What happens if – ?'

'We lose a wicket now?' Keith finished his question for him. 'It's a tie. Neither side wins – but then, neither side loses. It's very rare. I don't think I've ever played in one, to be honest. Let's hope this isn't my first.'

Tom had hoped he wouldn't have to face another ball. In

all the excitement, he'd forgotten his bruised chest. Now it started aching badly. He felt his breath coming fitfully.

'Do you want a guard?' the umpire was asking.

'Middle. Please.'

'Hold your bat up straight.'

The entire Thurston team had gathered round in a menacing circle. He made a mark on the crease and settled over his bat. The bowler sprinted in, far faster, it seemed to Tom, than he had before. He was obviously giving it his last ounce of effort. With a terrifying grunt his arm swung down. There was a supplementary yell, and then complete pandemonium as the ball crashed into the stumps.

Tom couldn't believe it. After all that heroic effort, he'd been clean bowled when they needed just one last run to win. Almost oblivious to the pats on the back and the handshakes from the Thurston team, he turned away and started to plod back towards the clubhouse. He felt he'd let down the whole side, and in particular Rob White and of course Keith who'd batted so brilliantly to get them that close to victory.

Keith caught up with him, and put an arm round his shoulder.

'Well done,' he said. 'You were great.'

Tom just shook his head. He was too disappointed to speak.

'Come on, you go first,' Keith said as they approached the clubhouse and the clapping crowd. Tom couldn't understand why everyone looked so cheerful. But then he was distracted by seeing his dad restraining his mum. Having her come up and kiss him in front of everyone would be the most cringe-making thing in the world.

'Well done, Tom – batted, Keith.' There were whoops and catcalls as they crossed the boundary, and there was Rob White waiting for them.

'I'm sorry, Rob,' Tom said, barely able to lift his head to look him in the eye.

'Sorry – what for?' Rob White then burst out laughing. 'You mean you didn't . . .' And then to Keith, he said, 'You didn't tell him?'

'Tell him what?' said Keith.

'About the no ball! He doesn't know!'

Keith started laughing as well. Tom looked from one to the other. Had they both gone mad? What was going on?

'He's walked all the way in thinking he'd thrown away the match. Look, Tom, look at the scoreboard.'

Tom did. It read 121.

'That last ball, the one that castled you, was a no ball. He overstepped the crease. One run to us, son,' said Keith in triumph. 'We won! And you thought . . .' He shook his head and laughed again. 'Come on, let's get into that bar – partner.'

The joke about Tom not knowing they'd won went round the clubhouse like wildfire. It was the icing on the cake. Tom didn't mind. He sat in a daze in the changing room as his team-mates happily cavorted in the shower. Lumpy George stood with nothing but a towel around his middle and stuck out an arm like a railways signal. 'No ball!' he shouted, and everybody fell about with laughter.

The door flew open, and Rob White came in carrying a tray loaded with pints of lager and one Coke for Tom.

'Well done, lads, that was outstanding. And well done, Tom – worth your place in the side even when your stupid captain doesn't bowl you. Tom Marlin: Man of the Match.' Rob White raised his glass and everybody else did the same.

Tom didn't think he could get any happier. There just wasn't any room in his system for more happiness to be registered. He acknowledged the toast with a shy grin and took a long refreshing pull on his Coke. And that, he reminded himself, was the match he hadn't wanted to play in.

# CHAPTER 7

THERE was no problem with not wanting to play cricket after the Thurston match. Tom was completely bitten by the bug and spent most of his time looking forward to his next game.

And he just kept taking wickets. Six wickets, seven wickets, eight wickets in a match – batsman after batsman departing for the pavilion with a shake of the head and a long disbelieving look at their shattered stumps. And on Monday morning Little Paul would appear with his folder under his arm and reel off the latest stats.

His extraordinary success naturally attracted wider notice. The local paper printed most of the photos they'd taken, and came back for more. Nearly every week Tom featured in the headlines. Indeed, so consistent was he that the sports editor introduced a special column: Tom's Tally, and at Tom's suggestion co-opted Little Paul to produce the figures. Mr Giles was delighted with his success, even though he resigned himself to losing Tom from the school XI. Mr McCulloch had obviously read the newspaper reports, as had Dr Gupta, and on one occasion they both came and watched a home match together. They seemed to find a lot to say to each other, though whether they were discussing the cricket or Tom's shoulder, he didn't know.

Tom attracted notice in other quarters too. One evening his dad called him to the phone.

'Tom Marlin?'

He couldn't place the voice at first, although he knew he knew it.

'Yes?'

'Bruce Cranley. We met over at Croton, if you remember, I sent you into the kids' changing room! Sorry about that. But you've certainly been putting me right ever since. Going great guns.'

'Thanks,' Tom said, still not sure where this was going.

'Don't mention it. No, you've been very impressive. Don't know how you do it, mind, but that's another story. Why I'm ringing is to see if you'd like to come on a scheme I run for the County. It's called Fast Track –'

'Fast Track? That was what Devlin was going to be on.'

'Yes, well maybe he was; but he's not now. His time will come, but not this year. No, I want to offer you the place.'

'Me? But –' He took a deep breath. 'But he's . . . he's much better than me.'

'At batting and fielding yes. Don't get me wrong, Devlin's a very promising cricketer. But compared to you – well, there's no comparison. None. I know you're young, and I know you're very new to the game, but I've never seen anyone like you. It's not just promise with you – you produce, week after week, wicket after wicket. You don't have to if you don't want to, but I've discussed it with Rob White and he thinks it would be worth your while.'

'Rob White thinks I should do it?'

'Absolutely. So what about it?'

'What do I have to do?'

What Tom had to do was turn up at the County ground along with a group of most promising young cricketers from all the local clubs. Compared to Kumble, the County ground was vast. There were stands round three sides of it and the pavilion dwarfed the Kumble clubhouse. The changing room was also enormous, and had a row of showers down one wall. After being made to feel at home with Kumble, Tom now felt

88

as much an outsider as he had in his first ever game. In a funny sort of way he would even have welcomed Devlin's presence. It would have meant he knew someone.

He changed in silence and was relieved when Bruce Cranley put his head round the door. 'Come on lads, I want you all down in the nets in two minutes. James, Barry, Ed, pad up.'

Tom finished changing as quickly as he could and slipped out.

Cranley met him at the nets. 'It'll all seem a bit new and intim-idating, but trust me you're here on merit. Some of the lads may not take you seriously at first, but they'll soon come round.'

Other cricketers were emerging from the pavilion in ones and twos, followed by the three batsmen who strode down the nets. Tom was in Barry's net. Two bowlers went before him, and he was dismayed to see how effortlessly and powerfully Barry dispatched them. Then it was his turn. Up he ran and ducked into his delivery. Out of the corner of his eye he just caught Barry leaving his ground with his bat raised high. In the last nano-second of his delivery he managed to make a tiny ad-justment and dragged the ball down by half a yard. It pitched and then spun viciously past the outside of Barry's bat.

'Have a look, have a look,' Cranley called out. 'You're on your bike if you do that in a match.'

Barry moved back to the crease. He hit the next ball very hard. In fact it nearly took Tom's head off. Fortunately he'd remembered Sherwin's rule about always watching the ball, so he managed to sway out of the way. Soon it was Tom's turn again.

This time Barry stayed in his crease, but the result was the same. Tom gave the ball his usual rip and as Barry pushed forward, it span in and hit his stumps with a satisfying clatter.

'You could have driven a coach and horses through that gate,' Cranley cried out. 'Get your bat and your pad together.'

To Tom he said, 'See, you're doing fine. Well done, lad. Keep it up.'

Tom felt slightly better, and was pleased that the other bowlers were beginning to take note. Barry smote two more balls out of the net before facing Tom again, and was obviously intent on getting his revenge. This time instead of coming forward, he rocked back and attempted a pull shot. Unfortunately for him, the ball spat off the pitch and hit him on the pads right in front of his wicket.

'You wouldn't even need to appeal for that one, Barry. On your bike again. If you're not going to take this seriously you can come out of there and I'll get someone else in instead.'

At the end of the session, after Tom had tormented and subdued all the other aspiring batsmen, Cranley took him to one side and gave him the County fixture card.

'These are the championship matches for the first team.' He showed Tom a column of County names with dates alongside. Then he flicked to the back. 'And these are the Colts matches. They'll be starting soon – pretty much when term ends. I can tell you now I'm going to want you in the squad, so if you wouldn't mind talking to your parents and making sure they don't have any plans to take you away on holiday or anything like that. Assuming you'd like to play, of course.'

Tom nodded. Yes, he thought he probably did want to play.

'Here, take it.' Bruce Cranley thrust the fixture list into his hand.


'So who's going to win the Ashes?' Keith said to him one day as they were stuck in a traffic jam on the way to a match.

Tom didn't have a clue. Indeed, he didn't have much clue as to what the Ashes were. He knew it was something to do with England versus Australia, but beyond that, nothing.

'Don't you follow it?'

Tom had a football team, because everybody had to have a football team, but he'd never given cricket a thought.

'Well,' said Keith, 'You should. Learn a lot watching the Test boys. Though having said that, it can be frustrating supporting England. They've all got the talent – but I don't know, there's a lack of competitive edge somehow. Whereas the Aussies, they'd sacrifice their grannies to win the Ashes.'

'Paul, what are the Ashes?'

Tom felt shy having to ask, but it was clear he was going to have to find out sooner or later.

Little Paul looked up from his folder and rolled his eyes. 'You've taken 83 wickets at 4.376 and you don't know what the Ashes are?'

He sighed in happy resignation. 'England? Australia? Test matches?' He looked at Tom and realised he was going to have to start from the beginning. 'They played the first Test match in this country in 1880.'

'Sorry, what's a Test match?' Tom asked.

'Pretty much what it says on the tin – it's the highest test you can get as a cricketer, playing for your country. Anyway, in 1880, England won, thanks largely to W. G. Grace, who was the best cricketer ever. OK, so far?'

Tom nodded.

'Two years later the Australians were over in England again, and there was another Test match. This time the Australians won.

'So?' said Tom.

'So?!' Little Paul squeaked. 'So everyone was in shock. We didn't expect to get beaten by a bunch of colonials. It was unthinkable. It was the most astonishing thing that had ever happened in cricket. Everybody was completely gobsmacked.'

'But where do the Ashes come in?'

'I'm coming to that. Because it was such a spectacular defeat, it felt like English cricket had been killed. Someone wrote a spoof obituary for the press saying that English cricket had died and that the body would be cremated – and, here we go, the ashes would be taken to Australia.'

'But there weren't any ashes really?'

'Not then. It was just a – a spoof. But then, when the next England team went out to Australia and won, some Australian ladies got together and burnt a bail and put the ashes in a little urn and presented the urn to the victorious England captain. He then brought the urn back to England and it's been here ever since.'

'So we've always beaten Australia ever since then?'

Little Paul laughed. 'As if. No, they've beaten us far more times than we've beaten them, but because the urn was a personal gift we've always kept it. But that's very different from who *holds* the Ashes. Like at the moment, the Aussies hold the Ashes. Which means we've got to beat them in the Test series to get them back. Whereas they don't have to beat us; they just have to draw, which would mean they keep them. Got it?'

'So, are we going to beat them?'

Little Paul puffed out his cheeks. 'It's anybody's guess. On paper we're as good as they are. But there's a big question mark about the captaincy. Eldridge has been around for a long time, but I don't know whether he's worth his place as a batsman any more. The Aussies may have lost some players, but the next batch'll be pretty good. And they simply don't understand about coming second. It'll be close, really close . . .'

Tom found himself hearing more and more about the coming Ashes conflict. ELDRIDGE FAILS AGAIN, Tom read on the back page of his parents' daily. He let his eye wander down the column. 'How can we justify keeping a man on as captain if he can't be relied on to score runs?' There was a picture of the England captain walking off the field after his latest disappointing innings. He looked tired and troubled, and Tom felt a bit sorry for him.

'Dah dah!'

Little Paul opened his folder with a flourish. '100 wickets! Well done, Maestro. And look at that average.'

Tom cast his eye over the latest print-out from Paul's computer. He was slightly bemused by all the fuss over his bowling. To him it seemed a natural thing. It was the way he did it, and if it bamboozled batsmen, that was great. But in fact, he took more pride in the 13 runs he'd managed to score, because batting was really really difficult. And, since his first to dismiss Devlin, he'd taken two more catches, one a stinger at mid-wicket.

'Got to email this over to the paper. I think they're going to do a bit of a splash.'

Little Paul was right. The whole of the back page was dominated by yet another picture of Tom, and a breakdown of Little Paul's statistics. There were quotes from Rob White, who said Kumble, sitting pretty at the top of the league, were having their best season ever thanks to Tom, and from Bruce Cranley, who said Tom was the most promising young bowler he'd ever come across. 'The sky's the limit for Tom. It's just a question of how much he wants it.'

Tom attended another session at the County ground. This time there were a few interested spectators – a middle-aged man in a sports jacket, a tall man in a tracksuit, and a younger man whose presence in particular caused quite a stir amongst the ranks of the fast-trackers.

Tom had no idea who these people were and went about his business – which was causing mayhem at the business end of the nets. After a while, he noticed that two of the spectators had disappeared, leaving the tall man in the tracksuit.

Bruce Cranley went over to him and Tom could see them deep in conversation, though he couldn't hear what they were saying.

'Can't we do something with that action, Bruce? It hurts to watch.'

'Des, what do you want to do – remodel it?'

'I'd like to start all over again from scratch.'

'Madness, absolute madness. Look, the boy's a natural.'

'That doesn't look like a natural bowling action to me. Talk about a frog in a blender.'

'But it works. And if it works . . .' Bruce Cranley broke off to admire yet another delivery which penetrated the batsman's flat-footed defences and struck the middle stump: 'I rest my case.'

'Sure. All the same, it's weird. And we're sure it's legal?'

'Des, he's been playing in the league and there hasn't even been a murmur. I've talked to some of the umpires personally, and they all give him the green light.'

'Good. Have to be sure, though. What's his batting like?'

'Appalling. Hopeless.'

'Fielding?'

'Not much better. He'll drop far more than he catches. But he does have an amazing arm. Wings it in, top of the stumps, from anywhere on the ground.'

'So, he can't bat, and he can't catch.'

'But the wickets, Des. It's carnage, every time he bowls.'

'Well, here's the man to check him out.'

A lone batsman emerged from the pavilion.

Tom recognised him as one of the group who had been looking on earlier, but still had no idea who he was. He was soon enlightened.

'That's Nick Appleton,' a tall boy who had been bowling quite fast said.

94

'Who's Nick Appleton?' Tom asked.

'Only the County captain,' came the reply.

Appleton walked up to the nets, and with a winning smile said, 'Good morning, gents. I hope you don't mind my crashing your practice session. Just felt like a bit of a warm-up before Thursday.'

Cranley came up. 'OK, Barry, off you go – and Jed and Paul, you go and put pads on. Right, on we go, the rest of you.'

Barry came out of the net, and Nick Appleton took his place. He put his helmet on, and waited easily for the first bowler. The tall boy came running in. The ball was on a good line just outside the off stump, and Appleton left it, and then gave a nod of respect before bending down and retrieving the ball.

'Go on, Tom,' Cranley said.

And Tom ran up and bowled. It was a ball he liked to start with – pitching just outside leg-stump and spinning dramatically towards the slips. He gave it generous flight, but it dipped late and savagely. This was what did for Appleton, who was wrong-footed and left making a last-minute lunge. The ball slipped past his outside edge and clipped the top of the off stump.

He gave Tom more than a nod of respect. He stood looking at the wicket, at where the ball had pitched and shook his head. 'Well bowled,' he said as he lobbed the ball back.

He played the next four bowlers with complete ease, and then it was Tom's turn again. This time it was a googly, with a lot of top-spin, which made it kick off the wicket. Appleton covered his stumps, but couldn't prevent the ball clipping his gloves and looping up to give a close fielder the easiest of catches.

When Tom's next turn came, Appleton called out: 'Hat-trick ball!' Everybody in the other nets stopped to watch.

Tom ran in and bowled his quick straight one. Tom's quick straight one was quick and straight, and it also kept low. It hit

Appleton's pad about six inches above his boot, plumb in front of middle stump.

The man in the tracksuit, who had been watching intently from behind the bowler said, 'That's out!' and put his finger up like an umpire.

Appleton took his gloves off and tucked his bat under his arm, as though in a real match. Then he laughed and threw the ball back to Tom.

'Not doing a lot for my confidence, this. But well bowled.'

At the end of the session, Appleton took his helmet off and wiped the sweat from his forehead. 'Thanks, lads,' he said to boys who had bowled at him, and then to Tom, he said, 'Come and have a word.'

As he led off towards the pavilion, he stuck out his hand. 'Nick Appleton. Sorry we didn't do the introductions earlier. And this is Des Chatwin, the County's coach.'

Tom shook hands with both of them, and then they continued over the smooth turf of the outfield.

'What do you think, Des? Bit of promise there?'

Des snorted. 'Promise! He had you out six times in a dozen deliveries.'

'Six?'

'Assuming a wide second slip.'

'Fair enough,' said Appleton.

Both men laughed.

'Look, there's Ted.'

The middle-aged man Tom had seen earlier was making his way down the pavilion steps to meet them.

'Ted MacClaren – Club Secretary – Tom Marlin.'

'Very pleased to meet you, young man,' MacClaren said. And then to the others, he added: 'You know I didn't believe half the hype in the local rag. But I've been watching through the binoculars for the last half hour, and – well, he's absolutely amazing.'

There was a pause. Tom saw the three men look at each other.

Des Chatwin broke the silence. 'You're not thinking what I think you're thinking – are you, Nick?'

'What do you think?'

'I think we need to think long and hard, that's what I think.'

'Ted, what about you?'

'I think it's unthinkable. But I'm very happy to think the unthinkable.'

'Tom, sorry, we must stop this,' said Nick, smiling broadly. 'You were fantastic today. We've all been really impressed.'

'Am I going to get a game for the Colts?' Tom asked.

For some reason the three men seemed to find that amusing.

'As you've just heard us say, we need to do some thinking, but I can promise you, you'll get representative cricket this summer.'

When the call came, it wasn't Bruce Cranley who made it. It was Ted MacClaren. And he dropped a bombshell.

'The first team?' Tom couldn't believe it.

'I know it's a huge step up, massive. But – the fact is, we have a problem in the spin department. Steve Draper's off with an injury, and the lad who's stepped up from the seconds, well, frankly, he's not good enough. I mean, he will be one day; but he's not now. And if we're going to make a credible push for the championship, we have to have someone who can take wickets for us once the shine has come off the ball.'

'But –'

'You're young, you're inexperienced, you've only just started playing; you can't bat, you can't catch. We know all that, Tom. Believe me, we have not come to this decision lightly – and we're all prepared to accept we were wrong if it doesn't come off. But I have to say, after your performance in the nets – well, none of us had ever seen anything like it. Nick's one of the best bats in the country, an England regular, and you tied him up in knots. On the basis of that – and the fact that you've been taking wickets by the dozen all season – we reckon it has to be worth the risk. So what do you think?'

There was a long silence. If Tom could have seen the look of consternation on the Club Secretary's face as he waited for a reply, he would have been impressed at how seriously he was taking this.

Eventually, he said, 'Yes. I suppose, so. If . . . if you really think I could do it.'

'That's my boy,' said MacClaren, with an audible sigh of relief.

'I'll have to ask my parents,' Tom added quickly.

'Of course, and of course I'd like to meet them, and I'm sure Nick would too. Just to talk it all through. We'll have a meeting at the Ground – tomorrow, perhaps?'

'OK,' said Tom. 'I'll tell them. And what about school?'

'Leave that with me. There aren't many schools that are going to try to stop one of their pupils playing first-class cricket. And besides, it's nearly the end of term.'

# CHAPTER 8

THE next twenty-four hours passed in a flurry of activity. There were phone calls and meetings; Tom had to be kitted out – new boots to replace Mr Giles's old pair; new pads and new bat. He met more of the County hierarchy, and some of the squad – huge, athletic men, who looked at him with friendly bemusement for the most part.

He had been sworn to secrecy while everything was sorted out, but at last the embargo was lifted. He had to talk to someone.

'Tell me you're not kidding, Tom?' said Little Paul, after his initial intake of breath. 'Jeepers! It's incredible. But it's so right, it's *so* right. I can't believe you had a net with Nick Appleton and didn't tell me.'

'I couldn't, Paul. Honest. Mr MacClaren kept saying it was all very hush-hush.'

'Oh boy. I can't wait to see Devlin's face. Look,' Little Paul continued as though just taken with an idea, 'why don't you come round. Dad and me are just going to watch the highlights.'

Little Paul's dad met him at the door.

'Congratulations, Tom,' he said, warmly. 'Absolutely brilliant. Come in. Make yourself at home. Paul, get some drinks.'

The three of them settled around the big screen in the sitting room. Almost immediately one of the England batsmen was out lbw. There was a replay which showed his blue pads being hit in front of his stumps.

99

'Absolutely plumb,' said Little Paul's dad.

A graphic showed the path of the ball. It hit the top of leg stump.

'Marvellous invention, Hawkeye. Not infallible, but a step in the right direction.'

There was another slow-motion replay which widened the focus to take in the bowler. He was a huge man with shaggy blonde hair.

'How'd you fancy facing him, Tom? Fastest in the world, they reckon.'

The screen flashed up the name Brad Dawson and some statistics.

'Look at that, 97 mph, that's seriously quick. Mind you, now you're playing with the big boys, you'll be rubbing shoulders with some speed merchants. Fortunately we've got two of the fastest on the circuit. Saw Charlie Cruze bowling the other week, and he was awesome. I'll be coming along on Thursday. And Paul can trot along after school.'

Tom biked home after the cricket to find the phone ringing. In fact, it rang more or less all evening. It seemed as though every sports journalist in the country wanted to interview him. Of course Tom wasn't used to people pushing him for quotes, and ended up saying the same thing about wanting to do his best and not letting the side down over and over again. Most of them wanted more than that. Who did he think would win the Ashes? Would Nick Appleton stay as England opener? Which of the Australian tourists did he think England needed to look out for? He could only name one, so he said Brad Dawson. How did he think he would do against first-class batsmen, even Test batsmen? Was he confident he could step up to the plate? In the end, his mum took the receiver from him.

He was pleased about that, until she said, 'Tom's got to go now. He's got his homework to do.'

Well, at least she didn't say it was his bedtime.

'Come on, Tom, bedtime. You've got a big day tomorrow. Off you go.'

Sleep was out of the question. Tom lay in bed trying to get his head round it all. He found his attention drifting off into fantasies of stunning deliveries and unbelievable catches. But then, instead of floating off into sleep, he would be jolted back to full consciousness by a panic attack. This time it would be a step too far; the batsmen would just be too good and he'd get clobbered all over the ground. The crowd would boo. The crowd! There would be people watching, people would pay at the turnstiles. That thought alone kept him awake for a full hour. Eventually, somewhere in the small hours, he made his last disastrous attempt at a catch, and dropped into sleep. But even once asleep, his mind was still fretful, and he had horrible dreams of finding Devlin playing for the opposition, Devlin grown monstrously huge and immensely powerful, Devlin who would dispense with his bat, and in a frenzy of hatred would grip him by his shoulder and shake him, shake him, shake him . . .

'We've let you sleep as long as we dared. You don't want to be late for your debut.'

Tom sat up with a start. The relief of escaping Devlin's clutches and finding his dad looking down on him was massive.

'Sleep all right?'

'Sort of.'

'Well get dressed. Mum's doing you some toast. We're leaving in ten minutes.'

The drive to the ground was familiar, but to Tom it seemed like a film. It looked real, but in a minute Little Paul would pass the popcorn. There were cars and people all heading in the same direction. When they got to the ground, Tom's dad didn't know where to go. The man on the gate wasn't being very helpful, when suddenly Mr MacClaren came up.

'I can't stop,' Tom's dad said. 'I'm late for work as it is. I just need to drop him off.'

'That's fine. Quite understand. Hope you'll come back in the evening and see how he's getting on.'

'Bye, Dad.' Tom hopped out.

'Come on, young man, this way.'

'Hey, Tom? Tom Marlin? There he is.'

Suddenly they were surrounded by photographers.

'Make it snappy gentlemen – no pun intended. Tom's got a cricket match to play in. OK, that'll do. Come back for more when he's taken a hatful of wickets.'

As he shepherded Tom through a gate marked Officials Only, he said: 'I'm afraid we've turned you into an overnight sensation. You'll get a lot of that but you'll get used to it, and then they'll get tired of it and go and pester someone else. Here's Nick. I'll hand you over. Good luck.'

Nick Appleton led the way up the stairs. Tom looked round the crowded changing room. There were huge coffins on every surface, spilling open with pads and gloves and caps and helmets, while their owners stood around in various stages of undress.

Nick said, 'Got to toss,' and turned back to the door.

'Come 'n squeeze in next to me, kid,' said a huge West Indian. He'd met Charlie Cruze the day before and watched him bowl in the nets. He was very fast. 'You and me better be friends, 'cos we're the tail, man,' he said, moving up a bit. 'Jeez, I sure do hope he win the toss. Charlie don't feel like bowling this morning.'

He stretched out luxuriously. Then he looked down at Tom and winked.

'Gotta be better than school, huh!' He laughed.

The idea amused him so much he was still laughing when

someone at the window called out: 'He's lost it. We're fielding.'

There was the general groan and everyone started rummaging in their coffins for their shirts. Normally Tom didn't mind fielding first, but today was different. He'd hoped to be able to settle in a bit, acclimatise to playing in a first-class match. But now he was scrabbling around in his bag for his socks just like everyone else.

Nick Appleton came back into the changing room. When the jeers and banter died down, he said, 'We've got to keep it tight, try to get the breakthrough, frustrate them. It's a lovely wicket out there, and if anyone gets set they'll cash in. Charlie's going to do the honours from the top end, Zeph from the pavilion end. I know you're all as keen to see Tom bowl as I am, so I will definitely give him at least an over before lunch. Right, let's do it.'

Down the steps they clattered and out into the sunshine. Tom blinked, and tried to work out what that strange noise was.

It was applause. He looked around at the stands. They were not full by any means, but there were little clusters of supporters, and rather more in the members' seats in the pavilion.

'Tom!' It was Little Paul's dad. He gave a cheery wave. Tom waved back.

People pointed at him, and he realised that everyone was looking at him. They did a brief warm-up, and then Nick led them all out to the square. Tom felt weak, panicky. There were two hours' fielding ahead of him, and the promise of a bowl before lunch. He realised that Nick Appleton had said that so that he didn't fret about when he would be called into the attack, but now he wished he hadn't.

'Fine leg, Tom?' Nick Appleton said, coming over to him. 'Look,' he went on, 'there's nothing to worry about. It's a huge step up, and no one's expecting miracles. But you're good, very good, and you've already proved that. This is the same game – only everything happens a lot quicker. You'll get used to it. The important thing is to relax and enjoy it.'

He grinned encouragingly and Tom trotted off to the boundary.

Not for the first time, Tom was amazed at the courage of batsmen prepared to face that hard red missile at a distance of just 22 yards. He watched Charlie bowl, and he felt a kind of awe. His run was far longer than Keith's, or any of the other quicks he'd played with or against in club cricket. He started from halfway to the boundary, and moved as smoothly as a train up to the stumps. The right arm flashed over and then . . .

It took Tom at least an over to sight the ball. He could tell where it had gone, but it was a real effort actually to see it. The opening batsman played one shot off his toes, which Tom thought was probably his. He charged off round the boundary, glad to be in the game. But the ball reached the rope 30 yards ahead of him.

One of the other fielders trotted down to take the ball, and Tom underarmed it to him on his way back to fine leg. Well, at least he'd done something.

At the end of the over, Nick Appleton waved him up to the wicket and directed him to very wide mid-on.

'Don't worry,' he said. 'If Zeph gets it right, you won't have much to do. And he's taken 70-odd Test wickets for Pakistan, so he knows what he's doing.'

Zeph was a left-arm bowler and came in off a shorter run than Charlie.

'Push round a little more,' he said to Tom when he came to give his field his final consideration. Tom noticed that he was one of only three fielders on the leg side. There were three slips and a gully. It was obvious that Zeph wanted to get the batsmen playing just outside the off stump.

Tom watched fascinated as Zeph glided in. His approach to the wicket was smooth but purposeful, and although he clearly wasn't as fast as Charlie, he was quick.

The opening batsman on strike played and missed at a couple. The third ball was dug in a little short, and the batsman jumped to keep it down. He played it past the man crouched under the helmet waiting for a catch, and for a moment thought about a single.

Tom raced in and scooped up the ball.

'Well in, Tom,' Nick called from slip. Tom felt ridiculously pleased, and at once much more at ease. He was the least good fielder on the team by a long way, but he wasn't completely useless. He just had to concentrate and do his best.

The morning session progressed on predictable lines. Charlie and Zeph beat the bat quite often, and once Charlie went up for a passionate lbw appeal, but it was obvious from the way the batsman rubbed his leg above his pad that the ball had been going over the top. There were few runs to begin with. Both batsmen went about their business cautiously, though when they saw a scoring opportunity, they hit the ball extremely hard, and mostly either side of a fielder.

Nick changed the bowling, bringing on two more seamers. They were not as fast as Charlie and Zeph, but they obviously caused problems in their own way. One took a wicket in his second over, the batsman misjudging a drive and giving mid-off a stinging catch which he took at ankle-level. Tom applauded, while knowing with absolute certainty that he would not have caught it.

And then, as the clock on the pavilion pointed to three minutes to one, Tom's moment came.

'Right, Tom, here we go.' Nick handed him the ball. 'I've had a word with Bruce Cranley and he told me the field you usually have.'

Tom looked around. Yes, that seemed about right.

'So, over to you. And if you can get Clive Easterby out I'd be extremely grateful. He's after my Test place.'

He gave Tom a friendly grin and trotted down to slip.

Where, barely forty seconds later, he threw up an easy slip catch with a little laugh of pleasure.

'What a jaffer!' he said, as he came up to Tom, his eyes glinting with pleasure. 'Had to play it.'

He threw the ball up again, and then lobbed it to the umpire.

Tom wondered what was happening. All the players were making a bee-line for the pavilion.

Nick Appleton saw his puzzlement and explained. 'If there's less than two minutes before the interval, the new batsman doesn't have to come out. But I can tell you, you've just spoilt his lunch for him. And you've done me a massive favour. Come on, in we go.'

Charlie and one or two of the other players came up to congratulate him.

'Brilliant, man,' said the big West Indian. 'Boy, have you saved us some toil with that one!'

Lunch was much better than school dinner, but Tom didn't eat much. All he wanted was to be back out on the square, finishing his over.

However, when the first two balls disappeared into the stands, he wasn't so sure. The new batsman had obviously decided on all-out attack. Tom had never seen hitting like it.

'Panic's set in early,' Nick said while they waited a second time for the ball to be returned. 'Don't worry, just keep going. I'm going to leave the field exactly as it is and see how long he wants to play this game.'

Tom bowled again. The batsman went for another calculated heave. He made contact, and at first Tom assumed he'd struck another towering six. But when he looked up, he saw

106

the ball steepling high above the wicket. It wasn't going for six after all. But where was it going to come down?

Tom squinted in the sunshine. There was a lot of shouting. The batsman was calling loudly for a run and several fielders were yelling 'Catch! Catch it!'

Tom realised they meant him. Just as his heart sank, there was a new shout.

'Zeph – yours. Leave it to Zeph, Tom.'

It all happened very quickly. Tom saw a figure coming towards him and backed off so as not to be in the way. And then with complete assurance, Zeph positioned himself with his hands together pointing upwards. And down the ball dropped, straight in.

'Well bowled, young man,' Nick said. 'One wicket for 12 runs – fair exchange. I'll be interested to see if anyone else wants to take you on.'

The other opening batsman who was now on strike certainly didn't. He played out the rest of the over as though his life depended on it.

As Tom walked back to his place at fine leg, there was a ripple of applause from the stand. Someone called out: 'Well bowled, lad, well bowled.'

He felt shy, but didn't like to pretend he hadn't heard, so he looked up and gave a grin. At least half a dozen cameras clacked into action. When he got to the boundary he was glad to be able to turn his back on them and concentrate on the cricket.

Charlie kept it tight with a maiden, and Tom followed with another one. The run-rate slowed to a trickle as both batsmen concentrated on survival.

'They've gone into their shell,' Nick said to Tom at the beginning of another over. 'I'm going to try crowding them. Ed, Josh – helmets, gents.'

With two men crouched so close to the batsman they could

almost have shaken his hand, Tom knew he had to be really accurate. The first ball bounced off the leading pad straight into Ed's hands. He swivelled and lobbed it back.

Tom bowled again. The batsman went back and played the ball down on the other side of the wicket. It bounced sharply and Josh gathered it one-handed.

It was tense, and although it didn't look as though much was happening, the crowd were very attentive. When the batsman managed to deflect the ball off his pad, there was an audible gasp of disappointment as the stalemate was broken.

Tom was completely absorbed. He'd never bowled at batsmen with the skill and patience simply to defend. It was a new challenge.

'It's a question of who cracks first,' Nick said: 'you or them. They're waiting for you to give them a bad ball to hit. We're waiting for them to get frustrated and try to force the pace. Batsmen hate not scoring. You're doing brilliantly. Just keep going.'

After a while Charlie got hit for a couple of fours. Zeph came back into the attack and again the runs dried up.

Not long after the bowling change, Tom noticed that the opener was making tiny foot movements that he hadn't made before. And a ball or two into his over, he sensed a change. Suddenly, down the wicket he came, and drove the ball faultlessly through the covers for four. Ed leapt into the air to avoid being hit, but the ball didn't really go near him.

'Don't worry about it,' Nick told him at the end of the over. 'Nice shot. Fair play to him. The important thing is he used his feet and left the crease. That's what we want.'

It was now apparent that there was a definite effort to increase the tempo. There was a wild slash at Zeph which resulted in a top-edge over the slips for four, and a rather ungainly sweep that had Josh hopping out of the way.

But then the breakthrough came. A slightly faster ball,

which surprised the batsman with its bounce, just took the inside edge and cannoned off the top of the pad to give Josh a sharp but straightforward catch.

The whole team crowded round Tom.

'You really worked for that,' Nick said, adding, 'Right lads, let's keep the pressure on.'

Tom's recollection of the rest of the afternoon was slightly hazy. This wasn't because he wasn't concentrating. He'd never concentrated so hard in his life before. It was the fact that he was concentrating so intently that meant he didn't have an overview of the game. Runs were scored, wickets fell, appeals for lbw rang out.

There was a break for tea, and Nick made him lead the team off. But all he could remember was eating a giant slice of sponge cake.

After the interval, Charlie came back on and got a straight fast one through. The middle stump flew out of the ground and the ball came careering down to Tom at fine leg. He ran back with it and the huge fast bowler leant down a little to do a high-five with him.

And then he was bowling again, bowling at the lower order who were caught between a rock and a hard place, as Nick Appleton put it. They didn't fancy Charlie's pace, but they couldn't play Tom's spin.

And then, after a huge slog had resulted in a great catch on the boundary, he found himself bowling at number eleven, with fielders all round the bat. Tom was almost sorry for him, as he played and missed, and pushed his pad down the wicket in the hope of keeping the ball out. It didn't take long before he got a thick edge onto his pad, and Ed threw up the ball with a yell. The number eleven's shoulders dropped, and he put his bat wearily under his arm and turned for the pavilion.

The applause as Tom led the team off the field was astonishing. There seemed to be a lot more people in the ground, and there, in the members' seats, Tom saw his mum and dad. He had a moment's stab of embarrassment when his mum stood up. But then everyone else did as well, so it didn't matter. He could just hear her call out, 'Well done, Tom,' and then he was through the door into the pavilion and running up the stairs to the changing room.

There was still an hour's play left, and Nick Appleton and Josh Lemmick went out to open the innings. Apart from the next two batsmen, who put their pads on, the rest of the team ripped off their boots, changed into tracksuit bottoms and lounged on the seats on the players' balcony.

'That's what I calls a nice day's cricket,' said Charlie, stretching luxuriously and then closing his eyes with a wide smile on his face. 'OK, guys. Don't wake me 'less there's a crisis.'

Tom enjoyed being on the balcony. Not only did you get a great view of the cricket, but you could look down on the crowds as well. Little Paul had made it over from school and was sitting with his dad. He'd go down in a while, but now he wanted to savour the moment.

A little later, Mr MacClaren stuck his head through the balcony door and called him for a quick word. Tom got up and joined him in the changing room.

'Remarkable, quite remarkable. The best bowling performance any of us has seen in years, Tom. We're really grateful. Couldn't have asked for more.'

Mr MacClaren smiled, but only briefly.

'The thing is,' he went on, 'well, you've turned into a bit of a sensation. Remember those snappers this morning when you got to the ground? Well, there's four times as many now, plus TV crews and more sports reporters than we've seen on the County Ground since Bradman was here in 1948. And they all want a piece of you, young man.'

He broke off to look out of the window at the cricket. 'Good shot. I really hope Appleton gets a century. Just to cement his Test place. That should have been the story, but I'm afraid you've stolen the limelight. It can be a bit unnerving, if you're not used to it. Or even if you are, come to that. We'll do our best to protect you. I've spoken to your parents – and they are so proud of you, and rightly so – and we've agreed that you will not speak to the media. Nothing, not a dicky bird. If you talk to one of them, they'll expect you to talk to all of them. But we're going to have to give them something, because otherwise they'll follow you home and set up a siege outside your house as though you were a pop star. So at the end of play there'll be what they call a photo-op, where you'll just have to pose and smile. I'll be there and I'll tell them they've only got ten minutes. Then there'll be a press conference, but not for you. All the press boys will be there, so that will be our opportunity to sneak you out the back and get you home safely without being mobbed to death. Meanwhile, your best policy is to stay up here. I know you probably wanted to go down and sit with your parents, but this is the one place on the ground where we can keep you out of the public gaze.'

Golly, thought Tom. Then he remembered Little Paul. He obviously couldn't go and sit with him if it would mean being mobbed by the media.

'Problem?' Mr MacClaren asked.

Tom told him. He nodded. 'Leave that with me, Tom. You go back onto the balcony and watch the cricket.'

Tom did so, and was just in time to see a nice late cut race past gully's outstretched hand. The score, he noticed, had gone up to 37 for none. Under the legend VISITORS, the scoreboard read 129. I did that, he thought.

A little later he noticed Mr MacClaren making his way along a row in the stand where Little Paul and his dad were sitting. After the shortest of conversations, they got up and followed him back along the row and out of sight. Five minutes after that, there was a knock at the balcony door and Mr MacClaren said, 'A couple of visitors for Tom.'

'Awesome, man, awesome.' Sherwin tilted his head. 'Wish I'd been there.'

'You should have come along.'

'Couldn't. Had to do a thing for my ma. Anyway, glad you had a ball.'

'A ball? It was just the best thing ever,' Little Paul said. 'Sitting up on that balcony next to Charlie Cruze, watching Nick Appleton batting. And there was me thinking Tom was getting too grand to come down and sit with me and Dad.'

'Too many media people. They were everywhere. They said I had to stay put. I couldn't even go and sit with Mum and Dad. And then at the end of play, I had to have this photo session –'

Little Paul took up the story: 'They had Tom posing, holding up the match ball, signing autographs.'

'Signing autographs – that's cool, man!'

'And then, when they found that Tom had been smuggled out of the ground during the press conference, they went crazy. They'd seen me and dad with him, so they turned on us – you know, for quotes and stuff.'

'I hope you didn't say anything.' Tom looked concerned.

'Just gave them a few stats. New page tomorrow: "First-Class Cricket". Can you believe this is happening?'

'As long as you didn't tell them where we live,' said Tom.

'As if. Dad told them to hop it, and so we came back home and I got your call, and here we are.'

The three boys looked down on the town from the hill in the park. Their bikes lay scattered untidily around a wastebin. After a day in the public glare, Tom had just wanted to wind down with his friends, catch up on the gossip, be ordinary again.

'Oh-oh,' said Sherwin. 'I think we got company.'

There was movement at the bottom of the hill, figures flitting through the trees. And then suddenly a moped broke cover and started to make its uncertain way up towards the summit. In addition to the helmeted driver, there was a photographer riding pillion.

'Time to go, folks,' he said, and the boys scrambled for their bikes.

'Out the back way?' Little Paul shouted, and they careered off down the track in the opposite direction.

Tom looked back and saw the moped cresting the brow of the hill. It would catch them up in no time.

'Let's split,' said Sherwin. 'Sew a bit of confusion.'

He peeled off, leaving the tarmac'd path and arcing across the grass towards the lake. Tom heard Little Paul say, 'They're everywhere!'

And sure enough, there ahead of them on the path, stooped like commandos, were five or six more photographers.

'Charge!' cried Little Paul, who was throwing himself into things. The photographers leapt out of the way, and the two boys sped on as fast as they could.

Tom risked a glance over his shoulder, and saw that the moped had chosen to pursue Sherwin. For a moment he tried to think what he would do, and then, when he saw him veer sharply to his right through some trees, he allowed himself a broad grin. Sherwin knew about the lake. Chances were that the guys on the moped did not.

Little Paul was obviously thinking the same thing, and as the path diverged, they swung left. Lake and Rose Garden, said the signpost.

They were only just in time. As they rounded the bend, they could see Sherwin wrenching his bike onto the little

113

ornamental bridge that hooped over the stream that fed the lake. He wobbled, but held his course – a manoeuvre every boy in town had perfected over the years. It was a new trick for the driver of the moped, and he didn't learn it first time.

As though in slow motion, the machine reared and then, with its front wheel swivelling violently, shot off the bridge. The driver clung on for dear life, but the photographer flew off and measured his length in the shallow water.

Sherwin saw them and headed over, stopping his bike with a neat twist. The three boys exchanged high-fives, their faces lit with laughter.

But they couldn't enjoy their moment of triumph for long. Figures were moving through the bushes. It was time to be moving again.

They pedalled furiously, steering a course between evening dog-walkers and late shoppers.

'You watch where you're going,' one woman shouted at them as Tom brushed past her bulging shopping bag.

'Didn't even touch her.'

'Silly old bat.'

They quickly left their pursuers behind, but Tom didn't want to give them the chance of getting back to their cars and following him home, so he kept up the pace.

'Let's split at the back gate. Thanks, guys, that was brilliant. See you tomorrow.' It was the last thing anyone heard him say for quite a while.

# CHAPTER 9

Tom never really managed to piece together exactly what happened next. He could remember flashing through the open gates and into the little crescent beyond them. He intended turning left and then cutting through the residential estate, using a cycle path to throw off the photographers in their cars. But he never made the turn. He remembered hearing a car engine starting up, and then he was blinded by the headlights and instinctively tried to twist his bike out of the way.

He hit the car, or the car hit him – he was never sure which way round it was – and the next thing he knew he was sailing over the car roof and onto the road.

There were fragments. He was fairly sure he heard Little Paul cry, 'Look out, Tom!' Another voice – very distant – said, 'Oh my god, the poor boy . . . Is he dead? Are you all right? Can you hear me?' That he was pretty sure was Sherwin. Then there were sirens, and then nothing, nothing at all. But there was something else, some little sliver snagged in his memory, but he just couldn't tease it out, try as often as he might . . . something familiar, he thought, some fleeting recognition. But it eluded him every time.

He came to in a hospital room. His first glance took in a tableful of cards and a bowl of grapes. Then he moved his head the other way.

His mother's face loomed over him. 'Say something to me. Oh, Tom.' She flung her arms around him and kissed him. Then she burst into tears.

'I've been so worried, we both have. It's been awful. Say something, anything.'

'How long have I been –?'

Tom suddenly sat up.

'The cricket . . . what day is it? How much have I missed?'

'It's all right. The cricket's fine.'

Gently she pushed him back on his pillows.

'They've done very well – Nick Appleton scored a century – what a nice man . Look, he brought a card – signed by all the team.'

She reached across and picked the largest of the many cards. The signatures were slightly blurry, so he stopped looking at them.

'But what happened?'

'No one's sure, but the police are still looking for the driver –'

'No, Mum. What happened in the match?'

'Oh,' she smiled. 'As I say, Nick scored a century, and the whole team made a very big score. And then they bowled the other lot out.'

'So it's over?'

'Yes, and they won.'

Seeing the look on his face, she laughed. 'You wouldn't have been allowed to go back and play even if you'd come round in time. Everyone was terribly worried about you. The doctors said you'd be all right, but you could see they were worried.'

Tom put his hand up to his head and felt a large bandage. He also realised he had a headache.

'You mustn't overdo it. Lie back and rest. I'll tell the nurse you've come round. I'm sure the doctors will want to see you. And I must tell your dad.'

She reached for the button dangling down beside the bed and then got her mobile phone out of her handbag.

*

'In the wars again, Tom? We're going to have to put him under house arrest, Mrs Marlin, to keep him out of mischief.'

Dr Gupta was his usual cheery self, and bustled around listening to Tom's chest through his stethoscope, shining a torch into his eyes and tapping his joints to test his reactions.

'We'll take you down for a brain scan this afternoon. Don't worry, Mrs Marlin, I am confident there will be nothing wrong in the brains department. But perhaps,' he said to Tom with a twinkle in his eye, 'perhaps we'll uncover the secret of this bowling prodigy's extraordinary skills. I am your biggest fan, Tom. And to see you in the County team – amazing, just amazing!'

'And look where it landed him – fighting for his life in a hospital bed.'

'You cannot blame the noble game of cricket for that, Mrs Marlin. It is the idiots in the media who think a photograph is worth risking a life. Why do they not learn after they kill the lovely Lady Di?'

'Well, it wouldn't have happened if he hadn't gone racing off on his bike without his helmet. Have you any idea what you put us through, Tom?'

'Shhh, Mrs Marlin, not now, I think. I'm sure Tom regrets the ordeal you've been through, but now I think we should let him rest. And so should you. Your vigil is over. Your lovely boy is back – back, undamaged. And you should go home, home to your bed, and have a proper sleep yourself. You can come back whenever you like, but first – home to bed. That's doctor's orders. Meanwhile we will keep our patient under observation until he is fully recovered.'

The hospital routine was familiar from the last time. The days passed in an undemanding round of drinks, meals, medication and examinations. Mr McCulloch looked in. 'Just to give my handiwork the once-over,' as he put it, but mainly, Tom thought, to sit and chat about cricket for a few minutes. 'I won't jeopardise your recovery by telling you the news from Lord's, but I will tell you young Appleton is about the only England batsman who looks the part.'

Later on the same day, the nurse came into his room to see whether he was awake.

'There's a call for you, Tom. All right to take it?'

'Who is it?'

'It's all right, it's not the press or anything like that.'

'Hello,' he said when she handed him the receiver.

'Tom! Nick – Nick Appleton. Hello?'

Tom was literally speechless.

'This is your captain speaking. Are you receiving me?'

Tom managed a shaky 'Yes.'

'Good. I was so pleased when I heard you'd come round. We were all desperately worried.'

Tom glanced at his bedside table.

'Thanks for the card – it's great. Can you thank everybody for signing it?'

'Sure. It was their idea. They were really gutted. But I'm not with the county at the moment – I'm at Lord's. Not going according to plan to be honest with you.'

'But Mr McCulloch said you were doing well.'

'Seventy in the first innings. Should have been a ton. Need a big one in the second innings. Look, I've got to go, but I'm really really pleased you're back in the land of the living. Oh, and one last thing. The committee have agreed with me that you should be awarded your 2nd XI cap. So congratulations – you deserve it.'

Tom stammered out his thanks and good wishes for the rest of the Test match, and then lay back on his pillows. Had he really just been speaking to Nick Appleton – from Lord's? Had he really been awarded his 2nd XI cap? He put his hand up and felt his bandage. Perhaps the bang on the head had affected him more than the doctors thought?

But no, there was the card from the county team. He picked it up and smiled at Charlie's huge signature right across the middle. Underneath he'd written, 'You get better, Pal – fast.'

No, it was all real. Now he needed to do exactly what Charlie said: Get better. And get back out on the cricket field . . .

Tom's parents were the only ones allowed to see him to begin with. He found their visits a bit of a trial. His mum cried quite often, and even his dad teared up on occasion. 'We thought we'd lost you,' he said very quietly, almost to himself. Then, as though to shake himself out of it, he said, 'If I ever meet the bloke driving that car, I'll wring his ruddy neck.'

Although he was pleased to see them, it was a huge relief when the nurse told him he could have other visitors. 'But only for a quarter of an hour. And they're not to over-stimulate you, doctor says.'

The first to come were Little Paul and his dad. Paul was the one you had to watch out for over-stimulating, Tom thought as he listened to his friend's dramatic account of his accident.

'I got two letters from the number plate. The police were really pleased with me. I mean, we went straight to you – never thought they'd just drive off. And I got the make. Peugeot. Peugeot 307 – saloon, not the station wagon. Blue.'

Little Paul's dad coughed. 'The police had mixed feelings about the whole episode, Paul. I know we've been through all this, and I know the paparazzi were after Tom, but you were all riding far too fast.'

'Dad! They were chasing us!'

'I know. But the fact is, if you hadn't been hurtling through the gates at 100 miles an hour, Tom wouldn't have been hit by the car. Anyway, water under the bridge –'

'And moped off the bridge,' Little Paul interrupted. He caught Tom's eye and they both laughed.

'And a very good story it made too. But we need to look forward now, and there's something I've been thinking about for a little while that I thought I'd mention to you, Tom. Have you thought about an agent?'

Tom looked blank. An agent? What was he talking about?

'You're the biggest news item of the summer. All the press, TV, radio – everybody wants the story.'

'Dad's right. I've had to start a whole new cuttings album. Look!'

Little Paul struggled with his rucksack and finally produced a large folder, marked 'Tom: Press Cuttings'. He unloaded it onto Tom's lap. It was heavy.

'Paul's right. It may not be what you want, but it's inevitable, and given that it's going to happen anyway, it might be sensible to have someone who can help you manage it for you.'

'And Dad's got a friend who –'

'Mike Field, his name is. Known him for years. I think you'd like him, and he's very good at what he does.'

Tom wondered what that was, but didn't ask. Instead, he said he'd think about it, and cautiously opened the cuttings album . . .

'An agent? Who on earth suggested that?'

Tom had decided to run the idea past Mr MacClaren rather than his parents. But he didn't seem keen.

'Well, I suppose it's not such a bad idea. It's just that some agents are – well, the line is they're only out to help their clients; but I have to deal with them, and most of them are really only interested in feathering their own nest. On the other hand, we can't have a repetition of that bun fight we had the other day. There's no way we can stop the media being interested in you. You're top of the hit parade at the moment. My phone has not stopped ringing, and of course if you had an agent, then they'd know there was someone to go to. This has all blown up beyond anyone's expectation.'

He broke off and looked directly into Tom's face.

'But the important thing is that you're alive and well on the way to recovery, Tom. I felt so bad about what happened, so awfully sorry for your parents. Perhaps we should have sent you away, just for a night or two – the whole lot of you to a hotel. Instead of leaving you to the tender mercies of the media.'

Here his face grew dark.

'Anyway, that nurse'll be in in a minute to tell me time's up, and I don't want to waste my visit on all the negative stuff. Everybody's absolutely delighted with your debut, and I took the liberty of asking your parents for the match ball back, and took it off to our engraver.'

Here he fidgeted in his jacket pocket, and produced the ball. Around the seam was a silver band, on which Tom's figures were beautifully engraved.

'Oh wow!' he said, as he held it up to inspect it. 'That's brilliant. Can I keep it?'

'Of course you can, Tom. And may it be the first of many. Now, I must get back to the office. I think we're going to lose the Test, worst luck, but Nick is playing a blinder. He's got a century. It's not going to be enough, but it shows the Aussies we're going to fight back and give them a good run for their money. Meanwhile, we're in with a chance of the championship for the first time in a decade. I haven't felt this excited about a season in years. Let's get you well and out of here and back on the pitch with a ball in your hand.'

The nurse put her head round the door: 'That's your fifteen minutes, I'm afraid.'

# CHAPTER 10

M IKE Field was a small, slightly chubby man with an open,
smiling face. He sat on the sofa in Little Paul's house
with Little Paul's cuttings album open on the coffee table before him. Tom had spent an amazed couple of hours reading the
hundreds of column inches devoted to his first – and only – day
as a first-class cricketer.

'They love him. Even though they nearly killed him.
SUPERKID SPINNER, SPIN SENSATION, SUPER STAR OF SPIN – the
subs are in seventh heaven. They must spend their nights
dreaming up headlines like those. And then you've got the
tragic side: KID CRICKETER IN COMA, TRAGIC END TO FIRST-
CLASS DAY, etc etc. You're the real deal, Tom. An absolute gift.
Potentially, it's a fortune.'

'We don't care about the money,' Tom's mum butted in.
'We want some way of protecting Tom, taking the pressure
off him.'

'Absolutely. I know where you're coming from, Mrs
Marlin. But if we get this right – if I get it right, if you want
me – then there will be a lot of money coming in. And I'm
quite sure that wouldn't go amiss. Set up a nice trust to look
after Tom's education. Charles could advise you on that side
of things.'

He nodded at Little Paul's father, who held up his hands
and said: 'Let's not get ahead of ourselves. If money comes in,
then of course it'll need looking after in Tom's best interests.
But first and foremost, we've got to tame this media frenzy.'

'Absolutely.'

He smiled his open smile and brought his hands together to signify that he'd laid his cards on the table.

'What do you think, Rick?'

'I don't know, Charles. It's all so – unexpected. You just don't imagine you'll find your family all over the news.'

Tom looked at his parents. They were clearly struggling to come to terms with it all. He could see it was hard for them, but he'd had to smile when he came across the family picture posed in the back garden on half the front pages of the nationals in Little Paul's album.

'We are where we are, Rick. And let's face it, there are huge positives. I mean, the lad's a genius! His bowling that afternoon at the county ground. Well, I've not seen the like of it. Ever. You can't pretend it hasn't happened. Or that it's going to stop – unless Tom gives up playing. And you don't want to do that, do you, Tom?'

Tom shook his head.

'Well, then,' Little Paul's dad went on. 'Would you like Mike to work for you?'

Tom liked Mike Field. He felt he could trust him.

'Yes – I would.'

He looked at his parents. They seemed to relax suddenly. It was now out of their hands. Someone else could take on the burden of trying to protect him from the media.

'Nice enough chap, Mike Field,' said Mr MacClaren. 'Though of course he's now badgering me for a contract for you, Tom. Still, that's his job, and I really do believe he has your best interests at heart. And he'll have my eternal gratitude if he can get the media off my back. I was going demented with the phone ringing non-stop. Now hopefully I can get back to thinking about cricket. Which is why I wanted to have a word, Tom.'

Tom looked at him expectantly. He felt fine. They'd taken

the bandage off and now he just had a large plaster over the wound where, the nurse told him, things were taking their course. The stitches, she said, would simply melt away as part of the healing process.

'Am I going to be able to play again soon?'

Mr MacClaren cleared his throat. 'The medicos have put you strictly "off games" for a fortnight But at least they're satisfied there's no serious damage up here.' He tapped his own forehead. 'That's the most important thing. The question really is at what level you should start playing again.'

Mr MacClaren saw the disappointment in his face.

'As I say, that's the question. It hasn't been decided yet. We are all really concerned that you don't overdo it by coming back too early or being placed under too much pressure.'

'But I'll be fine. I promise,' Tom said.

'I'm sure you will be, Tom. But we've got your parents to consider. They've had a pretty rough ride through this. Your mother was in a terrible state. And for a while was dead set on your never playing again. It's all right' – he spread his hand in a calming gesture – 'your father and I talked her round. But if we put you out there' – he indicated the empty outfield spread so invitingly beneath his office window – 'in a County game, and you find it too hard going, she might change her mind. And then where would we be?'

Tom let his head drop. He hated things being decided for him like this without anyone asking him.

'As I say,' Mr MacClaren went on, 'it hasn't been decided yet. I can tell you that Nick is really keen to have you back in the side. Even with Steve Draper fit again, and not bowling badly, Nick wants you. He thinks it our only chance of winning the championship. Not that he'll be playing much for us, now that the Tests have started. There's one round of County matches just before the last two Tests and the word is that all the England boys will be released to play in them. We've got

Phil Eldridge's lot, which could be interesting, the way things are going.'

Mr MacClaren looked out of the window.

'Yes,' he resumed, 'very interesting. I think we'd like to have you match fit for that, but if we can get you in a game earlier, so much the better.'

Tom's mum was waiting for him when he came out of Mr MacClaren's office. She was enjoying the sunshine in the members' enclosure. But Tom wasn't feeling very sunny and he sat in stony silence for the short drive home.

The weeks that followed were frustrating rather than boring. There was too much going on for Tom to be bored. Mike Field spoke to him every day and told him how he was getting on with sponsors – a surprising number of firms wanted to be associated with the One Day Wonder, as some of the press had christened him. He also outlined his media strategy. 'I'm finding your convalescence quite useful,' he chuckled. 'They're all deeply sorry about what happened and content to hold off for the time being. But that won't last. You'll have to come out of hiding some time. But in the meantime, we're not going to let them get close to you.' He laughed again. Tom liked the laugh. It sounded reassuring.

In the meantime, Mike Field issued press releases on Tom's recovery, and then there was the great day when it was decided that Tom should go and watch a bit of cricket at the county ground. A very limited number of photographers were allowed a five minute session, but no one was permitted to ask any questions.

He felt hesitant outside the home changing room door, but as soon as he opened it he was greeted with a warm reception. Charlie came up and practically smothered him in a bear hug, and Zeph held out a friendly hand. There were one or two new faces, and a rather lean man in his late twenties came up and said, 'Hi, I'm Steve Draper, the guy you're putting out of business.' Then he smiled and offered his hand. 'I heard all about it – sensational. I'm really pleased for you. Hope I'll get to play with you at some stage. The two of us can give these guys a rest.' He tilted his head to indicate Charlie and Zeph.

'Hey man, he can do all the bowling s'far as we're concerned. Ain't that right, Zeph?'

'Sure thing. But maybe you won't be playing County, Charlie – maybe you'll force your way into the England team.'

'Come on, man, they got their bowlers. They're not going to break that lot up.'

'Might have to. They're not taking many wickets. Another couple of five-fors and they'll have to take you seriously.'

It was certainly true that the England bowling quartet were not making the headway that was needed. England made a spirited showing in the second Test, piling up the runs – Nick Appleton scoring his second century of the series – but the Australians simply dug in on an easy-paced pitch and ran up an even more impressive total. The match petered out in a dull draw, and sections of the press started calling for wholesale changes.

Tom's life remained busy. There were meetings with his new sponsors. One of these was a local clothing firm, and he had to spend a morning being photographed in things he would never have chosen to wear himself. He also had another interview with the police, just in case he could add anything to what he'd told them immediately after he came to. But although he was still nagged by the thought that there was something, it remained beyond recall.

'That's OK, son. Don't worry about it. But if anything does come back to you, you've got our number.'

The man got up to go, but then hesitated. He got out his

notebook again and said, slightly shamefaced, 'Could I get your autograph for my boy?'

Tom stared at the notebook, opened at a blank page, and took the pen that was offered with it. Then he wrote: 'Tom Marlin'. It looked rather unimpressive, so he then put a line under it with a half-hearted flourish.

He could tell the policeman didn't think much of it either. But he said thank you, very politely, and strode off down the garden to his waiting squad car.

The subject of autographs came up at his next meeting with Mike Field. 'Probably worth practising, you know. Just get a blank piece of paper and try out what feels right. Aim for economy but make it look slightly – I don't know, flamboyant.'

Tom thought back to the signatures in his get-well card from the county team. He could see what Mike Field meant.

'Because,' Mike Field said, 'you're going to be asked for an awful lot of autographs. I've spared you the post-bag, but you've had thousands of letters.'

'Thousands?'

'Letters, cards, invitations, offers, requests. And they're still coming, thick and fast. But don't worry, you don't have to answer them. My PA's onto it.'

It was amazing that complete strangers were writing to him.

As though reading his thought, Mike Field said, 'It goes with the territory, Tom. You are now public property, a celeb. And unless you want to announce your retirement, that's the way it's going to be for the foreseeable. Look, I've got to dash. But you get practising your autograph. We're going to need it.'

'That one,' said Sherwin. 'Definitely that one.'

He pointed to one of about a dozen signatures that Tom had tried out.

Little Paul said, 'He's right. That one's cool. Now you just have to do it over and over again till you can do it right every time. Here, I'll get you some paper. You can stay in my room if you like.'

'What are you going to do?'

But the door had already slammed. Tom looked at the blank page and sighed.

The day came when Tom was allowed to start training again. Mr MacClaren tried to keep it quiet, but somehow word got out and there was a scrum of photographers milling round the entrance to the ground when Tom was driven through.

'Don't take any notice of them,' Mr MacClaren said. 'Just concentrate on your bowling.'

Tom didn't mind too much. He was just thrilled to be allowed to play again. When he opened the changing room door he found Nick Appleton putting his pads on. He got up to greet him.

'Tom – you're back. That's great.' He pumped Tom's hand. 'Are you all right? Let's look at you. H'm. You're going to have a bit of a scar, aren't you?' he said, inspecting the healed wound. 'Still, it's mostly under the hair line. Just don't go bald early like Dennis!'

Dennis Harmon, the other player padded up, aimed an air punch at him, and said, 'You wait, Skip, many more Tests against the Aussies and you'll lose yours.'

'Well done on your batting,' Tom said. 'It was brilliant.'

'Thanks,' said Nick Appleton. 'But it wasn't enough. I still need practice. You come in my net when you're changed.'

Tom was rather nervous as he stood at the end of his run waiting to bowl his first ball. What if he'd forgotten how to do it and he was just a useless kid that everyone had made a silly fuss over? He ran in and released the ball. It pitched outside leg stump, turned sharply, lifted and took the top of Nick Appleton's bat, flying at catchable height into the back of the net.

'I bat for six and a half hours against the Australians, and you clean me up first ball after a three-week layoff,' he said as he retrieved the ball. 'I ask you.'

After he'd finished his session, he came down the net pulling his helmet off and throwing his batting gloves into it.

He nodded to Tom to join him and the two walked across the outfield to the pavilion. 'Honestly Tom, all the time I was batting against the Aussies I never had to work as hard as I have for the last twenty-five minutes. I've made my mind up. Provided you feel up to it, I want you back in the 1sts straight away. Cricket's cricket whatever level, so if you're fit to play, you might as well play at your level. Which is definitely the first team.'

Yes, Yes, Yes!!! Tom yelled to himself inside his head.

'Thanks, Nick,' is what he said. 'Thanks a lot. That's great.'

'Good. The big question is, will your mum wear it?'

'She'll be all right.' She was certainly getting pretty excited about the sponsorship deals Mike Field kept bringing in. She'd even started talking about ditching her job at County Hall.

SUPER SPIN KID BACK WITH COUNTY blared the headlines.

The match overlapped with the third Test, and there was much texting between the two grounds. Both teams fielded first, but there was a stark contrast in their fortunes. Australia made a sound start and then consolidated. Although the England bowlers had their moments, their efforts were sabotaged by poor fielding.

'4 cts drpd [unsmiley face] how u do? N,' Tom read in the tea interval at the County ground. He was able to reply: 'gd tanx. 8wkts. Tom', to which the reply was 'u or team?' He wrote back: 'team'. Twenty minutes later he was able to send a further text: '+ me'.

It had been a great day, starting with a spectacular over

from Charlie in which the opening batsman had his off-stump knocked clean out of the ground. Zeph bowled well and kept it tight at his end. Dennis Harmon let them bowl in tandem for an hour, then summoned Tom.

'Just do what you do for Nick. Good luck.'

After a shaky start – his first ball slipped out of his hand and failed to pitch, but the batsman was so surprised he missed it – Tom settled into his rhythm, and the wickets started to come: two before lunch, with one borderline lbw appeal turned down; and then four in the afternoon session. Zeph nipped one out just before tea to reduce the visitors to 140 for 8.

That went up to 160 as the tail-enders had a go, but with an easy stumping and a brilliant catch by Charlie in the deep, Tom wrapped things up and took his personal tally to 8 wickets.

He was sitting on the balcony watching the last over of the day when his mobile vibrated in his pocket. It was a message from Nick Appleton: 'Well done. Better than us. Wish u were here. N'.


'They're going to have to consider him,' Mike Field said as he waited with Mr MacClaren before the onslaught of the press conference.

'Well, Bozzer's been here all day.'

'I thought he was interested in Charlie Cruze.'

'Ostensibly. But he's just seen Tom take 8 wickets for about 30. He's going to have to report that to his fellow selectors.'

Mike Field nodded.

'It's far too soon for him, of course,' said the Secretary. 'It would be ridiculous to throw a boy into an Ashes series.'

Mike Field looked at him and raised an eyebrow. 'He's the people's choice. And the current lot can't buy a wicket at the moment. If it wasn't for his age Tom'd be a shoo-in.'

130

'I know,' said the Secretary, 'but the fact is, he's just a kid. Can you imagine him facing Brad Dawson with the entire Australian team round him sledging him. They've come here to retain the Ashes, and they're not going to pull their punches.'

'I'm not saying you're wrong. All I am saying is that the press boys are going to be calling for Tom's selection.'

'I don't want anyone to think it comes from us. So if you can avoid stoking the flames I'd be very grateful. Oh Lord, here they come.'

The door at the far end of the room burst open.

'Mr Field, Mr MacClaren, do you think Tom Marlin has done enough to be called up for England?'

Ninety-five miles away, Philip Eldridge, the England captain, was asked the identical question.

'No, no, no, no, no,' he said. 'Which word do you not understand? We are engaged in the toughest challenge in world cricket, and this is not the time to be distracted by ridiculous fantasies. There is no easy solution, no magic wand. We have a good team capable of doing the job, but we are not playing as well as we know we can. What we need is to start taking our chances, not pander to some silly, sentimental wish-fulfilment on the part of the public.'

'Well, he did rather lay himself open to it, didn't he?' Mike Field said as he spread the papers across Mr MacClaren's desk next morning.

One tabloid printed photographs of the five England players regarded as being the weakest links in the team. SHOULD THESE MEN STAY IN THE TEST TEAM? read the headline, and under it came the answer: NO, NO, NO, NO, NO. The first picture was of a scowling Philip Eldridge himself. Another sports editor simply devoted his back page to a large photo of Tom and his bowling figures under the banner headline YES, YES, YES, YES, YES.

'Nothing I could do about it. I mean, they were going to go with that line anyway, but Eldridge just gave them a stick to beat him with.'

MacClaren sighed. 'He's right, though. The Aussies would have Tom for breakfast.'

The phone on his desk rang. As did Mike Field's mobile. They exchanged glances. It was going to be a long day.

But it was also a wet one. No play was possible at the county ground, and the Test was an on-off affair with the players coming out for a few overs between the showers. Australia piled on more runs while the England bowlers toiled without luck. Two more catches went down. The crowd, who were bored by all the interruptions anyway, decided to give vent to their feelings by booing vigorously. A few signs were held up for the television cameras: 'Sack Eldridge' got a cheer, but the first 'We Want Tom' went down very well. And soon the crowd were chanting: 'We Want Tom, We Want Tom!'

Next morning it seemed the whole country wanted Tom. One tabloid printed a 'We Want Tom' poster for people to stick up in their windows. Another offered car stickers and a third, tee-shirts. In the quality papers the debate raged fiercely. Yes, Tom Marlin should be promoted to the England team, said one ex-Test player. Another was equally adamant that no, Tom Marlin shouldn't be picked. Philip Eldridge refused to talk to journalists. When they cornered Nick Appleton, the questions didn't leave much room to hide: 'Would you pick Marlin if you were captain?'

'I thought he wriggled out of it pretty well,' said Mike Field with a laugh. 'What was it? "I have every confidence in the wisdom of the selectors, and I and the rest of the team are a hundred per cent behind Phil Eldridge, who has been and remains a great England captain." Clever. He could see they were trying to use him to put another nail in Eldridge's coffin – but that would have exposed him as disloyal.'

'Nick can look after himself. It's Tom I'm worried about. The hue and cry is simply going to get worse and worse,' said MacClaren. And then, looking straight at Mike Field, he said: 'It may be time for Operation Blank Screen.'

Mike Field suppressed a smile. He'd been amused by Mac-Claren's wish to give the plan a military title.

'I'll put everyone on stand-by.'

'Thank you. Now, if only it would stop raining, we could get on with the business of trying to win the County championship.'

There were only intermittent breaks in the rain – enough for the Australians to go on to a total guaranteeing them safety, and for Dennis Harmon to lead a successful assault on batting points before immediately declaring and asking his bowlers to do a job for him in the limited time available. This time it was Charlie Cruze's turn to hog the limelight. With Zeph as his constant foil, he ripped through the top order, taking the first five wickets.

In the end, the weather won. But the other County matches had also been affected, so they hadn't lost out. England, on the other hand, were in trouble. After their disappointing bowling performance, they looked distinctly shaky in the one innings there was time for. For once Nick Appleton failed, and with a clatter of early wickets, it fell to Philip Eldridge to put in a captain's innings.

His dogged 90 under difficult conditions was enough to kill off talk of replacing him. But the drawn match meant England remained behind in the series. Eldridge still re-fused to answer questions about Tom, so the press asked the

Australian captain for his view. Don 'Don't call me Bradman' Spiers, was amused.

'Yeah, sure, if they want to put him in the team, that's up to them. It won't worry us. If he's good enough, pick him. But, look, England aren't out of it yet. And to be frank, the last thing they want now is a gimmick. But if they pick the kid, we'll certainly autograph a bat for him.'

'Cheeky blighter!' was Mike Field's response to that. 'He thinks he's got the Ashes in the bag.'

'Maybe he has. What are the selectors going to do?' the Secretary said. 'Bozzer wouldn't say a word, but it must have come up at their meetings. You haven't heard anything on your grapevine?'

'No, everybody's playing it very close to their chests. But they are going to have to talk to us before they do it. They wouldn't risk picking him and then being told he couldn't play.'

BACK-TO-BACK TESTS: ENGLAND MUST WIN BOTH bellowed one headline the following morning. MAKE OR LEG-BREAK TIME FOR ENGLAND another suggested. TEST COUNTDOWN FOR TOM stated a third.


Operation Blank Screen went smoothly. Instead of going home after nets one afternoon, Tom was smuggled out of the ground in an anonymous white van. Twenty miles out of town the van pulled in off a B road, and Tom got out. Next to the van was a black limousine with smoked glass. The driver's window slid down.

'Hello,' the driver said. 'I'm Des. Hop in.'


MARLIN'S MYSTERY DISAPPEARANCE; TOM, WHERE ARE YOU? the headlines wailed.

'You're just going to have to be patient,' Mike Field told a room full of baying journalists. 'You make the kid's life hell,

134

what do you expect? We had no option. That's all I have to say
– except that he will be playing in the County's next match.'

'So he'll be up against Eldridge?'

'If Eldridge plays, he'll be playing against Tom Marlin.
That's all folks. Thank you.'


Clunk. Ping!

Tom had scored 12,000 points, the Pirates of the Caribbean
pinball machine told him. He grinned and released the silver
ball once more. Up it shot, and round it whizzed, rebounding
off the various features, until it finally dropped down towards
his flippers. He pinged it up the board again. When he got
tired of that, he'd go for a leisurely swim. He could hear his
mum and dad in the pool now.

They were enjoying the best holiday of their lives at a stun-
ningly well-appointed hideaway Mike Field had found for
them. 'Elite Retreats': he'd producing a glossy brochure with
a flourish. 'You're not the first celebrity who's needed a bit of
a break from the press pack, Tom, and these people look after
you extremely well, while keeping you out of the public eye.'

'Is it expensive?' Tom's mum had asked.

'Fabulously,' Mike had replied with a laugh. 'I had the
sponsors fighting each other to pick up the tab. You just go
and enjoy yourselves. Leave the rest to me.'

And they were certainly enjoying themselves.

Later that evening Tom sat back on the sofa in front of a
TV screen even bigger than the one in Little Paul's house and
watched his own picture on the news. 'Marlin, Master of Spin,
Mysteriously Vanished' the little subtitle that ran across the
bottom of the screen said.

'We have been reassured,' said the newsreader, 'that Tom
Marlin and his family are perfectly safe, but have decided to
have a complete break from the public exposure that has made
their life so difficult in recent days.'

Here there were pictures of a scrum of reporters thronging the crescent outside their house.

'Oh Rick,' said Tom's mum happily, 'What will the neighbours say?'

'You know, love,' he replied, 'I don't give a fig.'

They both laughed happily, and Tom felt glad that after all they'd been through they were getting something back. Then he knelt down and put on the DVD he'd selected from about 200 in a special cupboard just to the right of the television.

# CHAPTER 11

O PERATION Blank Screen provoked media uproar. The headlines now wailed: WHERE IS TOM?

Night after night Mike Field would issue another bland statement. Tom and family were safe and happy. They would return to normal life when the fuss died down. 'The ball is in your court,' he told journalists, before slipping away with a smile.

Tom came in to the county ground to practise with the rest of the team. There was no secret about that. The secret was how he came in, and where he came from, and where he went after the training session. Some surmised that he was moved around from one safe house to another. Others imagined him being passed around members of the county team, and set up surveillance on everyone who played, or could conceivably play, for the first team. This produced some high-octane exchanges between cricketers' wives and the paparazzi, and one sequence of photographs which sparked a lively exchange of solicitors' letters and the threat of court action. But that was just a side-show.

'Have you got him in the boot, Nick?' they shouted at Nick Appleton as he drove through the gates. He smiled and gave them a cheery wave.

'Charlie, have you got him in the boot?' they yelled at Charlie Cruze as he drove in. Charlie put his head back and laughed. It drove them mad.

But it also drove them to pool resources. There were only so many vehicles entering the ground and Tom had to be in one of them. There was a concerted effort to follow every vehicle that came out of any of the gates, until a posse of press and paparazzi ended up driving halfway to Cornwall behind a lorry stacked with portaloos.

Mike Field was more genial than usual at the next day's press conference, making several references to the joys of the open road and the health benefits of sea air.

'You're torturing us,' one experienced hack said to him when he managed to take him to one side. 'I know it must be tough for his parents, but the boy's pure gold. You're making us look utter prats, but we have to have a story. The public are going mental. What are you going to do if he gets picked for the Test team? The entire country will go nuts.' He broke off and looked at Mike Field. Not a flicker of a response. 'Ah . . . and if they don't pick him the entire country will go nuts.' He stopped. 'It's win-win all the way to the bank isn't it? Mike, you're a genius. I admit it. It's pure genius. The goose that lays the golden egg.'

Mike Field smiled, pityingly. 'Bill, get a life. Go home. I've got nothing for you.'

'Please,' said Bill, 'give me something. Anything. What's his favourite programme? Which football team does he support? I've got to have something. My editor's on my case morning noon and night. Does he like bananas? Mike, please . . .'

Tom was having a wonderful time, and the rest of the team were enjoying the drama as well.

'What is it tonight, Double O Seven? The helicopter or the midget submarine?' Steve Draper asked.

'Oh, just the portaloo as usual, I expect,' Tom replied with a grin.

The two spinners were becoming friends and Steve was always happy to talk to Tom about bowling.

'I can't compete with genius, mate,' he'd say, 'but I do have experience.'

Whether it was field-placing, mixing it up so as to keep the batsmen guessing or dealing with someone trying to hit you out of the ground, Steve certainly knew his stuff, and Tom hung on every word.

'Just a shame you can't tell me how to turn it square, make it dip at the last minute and then take off like a rocket,' Steve would say with a grin.

Tom was glad Steve had been back in the firsts during his convalescence. But what he really wanted was for them both to play in the first team. And when it came to the crunch match against Philip Eldridge's Leicestershire, that's what happened.

Nick Appleton called them aside a couple of days before-hand and said, 'Right you guys, we're going with two spin-ners. The pitches are drying out now. That'll be a belter for the first two days' – he indicated the square with a nod. Tom looked out to where the groundsman was sitting on the heavy roller. 'But after that, it'll favour spin, so let's have two!'

He smiled at them as their faces lit up.


'T. Potter – Electrician' was the legend across the back of the van doors. Terry Potter opened them to let Tom climb in. He wedged himself into a little gap between racks of tools and equipment, coils of wire, and a jumble of fittings.

'They don't give up, do they?' Terry said as they slipped out of the back gate. Tom had pulled a sheet over him to be sure of frustrating the cameras that clicked and clacked at every car, van, lorry and milk float that ran the gauntlet into or out of the ground.

'Or Lor!' Terry said after a few minutes, 'I think they're following us.'

Operation Side-step, Tom said to himself. Instead of meet-ing Des as usual, Terry drove to a second location, a farm at the end of a gated road. There Tom transferred to a tractor and was smuggled off the farm to a new rendezvous. It meant getting back a bit late for his early-evening swim, but he enjoyed the game of cat-and-mouse with the press.

The trouble was, there was no one to share the excitement with. He was missing his friends. He decided to ask Mike if Sherwin and Little Paul could come over. They'd love it, especially being picked up by Des.

'Wicked, man!'

'Unbelievable!'

The boys romped noisily and splashily in the pool. After that they took it in turns at the pinball machine and then had a tournament of air hockey. Tom won.

'You've been practising,' said Sherwin.

Tom shrugged.

'And you can come down here any time you like?' Little Paul narrowed his eyes as though if he looked closely enough he could find the fatal flaw. Then, with a shake of his head, he gave it up. 'Died and gone to heaven!' he said with a sigh.

'That was the best pizza in the world, man,' said Sherwin after their supper.

'Glad you enjoyed it,' said Mike Field who had come over for a drink and a chat with Tom's parents.

'You boys are going to have to be off in about half an hour,' he added.

There was a groan.

'You can come again,' he said as he went back to his drink in the lounge.

'Before we go,' Little Paul said, 'I bet you're not signing any autographs at the moment, are you Tom?'

Tom shook his head. He never got close enough to anyone to be even asked for an autograph.

'Here,' said Little Paul, producing some sheets of blank paper and a pen.

Tom looked at him wonderingly.

'Practice makes perfect. You need to keep your hand in. Look, you may get picked for England. Think about it.'

'Where are you two going?'

'Air hockey. We need the practice!'

On the morning of the match Tom arrived early – in one of the catering vans. But even at half-nine there were so many media people milling about that they needed the police to force a passage through for them.

'Out you hop, dearie. See you at lunch,' said one of the waitresses as the side door flew back and he hopped down some steps into the pavilion basement. Even that brief exposure was caught by a well-placed snapper.

'Good morning, Tom,' said Mr MacClaren. He ushered him quickly upstairs and into the secretary's office. Tom saw the daily papers strewn over the desk. STAND-OFF BETWEEN STAR AND STICK-IN-THE MUD was one headline, but Mr MacClaren quickly covered them with a file.

'Don't let that rubbish distract you. But it is relevant to what I have to say to you. We're in a potentially difficult situation. We're hosts and I do not want boorish behaviour stirred up by the tabloid press to taint our reputation. Phil Eldridge is a decent man, a fine cricketer, and a successful England captain. I do not want him humiliated. I know none of this is your fault, but I would just ask you to be extra careful not to do or say anything that might possibly inflame things.'

He broke off, and then smiled. He waved his arm at the ground beyond his window. 'Look out there. We're going to have a full house, every seat taken. And that's thanks to you, young man. So, go upstairs and get changed. And then go out and enjoy yourself.'

As Tom walked along the corridor, he was aware of noise

on the stairs up to the dressing rooms. Loud, but unfamiliar voices. He turned a corner and found the visiting team looking at him with interest. One face in particular looked familiar.

'There he is, Phil, the People's Choice,' someone said to the man he half-recognised. It was only after the men had set off up the next flight of stairs that Tom realised he had just met the England captain.

Nick Appleton won the toss and decided to bat. Phil Eldridge fielded at first slip. He wore a cap and kept very still most of the time. While the Leicestershire wicket-keeper was pretty vocal, Eldridge was much more restrained. He clapped the occasional delivery, but was far more reserved than the rest of his players.

There was a groundswell of partisanship in the crowd, some of whom waved WE WANT TOM pages torn from one of the tabloids. At one point, Dennis Harmon snicked a ball low and wide of Eldridge. It wasn't a catch, but some wag in the crowd called out: 'Wakey Wakey, Eldridge!' which in turn provoked a bit of a laugh and one or two faint-hearted chants of 'We Want Tom!' Tom felt his ears tingle.

After lunch Eldridge had the satisfaction of taking a really sharp chance and Nick came back to the dressing room with 64 to his name.

'Should have left it,' he said bitterly. But he'd laid the foundation of a good score, and spent the rest of the day happily clapping his batsmen as the total headed past 350.

Tom enjoyed the day too, though he was confined to the Home changing room.

'But if you'd like your friends to come up, I'll happily invite them,' Mr MacClaren said.

Tom had told Sherwin and Little Paul he'd get them in. They were very excited. Sherwin was speechless when Charlie

Cruze shook him by the hand and ushered him onto the players' balcony.

Tom exchanged glances with Little Paul. As he did so, he noticed something. Something was different. But he couldn't tell what.

'New shoes,' Little Paul said, as though guessing what was going through his mind.

Sure enough, Little Paul was wearing new shoes. And, Tom realised, they had slightly raised heels. That was it – Paul seemed slightly less little. He grinned and nodded his head in recognition.

'Very smart. They look expensive.'

'They were. And the jacket.'

This was new, too, Tom now noticed.

'Come into money?'

'Not really,' came the reply. 'I'm getting a bit for the stats. Your stats. The paper's syndicating them, and I get a percentage. I thought Mike was going to talk to you about it.'

'He did. It's fine,' said Tom, still admiring the new look. 'Let's watch the cricket.'


Nick declared shortly after lunch on the second day. They'd secured maximum batting points and now he wanted to make inroads into the Leicestershire innings. Charlie Cruze obliged by taking two quick wickets which brought Phil Eldridge to the crease. 'We want Tom! We want Tom!' chanted a section of the crowd, but Nick walked over to them with his hands raised, and they quietened down. Most people wanted to watch the battle between the England captain and the fast bowler everybody was talking up as an England prospect.

It was a fascinating duel. Charlie gave it everything – real pace, a bit of movement, some short stuff. But Eldridge was equal to it. He left the ball when he could, blocked it if he

143

had to, and occasionally worked it for a single. Tom was impressed at how much time he seemed to have. Even when Charlie bowled him a bouncer and he had to duck, his dignity remained intact.

After a while the runs began to come more quickly, and it gradually became clear that Eldridge had won that round.

'Tom!' Nick raised his hand and beckoned him up to bowl. There was cheering, and a ragged chant of 'To-om, To-om!!' Then a lone voice cried out: 'No, No, No, No, No!' at which the crowd roared back: 'Yes, Yes, Yes, Yes, Yes!'

'Just ignore them, Tom,' Nick said as he gave him the ball. But still the noise went on. Tom looked down the wicket at Eldridge and could see he was trying to ignore it too. But still it went on: 'No, No, No, No, No!' – 'Yes, Yes, Yes, Yes, Yes!' Tom felt awful, and Eldridge was obviously fuming. But what could he do?

Then the public address system crackled into life. It was Mr MacClaren, and he sounded furious:

'Can I please remind you all that this is a game of cricket, and ask you to extend the usual courtesies to our guests. Thank you.'

The crowd shushed like told-off school children.

Then Tom ran in and bowled Eldridge first ball. It was a stunning googly that tore through his defences and cuffed the leg bail a dozen yards. Eldridge looked at the wicket in disbelief and then up the track to Tom. And then all hell broke loose. Tom was mobbed – indeed, he was fearful his shoulder was going to go again, Charlie pummelled it so hard – and the crowd were delirious. Eldridge was simply hooted from the wicket, and walked back under a barrage of 'No, No, No, No, No!' and 'We want Tom!' which modulated in due course into 'Please pick Tom! Please pick Tom!'

'I wasn't supposed to do that,' Tom suddenly remembered.

'Do what?' Dennis Harmon asked

'Anything to make matters worse. Mr MacClaren said –'

At which point the entire team went into a group convulsion. It was like the no-ball episode, but worse.

'Don't laugh – don't laugh,' said Nick. But his own face was split with a grin. Charlie was completely gone. 'I wasn't supposed to do that,' he mimicked and clutched his stomach. That just started everyone else off again, and by the time the next batsman arrived at the crease, nearly everyone was wiping their eyes with their sleeves.

There were only a few more overs till tea, and the mirth gradually subsided. Nick brought Steve Draper on, and he and Tom bowled tightly together until the interval.

'Uh oh', somebody said as they followed the not-out batsmen towards the pavilion. Mr MacClaren was standing at the top of the pavilion steps. It was obvious that he was very angry.

'Upstairs, upstairs into the dressing room. Now. All of you. Never mind tea.'

They climbed the stairs in silence. As soon as they were all in, Mr MacClaren shut the changing-room door and launched into them.

It was bad enough that the crowd showed disrespect, but for the team to behave like that was appalling. They were not schoolboys, but grown men with responsibility to give an example, had they any idea what the press would make of their behaviour, the season was in a delicate enough state as it was without . . . and on and on it went.

'I have never, in my entire working life felt so ashamed. Not only did I have to go and apologise to the England captain for the behaviour of the crowd; I had apologise for the ungentlemanly conduct of the team. Can you imagine what the papers are going to make of this? It's the worst possible publicity just when we were doing so well. I'm at a loss, at a complete loss what to say. I know the committee are going to take a very severe view on this. A very severe view indeed. Nick, before you take the team out again, you're going to knock on the Visitors' door and apologise on behalf of everybody for that disgraceful behaviour.'

He held the door open and Nick walked out. There was complete silence. Tom felt as bad as he had ever felt about anything. There was a moment when he thought he ought to speak, but Zeph caught his eye and made a little negative hand movement, which he took to mean it could only make a bad situation worse.

'Right,' said Mr MacClaren. 'You haven't had any tea, but then you don't deserve any. Go out there and do the job you're paid for without doing anything further to stain the reputation of this great cricket club.'

Nick came back from his mission stony-faced.

Without a word, he led them in down the stairs. Tom wanted to peel off and hide. As if sensing that, Steve came up behind him and whispered. 'We're all in this together, kid. It'll blow over.'

He'd almost forgotten the crowd waiting for them, but when they emerged into the sunshine there was a huge cheer. No one in the stands knew they'd been given a spectacular dressing-down.

'Charlie,' Nick called out, summarily ending Steve's spell. Tom fled to the safe haven of fine leg. He could see Nick talking to Charlie and the big fast bowler nodding his head.

The ensuing over was fast and uncompromising, and resulted in a wicket, Nick taking the catch at slip.

Tom decided not to go up for the team celebration. He felt he was in disgrace, that it was all his fault. And anyway, he didn't want to set anyone off again with some naive remark. He was sure Nick was cross with him, convinced that Mr MacClaren would be livid with him if he knew the full story.

At the end of the over, he did walk in, not knowing if he was still part of the attack. Nick threw him the ball without a word. The fielders were all focused on the batsman, and walked in with steely focus. He determined to do his absolute best for them.

An hour later, the Leicestershire innings was in ruins. With Charlie's hostile pace and Tom's unpredictable bounce and turn, the batsmen were all at sea. If anybody tried to become aggressive against Tom, Charlie gave them a horrible working over. Hardly a word was spoken. The intensity was electric. Tom felt everyone had changed up a gear. And he could see that it affected the batsmen. There was no easy chatting between overs. They seemed nervy, defeated.

The crowd sensed the change of atmosphere too. They clapped loudly when wickets fell, but there was no cheering, no barracking, no chanting.

And still Tom and Charlie bowled on. When the visitors were 8 wickets down, Nick talked to his fast bowler. He was obviously asking whether he could go on. Charlie waved him away and steamed in once more. The middle stump flew out of the ground and the crowd found its voice.

Three overs later Dennis Harmon took a diving catch off Tom in the gully. Leicestershire were all out. Nick led the team off to rapturous applause. As he entered the pavilion compound, Tom saw him look up to the visitors' balcony where Phil Eldridge stood with a grim face. Nick nodded to him and the England captain turned away into his changing room.

'Right,' said Nick, when they got back to their changing room. 'We're going back out there and we're going to do it all again.' He had enforced the follow-on, and Leicestershire would have to bat again for the last thirty-five minutes of the day.

Zeph took the new ball and made beautiful angles with it

in the evening sunshine. Despite his determination to give his all, Charlie was at last tiring, but he still proved a handful, and neither opener was comfortable against him.

Zeph took the first wicket, with a ball that jagged away, just nicking the top corner of the bat. It flew to third slip who took it above his head. An over or so later, he brought one back in to the pads and the slip cordon went up as one man. The umpire had no hesitation in raising his finger. Two down, and all eyes were on the pavilion.

Philip Eldridge was the next man in, but with barely ten minutes to go would he come out himself or send in a night-watchman? When the crowd saw that it was the England captain trotting down the steps, they applauded generously. He walked briskly to the crease and took guard. He hit his first ball from Zeph crisply off his toes for four, and followed this in Charlie's next over with a sumptuous off-drive which rattled against the advertising boards. It was a clear statement of intent. How would Nick respond?

Zeph bowled the penultimate over of the day, a maiden. Eldridge would face the final over. Nick took the ball and it was obvious he was thinking hard. In the end, he raised his hand to Charlie, and beckoned up Tom.

The crowd gasped. Nick brought two men in close to the bat, and then threw the ball to Tom without a word.

Why? thought Tom. Why not just let Charlie bowl the last over? Why me?

Perhaps there was a vestige of doubt still running through his veins when he released the ball. It was certainly the worst he bowled all day. It was short and aimed down the leg side. Eldridge picked up its co-ordinates immediately and moved back and across his stumps to dispatch it. Short leg ducked and began to move out of the firing line.

But instead of coming up so that it met the arc of Eldridge's bat, the ball spat through, keeping low. The England captain was good enough to adjust his stroke at the very last minute, but only managed a thick edge which guided the ball into the base of the middle stump.

There was a stunned silence. The crowd seemed for once incapable of expressing themselves. Perhaps their emotions were too mixed for them to know what they felt. Eldridge looked up the wicket and gave Tom the filthiest look he'd ever received from anyone, and then turned on his heel and marched off back to the pavilion. There was complete silence. It was as if the crowd were digesting the enormity of what had happened – the England captain bowled out first ball twice in a day by the boy he said he would never have in the England team. In a way the silence was more damning than the hoots and catcalls that had met his earlier dismissal.

It was late, and the umpires peered at the clock and decided that that was enough for the day. They removed the bails and Tom, the not-out batsmen and the other fielders followed the retreating figure of Eldridge back to the pavilion.

Tom felt shattered. He hadn't realised how much his long spell in the afternoon had taken out of him, but now he felt weak and jittery. He just wanted to go home – his real home. He'd have liked an ordinary evening, a walk to the chip shop with his dad, an evening watching telly on their beat-up old television set.

He could see Mr MacClaren hovering at the top of the steps. Eldridge pushed past him without breaking stride. A hurt look flitted over the Secretary's face. But then it was gone, and he looked sternly down at his players as they climbed the steps. He wanted a word with Nick, and led him away to his office.

'Why, Nick, why?' he asked as soon as he'd shut the door. 'Whatever possessed you?'

'It was the right thing to do.'

149

'No, it was the wrong thing to do. Utterly the wrong thing.'

'It was the right thing to do in cricketing terms. He got him out, didn't he?'

'He got him out with the worst ball I've seen him bowl. Eldridge was pumped up and as soon as he saw it was a long-hop decided to post it half way back to Leicester.'

'And he missed it, and we got the wicket which will almost certainly mean we win the match, tomorrow, before the weather has a chance to intervene. As captain, that is what I'm meant to aim for.'

'There's more to captaincy than winning cricket matches. Think of Douglas Jardine and the Bodyline series.'

'Oh come on, Ted, that was completely different.'

'You're right.' The secretary slumped down in his chair. He suddenly looked very tired. 'I'm sorry Nick, these last two weeks have been stressful beyond belief. I shudder to think what the press are going to make of today. I know Eldridge is a bit of a cold fish, but you have to admit we've treated him shabbily. And we've weakened him as England captain. The Australians must be laughing into their beer. How was he when you went to apologise?'

'Cold, aloof. He really hates Tom. That's what's got under his skin. I don't know what'll happen if the selectors pick him. As they should. And Charlie, come to that.'

'The press will be baying for us. Mike Field is holding them, but I'm going to have to face the music. Are you going to come like that or do you want a shower?'

'I'll come like this. Let's get it over with. How's Tom getting out tonight?'

'The police say they'll take him. We seem to have run out of electricians and caterers.'

The two men left the Secretary's office and went downstairs to face the music.

The papers predictably had a field-day, with the story dominating both front and back pages. LAUGHING-STOCK! boomed one above a picture of the whole team doubled up as Eldridge walked away from the crease. ENGLAND CAPTAIN HUMILIATED claimed another. ONE OR THE OTHER posited a third, matching half-page pictures of Tom and the England captain. WHO'S MY BUNNY? jeered another, with pictures of both dismissals side by side.

The secretary groaned as he viewed a particularly embarrassing picture of Charlie Cruze clutching his stomach. 'Well, there goes his chance of a test place,' he said, before skimming through an account of Nick Appleton's apology to Eldridge: 'an unforgivable and wholly regrettable lapse in standards,' he was quoted as saying.

He looked out of his office window. At least there shouldn't be anything like as many people coming in as on the first two days. They only needed seven more wickets and the match would be over. After the battering they'd taken, he didn't rate the visitors' chances of putting up a fight.

And he was right. Nick Appleton set about the job with remorseless efficiency. Tom still had five balls of his over to bowl and took another wicket with the fifth. After a night's rest Charlie steamed in from the pavilion end, and between them they polished the visitors off before lunch.

Desultory clapping echoed round the largely empty stands. The visitors declined to stay for lunch, and Phil Eldridge left the ground without saying a word to Nick Appleton. The home team felt deflated, even though their win had catapulted them to the top of the championship table. Even the press seemed sated after their orgy of sensationalism. It was even decided that Mike Field would take Tom home to pick up a few things, before heading back out to the swimming pool and the games room.

There was one journalist staking out the house. 'Do you think you've done enough to get into the Test side?' he asked as Tom unlocked the front door. 'Should Phil Eldridge stay as England captain, Tom?' he asked as Tom left.

Mike Field said, 'You've got some nice exclusive pictures, so be thankful for that and leave the lad alone. The selectors will choose the team for the fourth Test, and I can't see any challenge to Phil Eldridge as captain. You're just going to have to be patient like the rest of us.'

# CHAPTER 12

THE speculation about Tom's selection for the Test team was the hot topic. For many, he represented the only chance England had of winning the Ashes. But how could he play under Eldridge? Some called for Eldridge to be sacked and Nick Appleton to be promoted to take his place. Others argued that that would be playing into the Australians' hands. For some, the very question of putting Tom in the England team was destabilising and likely to lead to defeat.

Don Spiers, fresh from an effortless double century against one of the few counties they played, gave droll replies to journalists' questions. It used to be thought that the Australians specialised in the dark arts of 'mental disintegration', but now it looked as though England were out-classing them. The trouble was, England were practising mental disintegration on themselves! He agreed that Phil Eldridge had been put in an impossible position and he couldn't see how it would do anything but weaken an already demoralised team.

The headlines read: DON 'DON'T CALL ME BRADMAN' SAYS 'DON'T PICK TOM.'

Not that Tom saw it. He and his parents had more immediate worries. They were woken early. 'You've got to get up. There's been a breach of security,' they were told. 'Don't bother packing, we'll do that. Just dress. There's a horse-box in the yard. It's all right, it's clean. We need to get you out now.'

Barely ten minutes later the Marlin family were peering out through the vents of the horsebox. The normally quiet lanes were busy with vehicles. At one point they got stuck in a traffic jam; a little later there was a squealing of brakes as they swerved to avoid hitting a motorcycle.

'Who let the cat out of the bag?' Tom's mum said.

'Any ideas, Tom?' asked his dad.

Tom shook his head. It couldn't have been Sherwin or Little Paul. They'd been booked in for a return visit and wouldn't have done anything to spoil that.

'I suppose one of the people that drove me might have said something.'

'But they only knew where they dropped you off. And when the press found out they just changed the drop-off. No one knew where you were taken next.'

'Well, they do now,' said Tom gloomily, and wherever they're taking us next, it won't be half as nice, he thought. He had been looking forward to a lazy day by the pool and had chosen the DVDs he wanted to watch later.

The horsebox pulled off the road and went down a concrete track. When it pulled up and the doors were thrown open, they found themselves in a run-down depot of industrial units. Across the yard was a large vehicle which suddenly lifted Tom's spirits hugely. It was an American motor home, the size of a small bus. And there was Des. He had a road atlas in his hands and a warm smile on his face.

'Morning,' he said, breezily. 'All aboard.'

Later that morning as they made light work of the main route out of England into Wales, Tom's mobile buzzed.

'All right?'

'Fine, Mike, thanks,' he said.

'I'm sorry we had to move you at such short notice, but life would have become intolerable if we hadn't.'

'I'm sorry,' Tom said. 'I'm sorry I've been such a . . . nuisance.'

'Nonsense. None of this is your fault. I'm just sorry our

friends in the media found out. They were always going to. Only a matter of time. Let's just hope we can keep you under wraps till the Test team is announced. Des will look after you all. Just try to enjoy what may be the last few days of privacy you will have for quite a while. Good luck.'

He rang off. Tom put his phone away and looked out at a field full of sheep. It looked encouragingly peaceful.

Two days later a small group of men sat round a table at Lord's cricket ground looking at a piece of paper with twelve names on it.

'Which of them are you going to ring first?'

The large man with greying sideburns shook his head: 'The joys of being Chairman of Selectors. It had better be the boy. We need to know his connections will let him play before we drop the bombshell on Eldridge. Where's that number?'

Someone passed it across and he pecked out the digits and put the phone to his ear.

'Nothing. Where did they say they were sending him?'

'Wales.'

The Chairman rolled his eyes. 'Don't they realise how bad reception is? I'd better ring MacClaren.'

After a short, rather terse conversation, he said, 'He's going to text me an alternative number which will work. But he assured me they were happy for him to play, subject to all the usual provisos about security. Better tell Phil the joyful news, I suppose.'

Five minutes later he put the phone down and mopped his brow with a handkerchief.

'Not happy?'

'Well, you heard it from my end.'

'But he's not resigning?'

'No. You've got to give him that, he's as stubborn as they come. Let's try his secret weapon again.'

Tom was looking out over a lake from the top of a deserted valley, watching a red kite drifting this way and that patrolling the hillside below. The sun was out, but there was a slight breeze. He stretched his arms out and closed his eyes. The break was doing him good. The countryside was so beautiful, so unlike what he was used to at home, that he found all thought of cricket and playing for the Ashes and all the madness of the media simply drifted away. He didn't mind whether they picked him or not. He was happy here, out of the limelight, without the pressure, just being himself.

'Tom.'

He turned and saw Des striding towards him. He was holding a mobile. Tom suddenly felt a shiver of fear. Was this it? Were they really going to throw him back into whirlpool of hype and expectation?

Des handed him the phone

'Hello,' said Tom.

'Ah, Tom, got you at last. Can you hear me?'

Loud and clear.

'This is the Chairman of Selectors speaking to you from Lord's and I'd like to be the first to congratulate you on being picked to play for England in the fourth Test at Headingley. Tom? Tom? Did you get that?'

Tom looked down over the lake, over the empty flanks of the valley where tiny sheep moved imperceptibly through the coarse grass.

'Yes,' he said faintly. 'I can hear you. And thank you. I just hope I won't let you down.'

There were a lot of instructions, where he was to meet the team, how he would need to be measured for his England blazer, and so on. Tom felt dizzy when it was over and he handed the phone back to Des.

'So, they did it? Good for them. Congratulations. Now, let's go and tell your parents.'

Tom's mum had cried, holding him at arm's length.

'We are doing the right thing, aren't we, Rick?'

Tom's dad wiped his eyes. Perhaps it was the wind, Tom thought. 'I hope so, love. As long as you're OK with it, son?'

Tom felt anything but OK with it, but he nodded to re-assure them.

Des appeared from the motor home. He was carrying a tray with glasses and a bottle on it.

'Champagne?'

He poured two full glasses and presented them to Tom's parents. He half filled the third for Tom.

'I think if you're old enough to play for England, you're old enough to have a sip of bubbly.'

'None for you, Des?'

'Driving. But I can propose a toast: to a successful Test debut, and victory over the Aussies!'

Standing high in the Welsh hills, they clinked their glasses and drank. Tom found the bubbles prickly in his nostrils, but managed to get a mouthful down. The effect was similar to what happened when he released a new ball on the pinball machine. Little bells and flashing lights went off all round his head. He felt whizzy and wanted to float off into the air, glid-ing effortlessly with the red kites.

'Why's 'e mekin' you run from one end o' ground to t'other? Was it something tha's said?'

The barracking had started early and showed no sign of let-ting up. On winning the toss, Don Spiers chose to bat, so Tom found himself taking the field with the England team on the first morning of the Headingley Test. He was glad. The wait-ing after his selection had been awful. He knew he represented a huge gamble and he was terrified of failing. Once the team gathered in Leeds, all he wanted was for the match to start.

But now he was out on the boundary he was the focus of attention for the Yorkshiremen who had queued to get into the ground. And of course Eldridge's – perfectly sensible – decision to field him at fine leg both ends soon attracted notice.

'Will 'e give thee a bowl, lad?' another voice enquired.

It was just the same at the other end.

'My lad's a dead ringer for you, so if you want a rest, just let us know, and 'e can stand in for you!'

'Hey up, tha's yorn!'

One of the openers had deflected the ball off his hip, and Tom hared off round the boundary to field it. Mercifully he picked up well and threw the ball back in to the top of the stumps.

'Tha's got an arm on thee! I'll give thee that.'

There was generous applause as he took up his position again. He stole a glance at the big screen in one corner of the ground. It showed the replay of his throw.

Another man called out, 'It's good, en't it, seeing it on't telly?' which got another wave of laughter.

Tom was very self-conscious, but felt that the spectators were prepared to give him a chance.

After half an hour or so, during which he had dutifully trotted from one end of the field to the other at the end of each over, a voice called out, 'Eh, Eldridge, I hope tha's going to bowl the lad – he's doin' a marathon for thee!' There was a lot of laughter at this, and Tom could see that the England captain was unamused.

England had four fast bowlers: Chas Luton, Ahmed Mohammed, Bernie Brent and Andy Sneed. Eldridge gave all four a go but, as in previous tests, the breakthrough wouldn't come. There were maiden overs, lots of playing and missing, a couple of huge appeals for lbw. But as the minutes to lunch ticked away, there was no wicket.

The crowd began to get restless. There were individual calls to 'Give the lad a go', 'Why pick 'im, if you won't bowl 'im?' And then the chanting started: 'We want Tom! We want Tom!'

Tom knew Eldridge would hate to be barracked like that. He just hoped his captain didn't suspect him of egging the crowd on. With ten minutes to lunch he saw Eldridge look out towards him from his position at first slip. Was he going to ask him to bowl?

Next ball Chas Luton got one to nip away, and Eldridge took a sharp catch at chest height. The crowd immediately got off his back, forgot about wanting Tom and started clapping the England bowlers as they ran in to deliver the last couple of overs before the interval.

The score at lunch was 78 for 1, and there was a satisfied hum among the crowd as they debated whether that represented a better morning for Australia or the home side.

Tom certainly felt it was a good morning for him. He'd fielded well enough, with two or three good returns and one full-length dive which saved a boundary. He didn't mind about not bowling. The truth was, he was intimidated by the Australians. For the last couple of days the two teams had seen each other as they took turns to use the nets and practise their fielding drills, and the Australians to a man had seemed bigger, brawnier, louder, more confident. They hadn't been hostile or unfriendly; it wasn't that they didn't respect the England players. It was just that deep down they clearly had an unshakeable belief in their own superiority. You could tell they expected to win the match, you could tell they were absolutely certain of retaining the Ashes.

'Unless you snuck in here to get some autographs, you must be Tom Marlin. I'm Don – Don't Call Me Bradman – Spiers.'

The Australian captain had met him outside the members' enclosure. His handshake was painfully firm, and his eyes looked unwaveringly into Tom's.

'You really are just a kid, aren't you? Well, good luck. And enjoy it. You may not get another one.'

And with that the Australian ran up the steps and disappeared into the visitors' changing room. The encounter had not left Tom with any desire to bowl at him.

The afternoon session followed the pattern of the morning session, except that gradually the runs came more readily. Eldridge rotated his four fast bowlers in the hope of getting another wicket, and was rewarded when Ahmed Mohammed secured an lbw decision against the remaining opener.

This brought Don Spiers to the crease. Tom marvelled at the breadth of his shoulders, at the vigour with which he whirled his bat around. He marched up to take his guard with a natural authority. This was his world, this was where he ruled.

The second ball he faced flew past a diving mid-off and rapped against the advertising hoardings at the far end of the ground. A few balls later, Spiers rocked back and smashed the ball past cover. Another four. No one even moved.

'Lewk out,' warned someone in the crowd, ''e'll be putting one down your throat next.'

Tom really hoped not.

But two overs later, he saw Spiers step back and across his crease and hook a bouncer from Ahmed. There was a stir in the crowd as they tried to gauge how well he'd made contact. For a moment Tom thought he'd hit it true and that it would sail over his head for six, but then he realised it was a towering top edge. Everyone in the crowd seemed to realise the same thing at the same time.

'That's yours, lad,' one of his regulars said helpfully.

'That's gone oop,' said someone else.

There was no argument about that. 'Oop' it had certainly gone. Tom could see it, a black speck far above him. He felt like one of the poor harmless creatures on the Welsh hillside, caught in the unforgiving stare of the red kites.

He ran to his left and looked up again. How far was it going to carry? Was it his imagination, or was it actually circling like a kite?

Then, with a terrible finality, it started to fall. It positively hurtled towards the ground. Tom positioned himself, praying that he was at least in the right place to stop it. But at the last moment, he lost confidence and moved again. It was like trying to field an incoming missile.

At least he got a hand to it, but no more. A terrible groan went up as the ball bounced away from him. Australia's captain had had a let-off. And Tom's humiliation wasn't over. In his desperate attempts to at least get hold of the ball, he kicked it on and over the boundary. Four runs.

'Never mind, lad, 'e probably won't do that again for a day and a half,' someone said behind him. 'Anyway, tha can bowl 'im out yoursen' – when you get a bowl.'

'Give 'im a bowl? Tha must be outa tha tree. Lad's just dropped the Ashes, man. Send him home back down south with his mam and dad. Give 'im a bowl? I wouldn't give him a bowl o' broth.'

Tom felt as bad as he'd ever felt. He'd not only let the team – the country – down, but he'd confirmed all Eldridge's suspicions that he wasn't up to it, that he was a liability.

He hardly dared to look up as he set off on his trek across the ground at the end of the over. The thought of catching anybody's eye was terrifying. But as he skirted the square, he heard a familiar voice call out 'Tom'.

There was Nick. 'Head up,' he said. 'It was really hard. Anyone could have missed it. Remember, we managed to drop six last time. So don't beat yourself up about it, OK?'

He gave Tom a broad, encouraging smile and briefly put an arm round his shoulder. It was a public show of solidarity that did not go unnoticed by the crowd.

'At least your County captain's sticking up for you, lad. And fair play to him.'

'If yer get another 'igh one, give uz a shout. Ah took a screamer on Saturday!'

One good thing was that after his let-off Spiers reined in his aggressive instincts. Runs still came, but it no longer seemed as though England had lost all control.

It was more than halfway through the afternoon session when Eldridge introduced a new bowler into the attack. But it wasn't Tom. Instead, Hector Maitland, an elegant middle-order batsman and brisk medium pacer, was given the ball. There was a restless reaction in the stands. Even though he'd dropped a catch, the crowd were still extremely curious about Tom's bowling. There was a ragged attempt at a 'We Want Tom!' chant. But Hector Maitland quelled it in his first over, inducing the slightest of nicks to the keeper and claiming the third Australian wicket.

The victim was not Don Spiers unfortunately, but at least it was a wicket. The new batsman was predictably happy to let Spiers take most of the strike. And the Australian captain was now well past his 50 and obviously set on a century which would seal his side's domination of the day. Tom anxiously watched the hands of the clock. Spiers clipped Maitland off his toes for a boundary. There was time for one more over before tea.

A traditional time to experiment with a spinner. Tom's heart sank as he saw Eldridge waving to him to come and bowl. The crowd hummed with excitement, clapping wholeheartedly.

'Do your stuff, Tom. Relax,' Nick said to him as they passed each other.

Eldridge gave him the ball without a word. It was clear from the field he set that all he wanted was for Tom to keep the new batsman on strike. He put no attacking fielders close in, but set his men back in the ring to stop the single.

This was a pity because Tom's first ball in Test cricket was perfectly pitched, span and popped. It took the inside edge of the bat and would have given short leg an easy catch.

'Run!'

The Australian captain charged down the wicket to take strike.

This was exactly what Eldridge had wanted to avoid, but his body language somehow suggested that he wasn't surprised. He wafted fielders away to distant corners of the ground then stood at slip with his arms crossed as though carved in stone.

What happened next was as astonishing as it was shocking. Tom bowled a good-length ball outside the off stump. But while the ball was in flight, Don Spiers changed his grip, lunged down the wicket and unleashed a furious blow which sent the ball sailing over the deep-cover boundary.

There was a gasp from the crowd and some raucous cheering. Tom had never seen a reverse sweep before. He looked at the umpire, who was holding up both arms to signal six to the scorers.

'Perfectly legal, lad,' he said, when he saw Tom's questioning expression.

Tom was so unnerved that his next ball was a full toss. Spiers hit it into the top tier of the grandstand. Eldridge put his hands in his pockets and scuffed the ground with his boot.

Nick trotted up while the ball was being retrieved.

'He's obviously decided to target you. Don't worry. It's happened before, and it'll happen again. If he tried to hit you for three more sixes, you'll get him out. But do pitch it.' He smiled.

Spiers only managed to hit the next one for four. He slightly mis-cued an off drive. The ball went up a long way, but fell safely between two fielders.

'Well bowled, Tom,' Nick called out, clapping his hands.

Eldridge showed what he thought of it by dropping back from slip to a vague position half way to the third-man boundary.

The Australian captain hit the fifth ball hard, straight back over Tom's head. It cleared the sightscreen, giving the men on the boundary no chance.

The spectators were thrilled by the big hitting, but also protective of their bowler.

''E's only a kid,' someone yelled. 'Pick on someone your own size.'

Another voice called to Tom: 'Don't take it lyin' down, lad. Get amongst 'im.'

The ball came back. He took a deep breath. This was clearly going to be the last delivery he would ever be allowed to bowl in a Test match.

He could see the Australian captain on the edge of his vision as he approached the stumps. At the last moment of release he dragged the ball down. Spiers advanced, bat raised, his intentions clear. But at the very last second, he realised he wasn't going to get there, not quite. With astonishing skill, he checked his drive, converting the shot from all-out attack to defence. He was well out of his crease, so he had to get a bat on the ball to save himself from being stumped.

The ball flew, at comfortable catching height, straight to slip.

But there was no slip. While the two Australian batsmen crossed for the easiest of singles, Philip Eldridge walked in to pick up the ball. Without breaking stride, he threw it to the nearest umpire and set off for the pavilion.

Tom gravitated naturally to Nick's side. He looked up and saw his face set hard.

'Are you angry, Nick?' he asked.

'Angry doesn't begin to describe what I'm feeling,' he said.

164

'I'm sorry, Nick. Really I am.'

Nick looked down at him, almost in a double-take. Then he stopped. 'Tom, I'm not angry with you. You got thumped, but you also produced two wicket-taking balls in that over. I'm not angry with you at all.'

Those words were the one thing Tom had to hold on to through the rest of the day. The England dressing room was not a happy place. No one said much, and the captain said it all by the depths of his silence. Tom sat as far away from him as he could. He'd dropped the crucial catch, and his one over had given back the initiative to the Australians while propelling Spiers to within a few runs of his century. He knew he would not be asked to bowl again. He was a nobody, an intruder, a waste of space.

Out they went after the break and Eldridge reverted to his fast bowlers. Spiers played with studied care, leaving anything he didn't have to play. His partner followed suit, and the contrast with the run-glut before tea was dramatic.

Eventually, almost reluctantly, the batsmen picked up the pace and Spiers hit a sweetly timed on-drive down the ground to reach his century. He raised his bat to his applauding teammates on the balcony before turning to acknowledge the crowd.

'Doan' tha' fret, lad. The real Don, Don Bradman, he scored 300 in a day here once. This one'll not reach 250, I'll bet tha'.'

There was a fair bit of laughter at that, but another voice cut in.

'Leave the lad alone. 'E'd 'ave cleaned 'im up if captain had set a proper field.'

Tom played through the little clip of Spiers being caught by Eldridge off that last ball before tea. How very, very different things would have been.

*

The press were divided on the issues of Tom's contribution to the team effort and his captain's treatment of him. For every WONDER KID OUT OF HIS DEPTHS there was an ELDRIDGE GETS HIS REVENGE ON UPSTART SPINNER. Tom's dad sat on the sofa in the family suite next morning glancing through the coverage without comment. Suddenly he sat up, holding one of the tabloids in his hands.

'Tom?'

Tom looked up from his Gameboy.

'Yes, Dad?'

'What's this . . .'

He waved the paper. Tom reluctantly went over to him.

'What?'

'Look.' He indicated a column near the bottom of the page under a headline: WHO DOES THIS KID THINK HE IS?

Tom grabbed the paper and read: 'Obviously living in the lap of luxury in a retreat for the super rich has given young Tom Marlin ideas for coining it in. Our readers will be astonished to hear that in addition to the lavish deals his agent, Mike Field, has been putting together for him, young Tom has been selling his autograph on eBay.'

'Is it true, Tom?

'No, Dad. Of course not. Only –'

He was looking at the inset picture.

'Are you saying it's a fake?'

'No,' said Tom. 'No, it's mine all right. I did dozens of them. I gotta make a phone call.'

Little Paul was contemplating his bank accounts on line. Another £500 from the current account into the Gold Saver? Why not? A couple of mouse clicks and it was done.

Then his phone rang.

'Tom! Great. Nice of you to call. Look, don't worry about yesterday –'

166

He didn't finish his sentence.

After listening with his phone held slightly away from his ear for about a minute, he tried to say something. But he had only managed a word or so before the line went dead. He looked at his phone.

Then he began to cry.

# CHAPTER 13

Des drove them to the ground. The police cleared the way and the paparazzi elbowed for the best shots of Tom on the back seat. There were a few journalists hanging around the pavilion. Out of habit rather than in any expectation of getting an answer, one of them called out, 'How much for an autograph, Tom?'

Instead of keeping his head down and disappearing through the side door, Tom stopped and went over to the man.

'That story's unfair.'

'He spoke, the boy spoke.' There was a murmur that gained in strength. Suddenly there were fifteen, twenty men with notebooks and recording instruments crowding round, asking dozens of questions.

'You say the story's unfair, Tom?' asked the first journalist. 'But you're not saying it's not true?'

'It's not true that I'm selling my autograph on eBay.'

'So they're fakes, are they?'

'No, they're not fakes.'

'Someone selling them for you?'

Tom put up his hand for silence.

'They are genuine. I did them all. But not for sale. For practice.'

There was a bit of a laugh at this, but it was shushed down.

'I'd never given an autograph in my life and someone said I ought to practise so when I was asked to I could do a good one. But with you lot after me the whole time, I've hardly had the chance to give my autograph to anyone.'

168

'So how did they get on eBay?'

'They got into the wrong hands. And I'm very sorry. All I can say is that anybody who bought one will get their money back.'

There was another hubbub of new questions. One loud voice climbed above the rest.

'Do you think you'll get a bowl today?'

'You'd have to ask my captain.'

'He looked pretty furious with you yesterday. What did he say?'

'I'm not going to discuss it. Mr Eldridge is trying his best to win this match, and we're all a hundred per cent behind him.'

'Including you?'

'Of course. Now, I've got to go and change.'


There were other plain words being spoken at the same time. In a small office in the heart of the pavilion, Phil Eldridge was confronting the Chairman of Selectors.

'Phil, you have got to listen to me. We did not pick "that boy", as you refer to him, to pander to the media; far less to put your nose out of joint. I accept it's a gamble. I accept it wouldn't have happened if we were three up in the series and sailing towards an open-top bus ride round Trafalgar Square. The plain fact is that Tom Marlin represents our last chance of turning this series around. Bozzer Bothwell was there last week, remember. He saw Tom bowl, and he said it was your chaps who looked like the schoolboys. It's a shame he cleaned you up twice, because I think if you'd had to play him you might have formed a better opinion of him.'

The Chairman of Selectors paused and looked the England captain straight in the eye.

'As selectors we have a very simple job. It just happens that it's fiendishly difficult to pick the best team to represent

England. But someone has to do it, and at the moment it's us. We have to make decisions – and you, I'm afraid, have to go with them, whether you agree or not. We selected Tom, and we did not select him to be humiliated in front of a packed house at Headingley. He's in this side for a reason. In our judgement he's the best chance we have of taking 20 Australian wickets in a match.'

'And you're happy to let the Australians have 20 runs an over are you?'

'Spiers had obviously made his mind up to blow the boy out of the water. That reverse sweep – first up against someone you've never faced before? Smacks of desperation to me.'

'Desperation? Did you see how hard he hit it?'

'Of course I saw. It was a magnificent shot. He's possibly the only man in the world who could pull it off. But you have to look beneath the surface. Why did he feel he had to make that gesture, why take the risk – of being cleaned up first ball by a boy? Spiers is no fool, Phil. He's not a showman, and he's not a mindless bully. He was playing you.'

'Playing me?'

'He reads the papers.The figures speak for themselves. If Tom were even five years older there wouldn't have been any debate. He'd be the accepted choice. Now, Spiers may have a low opinion of English county cricket, but he's going to take seriously someone who goes through sides like a knife through butter. He's a threat – pretty much the only threat we've come up with. But he knows you don't rate him. So, the best way to neutralise our best weapon is to confirm your opinion that he's useless. Hence the all-out assault. Didn't you notice how sedate it all went after tea? No 20 runs an over then, not like when Tom was bowling. He wants you to leave Tom to rot down at fine leg and then be quietly dropped for the Oval. But the fact is, Phil, the boy bowled two wicket-taking deliveries in his first over in Test cricket – and if you'd given him the field he should have had, we wouldn't be having this conversation now.'

'Oh, so it's all my fault now, is it?'

'Phil, I'm losing patience. We picked you because you are the best captain for England. But that's provided you keep on doing the job well. It's not about your ego. It's about getting the best out of the team we give you. The only chance we have of turning this match round, and therefore the only chance we have of winning the Ashes is if we get Spiers out in the first session of play. I want you to use all the weapons at your disposal to achieve that. All – do you understand me?'

'Sold any autographs then, Tom?'

'I put mine on eBay. Didn't get nought for't, though!'

The banter started in the first over. Eldridge opened with Ahmed. Spiers was on strike. Tom prayed that there wouldn't be a repeat of yesterday's calamity.

Ahmed on the other hand seemed positively to invite it. His first three deliveries were short of a length. One was shorter and faster than the others and Spiers got into position, but at the last minute changed his mind. The ball seemed to brush his helmet and the crowd gave a great *Ooooh!*

Spiers took an unflustered single off the next ball and with his partner leaving the last couple, he was on strike for the second over of the day. There was a ripple of genuine surprise when Eldridge called up Tom to bowl it.

'You got it in for him or what?' Spiers said as he wandered down the wicket prodding the surface with the toe of his bat.

'Ignore him,' Eldridge said to Tom. 'Let's see how he likes a bit of pressure.'

As the field was set, Tom felt his confidence growing. Eldridge seemed to believe he could actually get Spiers out. He brought up two men close either side of the bat – helmets had to be rushed on by the twelfth man – and put Nick in tight at gully. Then he looked Tom straight in the eye and said: 'Now's the time to pull one out of the bag.'

'Come on, Tom,' Nick encouraged him. Up he ran to the stumps. Spiers pushed his left leg forward with his bat raised, but then decided against a big stroke. He tucked the bat behind his pad and got his head well over the ball, which span away and smacked into the wicket-keeper's gloves.

'Well bowled, Tom.' It was Eldridge. He clapped briefly, his hands high, then hitched his whites and bent forward for the next ball.

This was a googly, which lifted and hit Spiers in the stomach. He played no shot and raised his bat out of the way. He made no acknowledgement that he had been struck, merely kicking the ball away for the close fielder to step in and retrieve.

Tom bowled again, and again Spiers was watchful, jabbing the ball down in front of him. Three more dot balls followed, and Tom had bowled his first maiden in Test cricket.

Eldridge clapped loudly, and looked around at his men with a passion in his eyes that had been wholly lacking the day before. Nick squeezed Tom's arm as they passed. 'Great. Keep it up.'

And when he got back to the boundary there was a great cheer.

Ahmed kept it tight, and Tom soon found himself with the ball in his hand again. Spiers looked around at the fielders and tapped his bat hard on the crease. That reminded Tom of something. Someone. Suddenly he knew who it was: Devlin. Devlin before he wound up to try for a six. Now he knew. Spiers was going to try to hit him out of the ground.

Nothing in his run-up betrayed the fact that he knew; nothing in his delivery showed it; but at the very last moment he whipped his arm through a fraction quicker than usual and also swung his torso a little further to his left.

Spiers was out of his crease like a caged animal suddenly released. He took a step and a half down the track, his bat flashing through with all the strength in those broad shoulders. The ball hovered, then dived to earth, gripped and turned – straight into the waiting wicket-keeper's gloves.

The noise when the crowd realised the Australian captain had missed the ball was tumultuous. They roared ferociously, as the bails went spinning into the bright morning sunshine and the square-leg umpire raised his finger.

The England players converged on Tom. Nick ran up from gully and embraced him. And then Eldridge himself, moving more sedately, arrived. Tom knew instinctively that he would not want to high-five, but was just as pleased with the warm handshake. 'Well bowled, young man,' was all he said. But when Tom looked up into his face, he could see hints of a complicated set of emotions at work.

'Left-hand,' said the umpire.

'Goosey,' Eldridge said, as the the tall man stood on the crease and held his bat up to take guard. He made a funny forward thrust with his jaw, which was what had got him his nickname. It was even more pronounced when he ran in to bowl.

But despite appearances, Goosey was a deadly serious cricketer. Not only did he share the new ball with Brad Dawson, he was a phenomenal hitter, who on his day could shred any bowling attack in the world.

'I think I see a pattern emerging here,' the England captain said and started posting his men to far-flung corners of the field.

Goosey had an ugly stance, with his right leg thrust down the pitch, as though he could barely contain his ferocious attacking instincts. As Tom ran up, he noticed the Australian's bat rising alarmingly, and the next thing he knew the ball had been struck with a mighty crack. Before he could even turn his head, he knew from the sound the crowd made that it was a big one.

There were another couple of powerful blows in the rest of the over, at the end of which Eldridge came up to Tom.

'That was great. Arguably the over that got us back into this with a chance of winning the Ashes. I'm going to take you off now, because they're obviously after you. If we had runs in the bank, I'd leave you on. But I just can't take the risk. I'll bring you back on as soon as I can.'

Goosey carried on lashing out. First Dave Luton, then Andy Sneed felt the considerable weight of his bat. But eventually Ahmed tucked him up and got him to glove a catch behind.

True to his word, Eldridge recalled Tom. '338,' he said, his hand on his chin. 'If we could peg them back to under 400 . . . Over to you, young man.'

Tom bowled either side of lunch and added four wickets to the treasured scalp of the Australian captain. He didn't think he bowled particularly well, but he had the crowd behind him, and the England players fielded as though their lives depended on it.

One rank long-hop hammered away for a deserved boundary was scooped up inches from the ground at square leg. Eldridge took a great diving catch at slip, and there was an lbw which Hawkeye later showed probably shouldn't have been given. Tom did finish the innings with a peach of a top-spinner which went straight through Brad Dawson's unconfident defence. The tall pace man looked down the wicket at him giving him a long stare. Then his face creased into a grin, and he nodded in appreciation.

Eldridge came up to Tom and presented him with the ball in recognition of his five wickets. He then invited him to lead the England team off – to a tumultuous reception from the crowd.

*

'Well done, Phil. Splendid job.' The Chairman of Selectors beamed.

'I feel a complete fool not having used him yesterday. Lord knows how many runs we might have saved.'

'Still, you gave them something to think about today, that's the important thing. Spiers' face when he came in was a picture. It's like boxing, Phil. You can lose every round in the match. But if you deliver the knock-out punch, you're champion. Now, you better go and get your pads on.'

There was a great bustle as the opening batsmen padded up and the bowlers discarded their boots and their whites for tracksuit bottoms and sandals. Tom sat in a corner in a daze. 5 for 73. On debut. And there was a man on a stepladder painting his figures up on the Honours Board at that very moment.

His mobile phone kept buzzing. There were a lot of texts. One from Charlie was basically all smiley faces. Others in the county team gave the score from their match along with their congratulations and good wishes to be passed on to Nick, who was now ready to go out and open the England innings. Then there was one from Little Paul. Tom opened it and got a blizzard of statistics and records – first this, best figures that, and always Youngest Player to have . . . He gave a bleak smile, but did not reply.

He put his phone away and went onto the balcony to watch the opening of the innings. Brad Dawson sprinted in with an assassin's purpose, and Tom looked on anxiously as Nick ducked and weaved out of the way before the ball pounded into the wicket keeper's gloves. Goosey from the other end was no less hostile. Tom had to smile at his head movements as he jagged up to the crease, but the deliveries he dished up were no laughing matter.

He had watched the first two overs – both maidens – when

someone came onto the balcony and handed him a note. He got up and slipped away, taking the stairs down to ground level.

'Tom!'

'What are you doing here, Dr Gupta?' Tom said in amazement, shaking the doctor's hand warmly.

'Oh, I had a few days off, so I thought, why not go to Leeds to watch my famous patient in action? Also,' he said, leading Tom round the back of the pavilion, 'I have a brother. Also Dr Gupta – working at Leeds Infirmary. Plus,' and here he ushered Tom into one of the stands, 'next generation of Dr Guptas!'

The second Dr Gupta stood up in welcome, and next to him five eager faces smiled up shyly.

'Tom will give you his autograph – at a very reasonable group rate I am sure!'

Tom blushed, but happily squatted down as the autograph books were passed down the row to him.

Other young spectators noticed, and soon there was an orderly queue. Eventually a steward came and put an end to it.

'Health and safety,' Dr Gupta said with a rueful smile. 'We don't want you to cause a stampede, do we?'

As he was making his way back to the pavilion, Tom heard a terrible groan from the crowd. Something had happened, and it wasn't good. He ran to find a gap between stands and saw Nick, his helmet already off, walking back to the pavilion. He stood and watched the replay on the big screen. Even in slow motion, Brad Dawson's delivery looked awesome.

He climbed the stairs back to the changing room with a heavy heart. Nick was normally the sunniest of people, but everyone gave him a wide berth for ten minutes or so after he was out.

176

'Stupid, stupid, stupid! Didn't move my feet,' Nick said, more to himself than to Tom.

'It looked pretty quick,' Tom said.

'Quick? Of course it was quick. He's the fastest bowler in the world. Quick is what he does. And it's my job not to get out. Sorry. Didn't mean to snap your head off, Tom. It's just that if we could have kept the opening partnership unbroken through to stumps . . .'

He smiled. 'But you've had a great day, haven't you? We're all really proud of you. Really proud.'

They lost one more wicket and closed on 63 for 2, with Phil Eldridge on 20.

Tom was exhausted and didn't join the team for supper. Instead the Marlins had food brought up to the family suite in the hotel.

'Well done, Tom,' his dad said, raising his beer. 'You proved them all wrong. We knew you would, didn't we, Suzie?'

'Yes,' she replied; but Tom looked up and could see from her face that she was not really thinking about his five wickets.

'What's up, Mum? We did all right. Nick says we're still in the game. We just need a good start in the morning.'

'They're awfully fast, those Australian bowlers.'

'Of course they're fast, Mum. They're the best in the world. We just have to play well.'

'*We?* I'm not letting you go in against them. They'd kill you.'

'I won't be needed. We just have to avoid the follow-on and then chip away at their lead as much as possible, bowl them out cheaply and knock the runs off!'

'Avoid the follow-on?'

'If we don't get within 200 runs of their total, they can enforce the follow-on, which means they make us bat again – like

Nick did with Leicestershire. But we will, I know we will.'

'I'm not having you going out there batting.'

'Whatever, Mum. Look, it's time for the highlights. Where's the remote, Dad?'

They relocated to the sofa and sank back to watch Tom's triumph. Later in the programme there was footage of Tom in the stand with the Guptas. He hadn't realised he'd been caught on camera.

'Wait a minute, isn't that –?'

'Dr Gupta, yes, Dad.'

'What's he doing up here?'

Tom told him. Then he yawned and went to his room for an early night.

*

While Tom was getting ready for bed, one of the journalists in the hotel bar felt his mobile vibrate. Seeing who it was from, he slipped off his bar stool and found a more private place.

'Yes, boss?'

'Have you seen the highlights?'

'What's up?' His editor didn't ring him to make polite conversation.

'I don't know why we put you onto this assignment, I really don't. First you nearly kill the boy. Then you take forever tracking down where they're hiding him. Then you lose him altogether. And now the autograph story's backfired on us.'

'He just denied it. People don't have to believe him.'

'But people want to believe him. He's a national hero. And he's only just appeared on prime time signing autographs for a queue of kids the Pied Piper of Hamlin would have given his right arm for. Either Mike Field's a genius, or the kid's coated with Teflon. I'm going to take you off this and let you get back to what you're good at, following celebs through the sewers.'

'Hold on, boss. There's still mileage in this. I know there is.

I've got a plan. Next Test. At the Oval. Trust me. I absolutely guarantee we can nail him.'

'"We can nail him",' the voice sighed down the phone. 'What is it, this plan of yours?'

'I can't tell you over the phone. But as soon as I get back to London I'll –'

But the line had gone dead. He shrugged, pocketed his phone and headed back to his pint of lager on the bar.

# CHAPTER 14

ENGLAND lost a wicket early the following morning, but then Phil Eldridge and Hector Maitland made a stand.

'Not pretty, but gritty,' the Chairman of the Selectors said to no one in particular as he sat with the players anxiously watching the battle of nerves out in the middle.

The England captain unleashed an aggressive cover drive to register the first four of the day. The crowd gave him a big cheer.

'And to think,' said the Chairman, 'there were serious calls for us to drop him.'

'But then,' he added, looking at Tom with a smile, 'Phil himself expressed doubts about a certain member of the team. Oh good shot! Good shot!'

Hector Maitland also found the boundary.

The pair remained together for the rest of the morning. They came back to the dressing room with sweat running down their foreheads, fierce concentration still etched on their faces. Eldridge had the expression you might expect to see on the face of a heroic climber as he battled against the elements, determined he would plant his flag on the summit.

The struggle continued in the afternoon. England were well past the 100 mark now and kept pushing on to reduce the Australian lead. Eldridge had passed his 50 before lunch, and was obviously intent on converting it into a century. When Hector Maitland jabbed a ball down through the vacant third slip area to bring up his fifty, Eldridge congratulated him with a pat on the back – but also, Tom noticed, with a few intense words.

Whatever he said, it didn't work. Spiers brought back his fast bowlers, and Goosey startled Maitland with his bounce. Second slip took the catch comfortably.

It had been a long stand, worth over 100. But the job was still not done. There were still 79 runs needed to avoid the follow-on. Keith Jaspers, the wicket-keeper, was on his way to the crease but, Tom couldn't help thinking, apart from Ahmed Mohammed, who was in after him, and who had already scored two fifties in the series, there wasn't a lot of batting to come.

Tom's mind went back to the previous evening's supper. What if he were needed? What would his mum do? She couldn't stop him going out there, could she? How embarrassing would that be. On the other hand – he saw Keith Jasper duck under a bouncer from Brad Dawson.

Andy Sneed came and sat next to him. He had his pads on and was holding a glass of water.

'If you an' me end up batting together, I'll take Dawson, don't you worry. You can take Goosey.'

He laughed. It was not an entirely encouraging laugh. Tom saw from the the water in the glass that the seamer's hand was actually shaking.

'Don't worry. I was only jokin'. Faced 'em both Down Under. And the wickets are quick there, I can tell you. Played 'em with a stick of rhubarb.' He took a sip of his water, but stopped with a splutter when Keith Jasper took a blow from Dawson.

'That'll have stung,' Sneed said in a statement of the obvious. Jasper had flung his bat down and was hopping about on one leg while the Australian fielders stood around, looking at him.

Tom felt queasy. Perhaps his mum would forbid him to bat.

Perhaps being embarrassed was not the worst thing that could happen after all.

But perhaps it wouldn't come to that. After his initial battering, Jasper started playing with more confidence. He even started tucking the ball off his legs for singles to rotate the strike and give his captain the chance to take a breather from the non-striker's end.

When he was facing, Eldridge looked completely comfortable. He always seemed to have time, however furiously Goosey or Brad Dawson bounced him. Whatever its line or length, he never took his eye off it. Even when you were sure it was going to hit him on the helmet, he would withdraw his head at the very last moment.

And when he was certain that a particular delivery posed no threat, he would play an attacking shot through the cordon of fielders and bring a roar from the crowd. As long as he was there, they had a chance.

The total crept up to the 200 mark. Eldridge himself was nearing his century. Tom was just about to allow himself to relax when Jasper, who had been batting so well, made a mistake. Goosey bowled what looked like a half volley, but it was a well-disguised slower ball. Jasper middled it. But he hit it just too early. It went like a bullet straight into mid-off's hands.

England were 191 for 6. Their immediate target was within their grasp, but the Australians' tails were up. Four quick wickets and the match – and the Ashes – would surely be theirs. And one of those four wickets was Tom's.

The question of whether Tom should bat had been discussed at some length.

'It would be totally irresponsible,' Eldridge had said. 'It wouldn't be fair on the boy. We're basically batting ten men.'

But at lunch Nick had a word. If the ninth wicket fell and only a handful of runs were needed to save the follow-on, surely it would be worth sending Tom in? 'After all,' Nick pointed out, 'you can declare at any time – the minute he gets on strike, even. And it's not as though he hasn't faced the quick stuff. He can't play it, but he isn't scared witless by it. He knows to watch the ball and to get out of the way to avoid being hit.'

'Well, you're his County captain. If I'm still out there, you decide. But pray God it doesn't come to that.'

As Ahmed Mohammed made his way out to the middle, Nick came and sat next to Tom.

'What do you think?' he said.

'I think I'd better go and put some pads on,' Tom said.

'Good man,' said Nick. 'Good man.'


Tom's parents were also focused on the same issue.

'We can't let him go out there, Rick. Look at the wicket-keeper. He's a professional. And you saw what happened to him.'

'Suzie, keep your voice down. Please don't make a scene. We've got halfway through a whole day without anyone paying any attention to Tom or us at all. There might even be a few sports pages tomorrow that don't have a picture of Tom. How good would *that* be?'

'Whereas if he's killed by an Australian fast bowler, he'll be on the front page of every single newspaper in the world. How good would that be?'

'The Australians aren't going to do anything stupid.'

'Like take out the biggest threat to them winning the series?'

'Nick said –'

'Nick is a very nice man. But there's something about him that seems to have escaped you. He, like everyone else involved in this crazy game, is mad – obsessed with winning the Ashes. He'd send his own granny out to face Brad Dawson.'

'She'd probably be up for it,' Tom's dad said under his breath.

Just then there was a great cry around the ground. They looked up to see a crestfallen Ahmed Mohammed making his way back towards the pavilion.

'You may have to deal with Mum, Nick,' Tom said.

Nick looked at him, and then at Hector Maitland, who had joined them.

'She could try to stop me batting.'

Andy Sneed's off stump suddenly shot up out of the ground like a jump jet taking off. Brad Dawson disappeared under a mob of delirious Australians.

'Maybe your mum's right. He's working up a head of steam.'

'Nick, he's the fastest bowler in the world. You said so yourself. But this is the Ashes. I didn't even know what they were a month ago – but now . . . We're so close. It's got to be worth trying. But you've got to head Mum off.'

Nick looked at him to make sure he meant it. Then he said: 'OK. There's a service lift at the end of the corridor. It'll take you down to the kitchens. You can climb the stairs up from there. You're in good company – it's the way American Presidents get in and out.'

'Before someone assassinates them,' Hector Maitland muttered under his breath.

'Tom,' said Nick. 'Good luck. You're a star.'

Dave Luton passed Tom's mum on the stairs as he made his way to the wicket. Nick was waiting for her at the top. Taking her by the elbow, he guided her into an empty office facing out over the car park and shut the door.

First he allowed Tom's mum to let rip, looking at her sympathetically and nodding his head to show he was listening.

Then he replied, 'Tom's simply going to go out there and give Phil the chance to save the follow-on. He's completely committed to helping the side in any way he can – and after his brilliant bowling, he just doesn't want us to come so close and then . . .'

He left the sentence hanging. 'Phil's in total control. He can declare at any time he likes. Tom may not have to face a ball.'

'But he doesn't like Tom.'

'I know things got off to a bad start, but that's all cleared up now. Phil thinks the world of Tom – he really does. He wouldn't do anything to compromise his safety. I promise you. His own son's only three years younger.'

'Can I see him?'

'To be honest, I'm not sure that would be the most helpful thing just at the moment.'


Tom would have said Amen to that. He was walking nervously up and down between the gleaming cookers listening to the radio commentary that the kitchen staff had on.

'*Oh, and Luton's got away with that one. Yes, I think that's going all the way. He didn't know too much about it, but four's four, and I'm sure the England captain will take them from any part of the bat. Just 12 runs to go for England to save this follow-on. And of course, the burning question is, will they bat Tom Marlin? We've heard conflicting reports – that Eldridge will declare at the fall of the next wicket whatever the score – or that, if there seems a chance of getting over the line Tom Marlin will come in, even if he doesn't face a ball. Alan, what's your take on this? Would you ask him to bat, if you were in Eldridge's shoes?*'

'*John, the first thing to say is that I'm very pleased I'm not in Eldridge's shoes. He may have got 120, but it isn't easy for him out there. But to answer your question, I don't see how you can ask a kid to go out and face the fastest bowler in the world, for whatever tactical advantage. I mean, where's that put Dawson? Is he expected to bowl underarm at him?'*

*'Oh, that was mighty close. How did that miss? I have to say Dawson is putting in a magnificent spell here. He's giving it his all to get this follow-on.'*

*'Of course, if they do enforce the follow-on, Spiers is going to have a couple of pretty tired opening bowlers.'*

*'I suppose the thinking is that they can give it a final spurt, then rest up overnight to be fresh in the morning. Oh, a magnificent stroke from Eldridge – he timed that to perfection. The man at cover didn't move, and it's just crossing the boundary now.'*

The kitchen staff had by now stopped even pretending to work. They stood round the radio riveted. No one said anything to Tom, but whenever he caught anyone's eye they smiled. Someone gave him a glass of water. He felt his hand shaking as he lifted it to his lips.

The minutes ticked by; the runs came agonisingly slowly.

*'England need five runs to save the follow-on. Everyone's on the edge of their seat – including Alan and myself up in the commentary box. What Tom Marlin must be feeling doesn't bear thinking about. We still don't know if he'll come out if a wicket falls. I suppose it could depend on who's out. Oh – it's all over for Luton, caught by Spiers at slip. Now we'll find out whether they're going to throw young Marlin to the lions. Eldridge is standing his ground. He's not going off with Luton. He's looking to the pavilion. I really think he doesn't know what's happening. There's no sign of Marlin on the players' balcony. Where are they hiding him?'*

'Art goin', lad?' asked one of the chefs.

Tom picked up his bat and his gloves. The entire kitchen staff burst into a great cheer and started beating pans with wooden spoons and ladles. Someone held the door open for him, and Tom marched out.

'Sorry, lad,' Dave Luton said as they met on the pavilion steps. The fast bowler tried to say something else, but at that moment the crowd spotted Tom and the noise became deafening. The cheering when he led the team in after his five-wicket haul had been impressive, but he now felt as though he were walking into a barrage of sound. As he looked around, he realised that the crowd were getting to their feet. They started to stamp. Underlying the clapping and shouting and cheering there was a deep boom of thousands of feet tramping in time as he made his way out to the crease.

Eldridge had taken his helmet off to greet him. Sweat was pouring down his face.

'Good man, Tom. You're a brave boy, and I really appreciate this.' He wiped his arm across his forehead. 'Any time you want out, just let me know. I can declare at any moment. I'd never forgive myself if anything happened to you.'

'I'm fine,' said Tom, though he didn't feel it.

'Unfortunately, there are still two balls of the over. If we can get a single, we'd better go for it. Anyway, leave that to me. If I call you, just run. Don't mind where the ball's gone. Just put your head down and get to the other end as quick as you can. Don't bother trying to get in line to Goosey. He's a bouncy bowler, so the chances are it'll go over the top of the stumps. If he cleans you up first ball, we're no worse off, are we? Good luck.'

Tom walked to the striker's end and held his bat up.

'Middle please,' he said.

The umpire waved his hand a little and Tom moved his bat accordingly. Then he made his mark on the crease and looked around him. Five Australian slips looked back at him. He swallowed hard.

'Does yer mum know you're out here?' enquired a deeply accented voice. This provoked a little ripple of laughter.

'She's coming in next,' someone else suggested – to more laughter.

Tom felt his ears going red, but showed no sign of having

heard. Instead he took up his stance and tapped the ground with his bat. Somewhere in the middle distance, Goosey raised his leg, like a horse about to charge.

Nick Appleton had been listening out for tell-tale sounds during his chat with Suzie Marlin. He hardly needed to explain the gigantic roar that greeted Tom's appearance on the pavilion steps.

'Is he going out there?'

She looked terrified.

'Let's go and see, shall we?' He held the door open for her, and she bolted through and started for the stairs down to the enclosure. Nick went with her.

There were murmurs of sympathy as she made her way through the crowd back to her seat. Rick looked up at her as she approached and said, 'Come on, he's just about to face.'

She slumped into her seat next to him, with Nick beside her. Her face was drawn and as Goosey began his high-stepping run, she could hardly bare to look.

Tom's first ball in Test cricket was an eventful one. Not that he saw it. Goosey leapt in the air, his left arm flung wide, his face contorted with effort and what looked like anger, and then his right arm appeared suddenly above his head with the ball cradled in his claw-like fingers.

The next thing Tom knew was that the ball had hit him unbelievably hard on his left pad. But he hadn't got time to worry about that. Eldridge was bellowing at him: 'Come one, come one!' Tom lost no time in haring up to the non-striker's end, where the umpire was calmly signalling a leg-bye.

It's doubtful whether a leg-bye was ever cheered so loudly in the history of the game. The crowd went wild, shouting, clapping, clanking beer tins together.

Eldridge walked up the wicket. 'Congratulations, young

man. Didn't know much about it, but you're still there. Well done. Now, I have to get myself back on strike.' He looked round. The fielders were on the move. Gone were the five slips. Everybody was now in a ring to save one.

'Well, we only need four. I might just . . .'

He walked back to his wicket. Tom stood next to the umpire and watched Goosey begin his run. Up he came and over went his arm. Eldridge stuck his left leg down the track and drove, hard. The blade flashed down quite straight and with tremendous power. But somehow the ball just slipped past.

The Australians went up as one man, but didn't appeal. The crowd groaned in frustration. Tom was on strike again. Facing Brad Dawson.

The two batsmen met in the middle of the wicket – the veteran of 80 test matches and the novice playing in his first.

'What are they saying? He's got to come in now, hasn't he?'

'Don't worry, Suzie,' Tom's dad said soothingly, putting a hand on her arm.

'They're so close,' Nick said. 'If only Phil had middled that one, we'd be home and dry.'

Out on the pitch, Eldridge was making the same point. 'Sorry, Tom. It was right there, in the slot. I must be getting tired. Anyway, we are where we are, which is with you on strike.'

Tom said, 'I've faced really quick stuff in the nets, and I'm not scared. Honest.'

Eldridge looked down at him. 'You are a remarkable lad,' he said, and raised his glove. Tom punched it gently with his. The crowd applauded him every step of the way back to the batting crease.

He took guard, and hunched down over his bat. There didn't seem any point in looking at the ring of close fielders.

'Come on, Brad. Fire it up, mate. It's nearly bedtime!'

189

Tom hardly heard the laughter. He was concentrating, concentrating as hard as he'd ever concentrated in his life. He tried to cut out the crowd, cut out the chatter of the Australian fielders, cut out thoughts about his mum, cut out thoughts about what would happen if he got hit. He tried not to be distracted by the magnificent sight of Brad Dawson beginning his run up. He wanted the ball, just a sight of the ball. As the arm swung over, the ball was the only thing, the only thing in the entire universe.

It was past him before he could react. It whizzed past the grille of his helmet. His feet remained leaden on the crease, and his bat hung heavy in his hands. But he had seen it. He had forced himself to find it and focus on it. He might be clean bowled next ball, but felt a tiny ember of confidence glowing deep inside. Focus on the ball. If short, duck; if wide, leave; if pitched up, try and get a bat on it. He might be the worst batsman in the history of Test cricket, but he had a strategy.

Eldridge looked worriedly down the wicket. Tom raised his hand very slightly to signify 'Fine, I'm fine.'

'Come on Bradley, story time, mate. Let's get the job done.'

Tom shut down everything again. It was as though his brain was a control panel alive with lights and screens and dials. And most of them were unnecessary distractions. Flip, flip, flip, he turned them all off – all except his little radar screen showing Brad Dawson sprinting up to the crease.

He picked the ball up early. It was short. Tom ducked. He heard it smack into the keeper's gloves. It was like the noise he imagined boxing gloves made when they hit. It was a frightening noise.

Brad Dawson stood a third of the way down the pitch with his hands on his hips, ignoring the crowd's raucous response to his bouncer. He looked at Tom, and then flicked his long, damp hair back, and turned to retrace the steps of his run-up, now clearly worn into the Headingley turf.

'Oh Rick, I can't watch this,' Tom's mum said.

'He's doing ever so well – isn't he, Nick?'

'Exceptional. Really impressive.'

'But he's just standing there. It could hit him any minute.'

'He's watching it. Watching it like a hawk. The first one, from Goosey, he didn't see at all. But now he's switched on. He has had some practice. Luton and the boys gave him a couple of net sessions.'

'I wish I'd never allowed him to play.'

Tom was back at the controls. In came Dawson and fired the ball down at him. It was past in a flash. He'd made a move, instinctive, hopelessly late. But he was still there.

Eldridge gave a little nod of approval. Tom's mum gave a little sigh of relief. His dad cracked his knuckles. Nick sat motionless.

Dawson came in again. This time the ball was a little shorter. It seemed to get awfully big awfully quickly, but Tom just managed to sway back a few inches, letting it fly harmlessly over the stumps.

There was a huge *Ooooh* from the crowd.

By now Tom's mum was taking a closer interest. 'Is he the fastest?' she asked Nick.

'Generally reckoned to be. Charlie Cruze could give him a run for his money on a good day. But of course it's not all about speed. Dawson's got control.'

'So he knows what he's doing, whizzing them past Tom's nose. I thought so.' She folded her arms and braced herself for the next delivery.

The fifth ball of the over did not whizz past Tom's nose; it whizzed past his boots. It was a leg-side yorker which he did well to leap out of the way of. In doing so, he lost his balance, and nearly fell. Many in the crowd assumed he'd been hit and there was another outcry. But Tom soon righted himself.

This time Eldridge called him for a conference.

'That was close, but well done, Tom. Really good. Now, there's only one ball left, so just keep watching it. If he's got any sense, he'll go for fast and straight. That's what I'd want my strike bowler to do. But don't, whatever you do, pre-determine your shot. You have to keep watching it. You're concentrating really well. One more ball.'

Again the glove punch and the walk back to the crease to face the next ball. What would Dawson bowl? Would it be short, would it be full? Don't think about that, don't pre-determine, he told himself, flipping off the switches again.

Dawson sprinted up to the wicket and bowled. Then he threw up his hands in frustration.

'Well left, sonny,' the wicket-keeper said as he marched past slapping the ball from one giant glove to the other. 'Coat of varnish, mate.'

Tom looked up at the big screen. By rights his off stump should have cartwheeled out of the ground. But somehow the ball had missed. He'd made it, a whole over against Brad Dawson. The crowd cheered and clapped and laughed. As Brad Dawson made his way down to the fine-leg boundary, they hooted. He gave a pantomime scowl and turned his back on them.

Eldridge came down the wicket with a spring in his step. He put an arm round Tom's shoulder. 'Well done. That was magnificent. Magnificent. Now the ball's in my court.'

As Goosey ran in, Tom was feeling rather strange. He felt elated and wobbly at the same time. Concentrate, concentrate, concentrate, he told himself.

The ball was almost identical to the last one Goosey had bowled, and this time Eldridge connected with it. There was a satisfying crack, and a deep sigh of satisfaction from the crowd – until they realised that there would be no runs. Spiers had pushed his fielders back, allowing an easy single. But of course

Eldridge didn't want an easy single that would put Tom back in the firing line.

He came down the wicket again. 'I hit that too well. There are a couple of areas where we might get two. It would be close, but you're pretty quick. You'll have to go like a hare as soon as I call – and don't forget to run your bat in as you turn.' He gave Tom a business-like nod and walked back to take strike.

Tom felt that the pressure was now on the Australians. Eldridge had five balls – surely that should be enough to get the four they needed?

Goosey unleashed a yorker which speared into Eldridge's toes. He got a bat on it, but with the bowler following through down the wicket there was no chance of a run.

Two down, four to go. Tom was like a sprinter waiting for the starting pistol. Crack! There was another fine drive, and, yes, there was the call from Eldridge. 'Run! Run! Two. We must get two!'

He shot off. The crowd crowed with delight, but the Australians were making a fair bit of noise themselves.

'Get it in, get it in – bowler's end.'

Tom turned after making his ground and was about to race back up the pitch when he saw that the fielder at long-on had actually got the ball in his hands. Goosey was standing over the stumps yelling like a madman. There wasn't a run. But either Eldridge hadn't seen the danger or imagined Tom could fly, for he was launching himself for the second.

'No!' Tom found himself shouting. 'I can't make it. Get back!'

Things suddenly froze into slow motion. It was like an accident in a dream. You could see what was happening, but you couldn't do anything to stop it. It took Eldridge a moment to realise that Tom was sending him back. He started to swing round to regain his ground. The ball was in the air now, and Goosey was bringing his great arms down to catch it and remove the bails.

Tom felt he'd given Eldridge enough time. But time wasn't the problem. As he turned, Eldridge simply seized up. As though shot, he went down with a cry of agony, clutching the back of his leg.

The ball actually hit the stumps – and Goosey, unaware of what was going on behind his back, yelled 'Owzat!'

The umpire raised his finger. The innings was over. England had failed to save the follow-on.

# CHAPTER 15

IT had been a terrible moment. Tom looked on helplessly as
Eldridge clutched his leg and collapsed. He glanced up at
the big screen which showed the ball coming in like a tracer
bullet. He was overwhelmed with guilt. Not only had they
failed, after all that effort; but far worse, he had caused his
captain such a bad injury that he would take no further part in
the game.

'Zipped him up a treat, kid,' one of the Australian fielders
said to him. Tom didn't know what to do, but forced himself
to walk up the wicket.

Eldridge was propped up on his shoulders. He had taken
his helmet off and his face was pale with pain and disappointment.

Tom knelt down beside him. 'Sorry,' he said. 'I just didn't
think –'

Eldridge closed his eyes, and shook his head slightly.

'Kiss me, Hardy,' one of the Australians said in a meant-to-
be-heard whisper. Don Spiers cut through the little ripple of
laughter.

'Here comes the stretcher. Give them some space.'

And, cheered to the echo, the England captain was trolleyed
off the field. He was taken straight to hospital, leaving Tom
to climb the pavilion steps on his own. Close behind came
the Australians, led by Brad Dawson on account of his five
wickets.

At the top of the steps, just inside the main room, was Tom's
mum. He assumed she was waiting for him, but he was wrong.

'Mr Dawson,' she said in the tone of voice she only used on rare occasions, but always with effect. The tall fast bowler stopped in his tracks, and wiped an arm across his sweaty forehead.

'I want a word with you.'

Oh no, thought Tom. He couldn't bear any more, not after sabotaging the team's attempt to avoid the follow-on, and condemning the England captain to crutches for the rest of the summer. He turned his back, just as he saw his mother waving her finger under Brad Dawson's nose.

'I know what you were doing out there,' she was saying to him.

'Look, I didn't kill him, lady,' he said, spreading his big hands wide.

'I know you didn't. As I say, I know exactly what you were doing, and I want to thank you.'

'Thank me?'

'Don't play the innocent with me. You were magnificent. You had everybody fooled. But in fact a child of eight would have been safe out there.'

'Well,' he shrugged with a slight grin, 'what could I do? He was brave enough to come out to face me. I had to put on a show.'

'I'm very grateful,' Tom's mum said, putting her hand on the big fast bowler's sleeve. 'Thank you.'

'Well, don't spread it around. I've got a reputation to keep up.'

'It'll be our little secret. You're a great bowler – and a great man.'

Unaware of this conversation, Tom was upstairs in the England dressing room keeping out of the way in a corner. Spiers had enforced the follow-on they had come so close to avoiding, and Nick Appleton and the top order were putting their pads on.

Then suddenly the openers were on the field and everyone else piled onto the balcony to watch. Tom miserably stripped off his pads and and put them away in his coffin. He threw the bat in on top of them, and his gloves, and slammed the lid down. It had his name in big letters on it, along with various sponsors' logos, but he gave it a kick before going to look at the cricket.

There was a space next to Hector Maitland.

'That was bad luck, Tom. But you shouldn't worry about it too much.'

'Is he going to be all right? I mean, he's obviously not going to be all right, is he?'

Hector Maitland puffed out his cheeks. 'He's been nursing that hamstring all season. Accident waiting to happen.'

'It wouldn't have happened if I hadn't said no.'

'There was never a run there, man,' Ahmed Mohammed said.

Brad Dawson steamed in and unleashed a bouncer at Nick.

'They must have given him extra rations of Vegemite for tea! Doesn't he know the meaning of "tired"?' Maitland said. And then to Tom he added: 'Just think, Tom, twenty minutes ago you were out there facing that. You should feel proud of yourself.'

What Tom actually felt was terror. All the fear he had managed to suppress when batting suddenly flooded through him. How could he have stood his ground against bowling that fast? He felt physically sick.

England staged a stubborn fight-back. An opening stand of 80 gave the innings a foundation. Nick Appleton had taken over the captaincy in Eldridge's absence, and seemed determined to take the fight to the Australians. Runs flowed more freely than they had in the first innings. It was also helped by the fact that the Australian bowlers had been at it all day, and even the mighty Brad Dawson started to fade towards the end. At stumps England had made a promising start: 131 for 2, with Nick undefeated on 74.

Although he had been actively involved only for about fifteen minutes, Tom was completely drained. As soon as he got back to the hotel, he went to bed. He didn't even stay up to watch the highlights.

Next morning was warm and sunny. Headingley was seething and there was a buzz of expectation around the ground.

Goosey deflated that with the third ball of his opening over.

'That nipped back,' said Hector Maitland as he got ready to bat. 'Wish me luck.'

'You don't need it, man,' said Ahmed, getting up to put his pads on. With Eldridge gone, everyone moved up the batting order. Tom hoped Hector and Nick could repeat their earlier heroics against the Australian bowlers. He still felt guilty about what had happened the day before. He didn't want to go down in history as the boy who lost England the Ashes.

He had glanced anxiously through the papers over breakfast. Most took a lenient view of the run-out, though in everyone's assessment the consequences of Eldridge's injury far outweighed the failure to avoid the follow-on.

One of the few papers that took a negative view – a picture of Tom with his hand up like a traffic policeman under the banner headline WHAT HAS HE DONE NOW? – also carried a blurred photo of Tom's mum talking animatedly to Brad Dawson. The headline was: WHIZZ KID'S MUM LAYS INTO AUSSIE QUICK.

Tom had pushed it away from him with a groan. His mum had pretended studied indifference, while his dad had rolled his eyes and then frowned at the message: 'Don't even *think* of going there.'

On the strict understanding that Tom would not be batting under any circumstances, his parents had decided to take the morning off. Des had dropped him at the ground and was then going to drive them into the countryside for a spin, ending up in a nice pub up on the moors. 'Get us out of the goldfish bowl for a bit,' his dad explained. Anything that got his mum away from Australian cricketers was good in Tom's book.

Now all he could do was gaze out at the cricket and hope. The thing about batsmen as good as Nick and Hector was that they hardly ever looked like getting out. They played defensively, body in line with the ball, or they left it, or they hit it for runs. But he knew all too well that against bowlers of Test quality even the best batsmen could be out at any moment. So even as the partnership developed and Nick confidently approached his century, Tom still found it nerve-wracking.

Don Spiers kept his quick men on, but half way through the morning session, Nick turned Dawson off his hip for a sharp two and then raised his bat as he acknowledged the cheers. Hector Maitland was also looking comfortable. When eventually the Australian captain brought on his left-arm spinner, Jazz Davis, the pressure seemed to ease. However, ten minutes before lunch, Davis got one to turn, clipping the edge of Hector's bat.

The second wicket in the session suddenly tipped the morning – and the match – in Australia's favour. England still needed to clear the deficit, and had lost 4 wickets. This was really 6 wickets, given that neither Eldridge nor Tom would bat.

'Good time for a ton, Ahmed,' Dave Luton said as the all-rounder stood up and reached for his bat.

'Is there a bad time for a ton?' he replied with a smile.

Ahmed and Nick saw it through to lunch, and Tom

enjoyed standing on the balcony clapping the century-maker in. A Test match was like a battle, he thought. It ebbed and flowed. You might win a skirmish here, but then take a crippling blow on your other wing. History was the only subject he really liked at school, and he was particularly interested in battles. Waterloo was his favourite. How close that had been. And thank God the Prussians had finally bothered to turn up.

He didn't eat much. In fact the only English players who did were the men who had already batted. Those who would have to face the Australian attack some time during the afternoon seemed to have lost their appetites, while Nick made no pretence of being interested in his food. He sipped a glass of water and toyed with a bread roll, but then went back upstairs to sit alone in the dressing room.

When play resumed Spiers brought back his fast men. Nick played them with dour determination, allowing himself no aggressive shots unless the ball was really there to be hit. Ahmed on the other hand played with a greater freedom. Twice he carved Goosey over extra cover's head for four, and once he drove Dawson for six. That brought the scores equal and the crowd to their feet. They knew in their hearts that England were clinging on by their fingernails, but the sight of the young all-rounder belting the fastest bowler in the world straight back over his head was a gesture of defiance they appreciated.

'Made 'em bat again,' said Dave Luton. 'That's something.'

'But it's not enough.'

The voice was familiar, and there in the doorway to the balcony was Philip Eldridge. He was propped up on crutches and his face looked drawn with pain, but he managed a watery smile as his team registered their surprise at seeing him.

'Didn't think they were going to let you out, skip.'

'It's only a hamstring, for goodness sake. My place is here, and the doctor – a friend of yours, I believe, Tom – Dr Gupta – was quite happy to let me come.'

There was a move to make room for him, but Eldridge shook his head. 'Don't want to distract anyone's attention from the job in hand,' he said. And then he added, 'Tom, can I have a word?'

Tom's heart sank. Now he was for it. 'Can I have a word?' was head teacher speak for 'Come into my study for the biggest telling-off of your life.'

Eldridge manoeuvred himself back into the dressing room, and Tom followed him.

'Shut the door, Tom.'

Tom did so. This was going to be really, really bad.

Eldridge leaned against the table in the middle of the room and motioned Tom to sit down. Tom opened his mouth. He had to say something, he had to apologise, try to explain.

But Eldridge raised his hand.

'You don't need to say anything, Tom. It wasn't your fault. There wasn't a second run, and you being run out would have done us no good at all. Sending me back was the right thing to do. You weren't to know I've been nursing this hamstring all summer. I was the fool to push it, and if I'd had any sense, I'd have allowed myself to be run out rather than risk' – he broke off – 'this.' He pointed to his leg.

'It's been a funny few weeks. The summit of my ambition was to captain a successful England side against the Australians. But the fact of the matter is, we're not good enough. We haven't got the bowling – or rather, we didn't have the bowling until you showed up. And I was too pig-headed to see it. I deserved to be laughed at – I'd set myself up like a fool and you brought me down to earth with a bang.'

'They weren't laughing at you,' Tom blurted out. 'They were laughing at me. It was something I said. It happens all the time. There was a club match which we won off a no-ball, and I didn't realise. I thought I was out and we hadn't won. They laughed about that for weeks.'

'Really?' Eldridge was taken aback. 'Well, it doesn't matter now. It clouded my judgement, and I have to take responsibility for that. The selectors were right and I was wrong. And I was even more wrong to treat you the way I did on the first day. That was inexcusable, and I would like to apologise unreservedly. Will you accept my apology?'

Tom looked at him and said, 'There's nothing to apologise for. I bowled rubbish.'

'That happens not to be true, though I was pathetically pleased to think so at the time. But you certainly didn't bowl rubbish on day two, and if only I'd used you properly on the first day, we'd be winning this test match instead of losing it. And then your batting.'

Tom looked at him, wondering what he was going to say.

'There are grown men – some of them top-order batsmen – who would not have faced Dawson with the courage you showed yesterday. It made me very proud to be batting with you. And the crowd loved it. Yorkshire folk really love their cricket and we gave them something to cheer about, even if ultimately we failed. It was wonderful. You've inspired me, Tom. I'm going to do something which everybody will regard as stupid beyond belief. And I'm going to ask you to help me. Because I think I can trust you to help me without trying to stop me.'

He looked at Tom. 'Am I right, Tom?'

I don't believe it, thought Tom. He's going to bloody bat.

*'Well, I'm afraid that's it. England lose their seventh wicket. Poor old Andy Sneed. Not had a great match – bowled Dawson for 2. There's just Dave Luton, now making his way to the wicket to join Nick Appleton, but with a lead of only 57 you'd have to say it's all over bar the shouting.'*

'*So there's going to be no repeat of Tom Marlin's heroics today?*'

'*No, Alan. We've been told officially that the young spinner will not be called upon. And with captain Phil Eldridge hors de combat, this is in effect England's last wicket.*'

'Hey up, he's back. But you've not got your pads on, lad.'

Tom smiled at the chef.

'I'm not batting today. But someone else is.'

He held the door open, and in hobbled Phil Eldridge, fully padded up, holding his bat and accompanied by Hector Maitland, also padded up, as his runner.

The kitchen staff were stunned. Then someone said, 'They oughta have the cameras down 'ere. This is where the action is!'

'What's up? Has someone closed the main stairs or what?' Eldridge said. 'Just let's say I'd rather go out there to do my bit without a blazing row with a lot of people trying to talk sense into me.'

'Good on yer. D'yer mind if I take a photo?'

'I don't mind at all,' said the England captain. And suddenly every member of the kitchen staff was rummaging for their mobile phones and cameras.

'*Oh dear, Alan. I don't think Luton is long for this world. He really didn't have much clue about that one. It's sad. Nick Appleton has fought so hard. 147 is a tremendous score, but he's just going to run out of partners, and England . . . Well, what can you say? If only – and the list is a long one. There it goes – Luton's middle stump flying out of the ground, leaving England with a meagre lead of 65 to defend. But hang on, Appleton is staying put. Is Tom Marlin coming in after all? We were definitely told he wasn't going to. What on earth's going on?*'

With the same rowdy send-off that Tom had enjoyed the day before, Phil Eldridge, supported by Hector Maitland, left the kitchen and made his way up the stairs. And right behind them came everybody from the kitchen.

'I'm not missing this. They can sack me, but I'm not missing this,' said one of the washers-up. She was speaking for all of them. The abandoned radio was left talking to itself:

'*I don't believe it. It can't be. It is. It's Philip Eldridge, who can barely walk, coming out to bat with Hector Maitland as his runner. It's like the last scene in El Cid. Who was the star in that? Charlton Heston, I think. Anyway, the crowd are going completely crazy. This is the maddest Test match I have covered in thirty-five years. This England side simply will not do the sensible thing and admit that they're beaten.*'

# CHAPTER 16

'HAS he any idea of the risk he's taking?' The Chairman
of the Selectors had come onto the players' balcony to
watch. 'He could be putting his entire career in jeopardy. How
can you bat when you can't move one of your legs? It's insane.
What's he think he's playing at?'

Goosey bowled a short-pitched ball on leg stump. Eldridge
let it hit him on the shoulder.

'They're not going to show any mercy,' the Chairman went
on. 'They're that close to winning' – he snapped his fingers –
'and they're not going to let sentiment stand in their way.'

As though underlining the point, Goosey stuck another one
in short. Eldridge again took it on his body. The crowd were
getting restive. 'Pitch it oop!' a voice cried out. Goosey ran
in and dropped another one short. It whizzed past Eldridge's
helmet. The crowd upped the volume. It was more like a boxing match than a cricket match – a boxing match with one
fighter on the ropes, simply taking the punishment.

But unlike a boxing match, there were two fighters on
the same side, and Nick Appleton was prepared to mete out
vengeance with a very heavy bat. He hit Dawson for 16 in one
over, flashing four after four. And then he faced Goosey, and
all hell broke loose.

Short – he pulled for six; pitched up outside the off stump
– one bounce into the advertising hoardings. When the ball
drifted marginally to leg it was whipped away through mid-
wicket. Baited by the crowd Goosey high-stepped up and
launched a bouncer. It went for miles. Small boys screeched

in ecstasy; grown men dressed up as Elvis hugged each other. On the players' balcony the Chairman stood up with his fists clenched.

Goosey ran in once more. Nick played the ball delicately to fine leg, and Hector Maitland ran an easy single. Eldridge hobbled in from his position next to the square-leg umpire. He had one ball to face. It was, predictably, short. He let it hit him. The crowd booed. Goosey snatched his cap from the umpire. England's lead was now past 100, and someone produced a trombone and started to launch great, fat, wobbly notes like balloons across the battleground of Headingley.

And so it went on, improbably, heroically, with Phil Eldridge using every ounce of courage and skill and experience at his disposal to foil the Australian bowlers; and at the other end, Nick Appleton unleashing a devastating counter-attack. The runs mounted, the crowd hit new heights of frenzy, and the Australians wilted. There was no two ways about it, the body language was unmistakable. They were rattled.

Nick Appleton was well past 150, and the question was, whether he would reach a sensational double century. Eldridge had made 2, but his contribution was not to be measured in runs but in minutes. The stand had long since gone past 50, and it seemed entirely possible that they would put on a 100.

But after an hour Spiers decided to bring back Jazz Davis. Nick got down to the striker's end and pummelled a couple of boundaries, but when Eldridge was exposed to the spinner, he was immediately in trouble. He stirred the crowd with a violent swat that sailed over mid-on. But unable to use his feet, it was only a matter of time before he popped up a catch to short leg. Supported by Hector Maitland, and cheered every slow step of the way, he hobbled back to the pavilion. Despite his urging, Nick waited with him, and the two were given a standing ovation that reverberated around the ground and must have been heard half way across Leeds.

'Well, that's given you something to bowl at,' Nick Appleton said to Tom as he sat exhausted in the changing room.

'Get one tonight, and they'll have their work cut out tomorrow,' added Eldridge, who had his leg stretched out at an awkward angle and was mopping his brow. '165 on that will be quite a challenge. Even Davis was turning it.'

The rest of the England team were waiting for the final effort of the day. Eldridge looked each of them in the eye and said: 'Nick has played one of the great Test innings today. And with Tom, we've got a really good chance of turning this match around. But it's not about individuals. It's about pulling together as a team, fighting as a team. I want you all to give Nick and the bowlers a hundred per cent. Make the Aussies feel they're up against it. And good luck.'

There was a knock on the door. Two anxious faces looked in.

'Ah, Dr Gupta,' said Eldridge. 'And –'

'Dr Gupta – my brother. We thought we'd better come and look you over. Two for the price of one.'

They made way for Nick to lead the team out, wishing everyone, especially Tom, good luck.

It was a tricky passage of play for the Australians. The bowlers were fresh, the ball was hard, the crowd almost delirious at the prospect of a historic upset. But if they felt the pressure, the two openers didn't show it. They marched to the wicket with their usual assertive strides and, not for the first time, Tom marvelled at their confidence, their natural assumption of superiority.

For all that, they played within themselves, taking no risks, making no grand gestures. There was no need: they had all of the fifth day to knock the runs off. They took a couple of fours off Andy Sneed, but otherwise were content to push the ball around and wait for stumps.

As he'd said he would, Nick called Tom up to bowl the last over of the day. He brought in his fielders, crowding the bat, and gave an encouraging clap from slip.

The taller of the two batsmen was on strike. He made it quite clear what his tactics were when he pushed his left pad a long way down the wicket and let the ball bounce off it. He did the same to the second. There was a stifled appeal, but no response from the umpire. Tom tossed the third ball up a little but, although the bat was raised high, it did not swing down. Again, the big front pad pushed forward.

Nick called for the ball and trotted down the wicket with it in his hand.

'Try him round his legs. I don't mind if you get hit. It's worth the risk. And if that doesn't work, I'd go for the top-spinner. Fast and straight.'

The leg-break was certainly effective. It leapt up out of the old foot-holes and beat everything: bat, pad, stumps and wicket-keeper. Four fielders hared after it to cut off the boundary. Ahmed proved the quickest and tipped it back just inside the rope. The Australians had taken three, but at least Tom now had two balls at the other batsman.

He didn't need them both. The top-spinner pitched in line, seemed to accelerate off the wicket and kept low. Every member of the team joined in the appeal, and as the umpire's finger went up, the crowd erupted. Game on!

To say the fifth day of the Headingley Test was an anticlimax would be absurd. It was one of the most tense and absorbing on record. But for the first time in the match, the main focus was cricket pure and simple. There was no repeat of the human drama that had dominated the first four days.

Each side had its task. Australia had to score 143 runs; England had to take the remaining 9 wickets before they did so. England started well, Ahmed having the surviving opener caught behind in the fourth over. But this brought Don Spiers to the crease and he played himself in carefully, taking no risks whatever.

'He's set himself to bat through,' Nick said to Tom at the start of a new over. 'Don't try anything too ambitious. Just be patient.'

Tom noticed as the morning went on that he was bowling more to Spiers than to his partner. The Australian captain had taken it upon himself to cope with what he saw as the main threat. Tom felt flattered, but also frustrated.

At last he had a chance when Spiers failed to take a single off the last ball of Andy Sneed's over. Nick saw it as an opportunity too and crowded the bat with close fielders. The ball turned and spat. It beat the inside of the bat, it beat the outside of the bat, it went straight through a hesitant defensive shot but missed the top of the middle stump by inches. And then the breakthrough came. A little snick onto the pad, and there was the ball flicked high in the air as the whole team whooped with pleasure mixed with relief.

53 for 3. 112 runs needed. The game was still there to be won by either side, but somehow the crowd sensed a tipping point. England, amazingly, had the upper hand. Another wicket fell in the morning session, leaving Australia on 82 for 4 at lunch with Spiers leading from the front on 45.

He reached his 50 straight after the interval, taking advantage of a couple of looseners from Dave Luton. But then Tom removed his partner, bowling him through the gate, and the pressure was right back on. Dave Luton got one to leave Jazz Davis, and Hector Maitland gratefully received the catch at second slip. This brought Goosey to the wicket.

'I'm going to leave you on, Tom,' Nick said. 'If he clocks you for a couple, good luck to him. But I think you'll get him.'

Tom didn't get him, but he made him look pretty stupid. The crowd, who had adopted Goosey as their pantomime villain, jeered as the tall man thrashed around without success. Despite his captain going down the wicket to talk to him, he allowed himself to be goaded by the crowd, and when he lashed out at Dave Luton, Ahmed took a great catch, leaping high to his left. It was a long and noisy walk back to the pavilion.

After that, Australian defiance dwindled to some over-cautious poking about by the rest of the tail-enders, while Spiers tried desperately both to keep the score moving and farm the bowling. It was a thankless task, and when Tom had a whole over at Brad Dawson, everyone on the ground was poised to begin the victory celebrations.

They had to wait a little longer than they expected. Dawson was not going down without a fight. He smeared the first ball high into the sky, and although there was a lot of top edge in the shot, it still just cleared the boundary. He connected far more sweetly with the next delivery. It sailed back over Tom's head and made a satisfyingly loud crash when it landed behind the sight screen. It brought Australia within 30 runs of victory. Nick pushed his fielders out, posting catchers to the long-on, long-off and deep mid-wicket boundaries.

'Just stay calm. He can't keep doing that.'

As Nick was talking to his bowler, Spiers was halfway down the wicket in conference with his number 11.

The effect of the two captains' words was immediate. Tom bowled a good-length googly which might have followed the previous ball over the ropes had Dawson continued to swing the bat. Instead he pushed forward defensively, fatally leaving a gap between his inside edge and his front pad. Tom could see the bails suddenly cartwheeling into the air.

The Australian captain let out an expletive, but then turned to Tom. Tom could see the disappointment in his eyes, but Spiers managed a crooked smile and stuck a sweaty hand out. Tom took it.

'Fair do's, kid. You beat us fair and square.'

The England team surrounded him, and then the players suddenly realised that the entire crowd were intent on joining in. Despite desperate pleas over the tannoy, thousands of spectators were racing across the grass. The players disappeared in the mass of humanity, only to reappear above it, hoisted on broad Yorkshire shoulders.

Tom found himself grabbed by two burly men in dresses and blond wigs, who set him astride their shoulders and pushed on through the melee towards the pavilion. Ahead of him he could see Nick, and Ahmed, Dave Luton, Hector Maitland and the others.

As they lurched through the crowd, Tom's legs were gripped, his hands sought, and his back slapped. 'Ee, lad,' said an older man looking up at him with tears in his eyes. 'Ah were 'ere in '81. That were a miracle. I never thought Ah'd see same thing twice. Let me shake tha hand.'

Finally they reached the pavilion gates and Tom was allowed to slip down to the ground. There was a blur of faces, but he picked out his parents, clapping like mad with the biggest smiles he'd ever seen on their faces. He saw his mum making a move towards him, but then his dad laid a restraining hand on her arm. At least the papers wouldn't have the big embarrassing kiss to slap over front page in the morning.

The next person he saw was Philip Eldridge waiting for him half way down the steps, supporting himself on his crutches.

'Splendid,' he said. 'I knew you'd do it. What a wonderful day. You've restored our pride, Tom. And Nick' – here he shook Nick's hand vigorously as his deputy joined them – 'Well done. Didn't put a foot wrong. Brilliant captaincy. And Ahmed, well bowled; Hector, brilliant catch . . .' As the England team climbed the steps, Eldridge greeted each one of them.

The crowd cheered their heroes and broke into a ragged rendition of Rule Britannia! And the kitchen staff, not wanting to be left out, waited just inside the doors displaying a huge cake with the scores hastily emblazoned across the icing and a tray of champagne.

It took a while for the crowd to be persuaded back behind a rope pushed out from the pavilion by the stewards so that the presentations could take place.

'Jeez, that was some match,' Don Spiers said when he was interviewed. 'Look, that was a great fight-back. I don't see what we could have done differently. If people are going to come out to bat with only one leg to save the game, all I can say is fair play to them.' He paused while the cheering died down. 'Nick Appleton's 184 has to be one of the best, if not the best, Test innings I've ever seen. And then out of nowhere you produce the Super Kid Spinner.' There was more cheering. Dave Luton gave Tom a friendly nudge in the back.

'You know,' the Australian captain continued, 'for a number of years we had the best bowler in the world. You all know who I mean. And, while it doesn't make you invincible, it sure as heck helps. And on the evidence of this match, you've got someone who's right up there.' There were more cheers.

'And good luck to him. He's proved himself not only immensely talented, but also dedicated and courageous. We respect that. Don't get me wrong: we hate losing. But we like a close-fought game, and we're going to pick ourselves up and go down to the Oval and give it our best shot. Thank you. Thank you all – you've been a great crowd.'

The cheering as Spiers climbed down from the podium was fantastic, but it went up several decibels as Phil Eldridge negotiated the steps up to receive the winners' cheque, and then hit a positive crescendo when Nick Appleton went up to receive his Man of the Match award. 'It must have been a tough decision,' he said, holding his cheque. 'It's not often someone's going to take 11 wickets in his debut Test and not get the Man of the Match. But whereas I'm probably never going to score 184 again, I'm quite sure Tom Marlin will take many more five-fors and six-fors, so I'm happy to accept it on this occasion!'

Even when the formalities were concluded, the crowd showed no sign of wanting to go home. 'We want Tom! We want Tom!' they chorused tirelessly after the players had retired to their dressing rooms to change. In the end the players had to go out onto the balcony and acknowledge the cheers. They waved and smiled, then one by one they slipped away, until Tom realised he was out there alone.

'Thank you!' he shouted above the hubbub. He hoped they could read his lips even if they couldn't hear him. Then he threw his arms wide as though to embrace all of Headingley and the wonderful crowd who had followed every ball of the match with such intensity, and then he disappeared through the balcony door.

There was an informal reception with more slices of cake and more champagne. Tom saw 'his' Dr Gupta again, and was able to say goodbye to the Leeds Dr Gupta. He noticed his mum talking to Brad Dawson. What was that about? He thought she'd declared war on him. But all the signs were they were getting on famously. She was laughing and trying at the same time not to spill her cake, which made him laugh in turn. Dawson caught sight of him and beckoned him over. He held out his huge right hand and gripped Tom's till he could almost feel the bones crack.

'I was just telling your mum, I knew I should have knocked your block off yesterday when I had the chance. Well played, fellah. That was awesome!'

'Thanks,' said Tom, massaging his hand. 'That was a pretty big six.'

'Yeah, then the skip comes down the wicket and tells me to

shut up shop.' He smiled, shaking his head. 'There's only one way I know how to play this game: attack on all fronts!'

Tom saw his dad signalling by the door. Time to go.

'Very nice meeting you, Mrs Marlin.'

'Suzie – please. It was a pleasure.' Then she put her finger to her lips and he winked back at her.

Grown-ups! thought Tom. It must be the champagne. He started easing his way through the throng, saying goodbyes and thank-yous as he went.

'See you at the Oval, young man,' said the Chairman of Selectors.

'Unless you've got a nice family holiday booked,' Don Spiers said with a tight grin. 'Well played.'

Des had brought the car right up to the back of the pavilion and eased it out through the gates and the waiting journalists. Mike Field had been onto some editors and had negotiated a truce, so that the Marlins could go home in the hope of being left alone for a short while before the final and deciding Test match.

# CHAPTER 17

THE days between the two back-to-back Tests were filled with renewed media frenzy. Praise was naturally lavished on the Heroes of Headingley, as they were quickly dubbed, and much excitement generated by the two dramatic entrances made from the kitchens, supported by many photos downloaded from the kitchen staff's mobile phones. But while the general mood was gung-ho, questions were asked about certain members of the team who didn't seem to be pulling their weight. Would the selectors stick with the winning team, Eldridge's replacement aside, or should they bring in fresh blood? Everyone seemed certain that Nick Appleton would take over the captaincy, but how much influence would he have over the team he led out at the Oval? One of the names cropping up was Charlie Cruze. FIGHT FIRE WITH FIRE, one headline suggested above a picture of Charlie looking particularly intimidating.

Tom enjoyed being back at home, sleeping in his own bed, surrounded by his own things, but life wasn't as it used to be. Even though the paparazzi were keeping to their side of the deal, he didn't feel free just to go out on his bike, in case there was someone with a camera waiting around the corner. And then there was the problem of Little Paul. He desperately wanted to see him, but he was still angry at what he had done. He caught up on the news with Sherwin, who had won promotion to the Kumble second team. He'd played against the demoted Devlin in the return of the match against Thurston.

'Man, he's still sore at you,' he said with a grin. 'Seems to think you're standing in his way everywhere he looks. I think he thinks you've got his place in the Test team!'

They both laughed. 'I got him out,' Sherwin added, tapping his chest. Then he moved his arm through the air in a sort of glide. 'Pitched leg, took off. You should have seen it.'

Tom suppressed a sigh. To be able to turn up at your club, play your game and go home with no fuss – what bliss!

'Come to the Oval. I'm sure I can get you a ticket. Bring your uncle.'

'Yeah?'

'I'd love to meet him.'


When the England side was announced there were two changes. Matt Green, who had been pushing for a place all season, came in for Eldridge, and Charlie Cruze came in for the out-of-sorts Dave Luton. Tom was very excited by this development, and texted the big fast bowler his congratulations. The reply came back instantly – all smiley faces and exclamation marks.

When the side came together for the match Charlie was the first person Tom looked out for. He wasn't hard to find, and immediately rushed up with a huge grin on his face. 'Can you believe this?' he said as he leaned over Tom. 'I think we were picked for our batting.' His peals of laughter made the rest of the team smile.

There was definitely a different atmosphere in the camp – lighter, freer, more bubbly. That was partly due to the wonderful win at Headingley, partly to Charlie's irrepressible good humour. But, Tom realised, it was also a lot to do with Nick as captain. He was younger than Eldridge, the same age as most of the players, and he was less detached, less head-teacherly. It was a united, happy and confident team that gathered on the first day of the Oval Test.

The upbeat mood was improved when Don Spiers called wrong at the toss and Nick chose to bat. Great, thought Tom, watching keenly from the players' balcony – at least a day, possibly more, with nothing much to do except watch the cricket.

Nick failed to reproduce his Headingley form, but Matt Green made a cultured century, and the rest of the batsmen enjoyed the fast pace of a classic end-of-season Oval pitch. The runs mounted, the crowd basked in the sun, and Tom managed to relax.

Well through the afternoon session on the second day Nick looked at Charlie and Tom and said, 'I think we'll spare the County's blushes.'

'Come on, Skip, a little bit of the long-handle from Charlie, no? Liven this crowd up – they gone to sleep, man.'

The atmosphere was certainly very different from Headingley.

'Charlie, you're going to liven them up – with the ball. I want you coming out of the traps for half an hour before tea. We've got to take 20 wickets, remember.'

'Tom'll take 15. He's just getting into his stride!' Charlie laughed.

Nick smiled. 'Anyway, I don't want you to pad up.'

'OK, boss.'

The eighth wicket fell at 478, and Nick waved to show he was declaring. In the time before tea Charlie Cruze put in three of the sharpest overs anyone had seen from an England bowler all year. He wasn't always accurate, and two wide balls were cracked past gully for four. Another shot deflected the ball at lightning speed towards the boundary to Tom's left. He sprinted after it, but couldn't cut it off.

But in between the boundaries Charlie made the Australians sit up and take notice. There were painful blows to the body, stinging raps on the gloves, and a dull clang when he hit a helmet. And then the breakthrough – a tentative shot outside off stump, and Keith Jasper was leaping in the air and then setting off on a great galloping loop of triumph. Despite the distance, Tom sprinted in from the boundary to add his congratulations. The big man put an arm round him and gave him a hug that crushed the breath from his body.

And then the new batsman was amongst them. Despite prefering to bat at four, Don Spiers had decided to promote himself. He now faced a torrid ten minutes before tea and Charlie, scenting the possibility of another even more glorious scalp, gave it everything.

But all his fire and passion were doused by Spiers' uncomplicated dead-bat forward defence. In between balls he looked away, unconcerned, chewing his gum. Charlie tried a bouncer, but it was too wild to be menacing. Spiers let it sail harmlessly by. There was something so assured about him that the whole England team drooped a little.

At tea Nick took Tom aside. 'Spiers is the key – we have to get him out, twice, to win the Ashes. He doesn't have to win this match. He can bat for the next three days. He doesn't care about making a game of it. He just needs a draw. Normally he'd be up for a duel with Charlie. But he's not interested. Which means you. Hope that shoulder's OK?'

'It's fine, Nick. Just give me the ball.'

The call came about forty minutes after the tea interval. The score was 73 for 1, and the batsman on strike was Don Spiers.

'We've got enough runs in the bank, so give it a bit of air and see if you can tempt him. I'll leave the fielders in the ring and if he wants to go over the top, fine,' Nick said.

But Spiers didn't want to go over the top. He wanted to go along the ground. He showed no hint of the furious aggression which he'd unleashed on Tom's first over at Headingley. Ball after ball he watched onto his bat or met with his pad.

Just once when served with a full toss, he opened his shoulders and cuffed it away for four. Occasionally Tom got one past him, but it was clear he was devoting his exceptional reactions and phenomenal batting skills to the core mission of staying put.

Tom fared better against his partner. The tall opener was more inclined to score runs, and certainly took the lure of the slower, tossed up, delivery. A couple of lofted cover drives had the fielders on their toes, and brought encouragement from Nick. But Spiers was always alert to the possibility of a single, and raced down the wicket at the slightest chance of a run, so Tom spent most of his time bowling at the Australian captain.

By close of play the visitors had reached the comparative comfort of 115 for 1. With three days of the match remaining, England still required 19 wickets, and it was hard to see how they were going to get them.

The situation hadn't improved – from an English point of view – by lunch on the third day. Ahmed had winkled out the opener, but Spiers had progressed quietly to within 10 of his century. As on the previous day, he faced Tom whenever possible. Over after watchful over passed, many of them maidens. And whenever the other batsman was on strike, Spiers was wound up like a spring to steal a single. He seemed to be a quarter of the way down the pitch by the time Tom had released the ball.

Then, when he did get a rare go at the number 4, Nick grassed a sharp chance, low to his left. He raised his hand in apology, obviously furious with himself. Tom tried something over-elaborate and paid the price of a well-struck drive to the boundary. It was the longest he'd gone without taking a wicket in his short career, and when he walked off at the end of the morning session there was no disguising his dejection.

Charlie came up to him and put a hand on his shoulder.

'That's why it's called *Test* cricket. You wouldn't want it easy, would you?'

'Guess not,' said Tom. But he wouldn't mind it a *bit* easier.

They clapped the two Australian batsmen in and then followed Nick up the steps.

'At least the grub's good,' said Charlie, and Tom realised he was hungry too – though he would gladly have traded lunch for Don Spiers' wicket.

It was after they had eaten and returned to the dressing room that Tom, as he usually did, checked his texts. Most were just good-luck messages, and he barely gave them a glance. But one was different. He read it very carefully, very carefully indeed.

'Come on, Tom, listen up.'

It was Nick, about to give his pep talk. Tom absentmindedly put his phone down on the locker next to him. He wasn't really listening to Nick. His mind was working overtime on something else.

The stalemate continued after lunch. Charlie and Ahmed made no impression on the impassive Australian pair. They were not interested in playing shots. They would bat for as long as it took to make the Ashes secure.

Down at fine leg Tom kicked at the boundary rope. After the epic match at Headingley, this was just boring, a betrayal of all the expectation that had built up over the last few days. The Australians didn't even care about winning the series. They just wanted to keep the Ashes, and all that meant was that they had to avoid losing. Pathetic. No wonder the crowd were entertaining themselves with Mexican waves.

To change things around a bit Nick brought Hector Maitland on, and then tried Andy Sneed. But it made no difference. The runs ticked up on the scoreboard, but the game seemed becalmed.

'Tom!'

He ran in, his heart racing. He had a plan. He was going to shake things up. His first over was against Spiers. It was just like the last over he'd bowled to him before lunch. Bat, pad, leave. Would nothing induce him to take a risk?

A couple of overs into his spell, he at last had the chance to bowl at the other batsman, who groped and missed. The crowd woke up a bit and gave some vocal support, and Nick clapped loudly from first slip. Spiers was as lively as ever, hungry for the quick single that would get him back on strike.

And that was how it happened.

On the fifth ball of the over Tom stopped dead instead of releasing the ball. Spiers was two paces down the track. With a simple sweep of his arm, Tom brushed off the bails and said: 'Howzat!'

It was another of those slow-motion, car-crash moments. Instead of simply putting up his finger, the umpire looked wonderingly at Tom as though he'd misheard. He's *miles* out of his ground, Tom thought. That's got to be out. And it was. With the reluctance of a soft-hearted judge passing the death sentence, the umpire raised his finger. Spiers stood where he was and stared daggers at Tom through the grille of his helmet.

'Why, of all the low-down dirty tricks . . .' he said. 'I thought your name was Marlin, not Mankad.' Then he turned on his heel and marched off towards the pavilion.

Tom heard him say something that sounded pretty offensive to Nick as he passed him. But that wasn't the most surprising thing. What was astonishing was that none of the England players seemed at all pleased at the dismissal of the Australian captain, and neither did the crowd. There were even a few boos. It took a moment before Tom realised they were booing *him*.

Charlie came up, but not bubbling with congratulations.

In fact Tom couldn't remember him ever looking so solemn.

'Now *that* you really shouldn't have done,' the big fast bowler said.

'He was miles out of his ground. He was doing it all the time.'

'I know, Tom. But you never, you just never do that. No. A guy called Mankad did that in a Test against the Aussies, and they've never forgotten it.'

He shook his big head sorrowfully.

'But if it's not allowed why did the umpire give him out?'

'Man, you really are green, aren't you? Ever heard the expression "It's not cricket?" – stuff that's not against the laws, but nobody does because it's against the *spirit* of the game. Come on, we got a new customer.'

'Better watch my step, hey?' the new batsman said unpleasantly as he took up his position.

Tom pretended he hadn't heard, but he had heard and it made him mad.

The last ball of the over was appreciably faster than the previous ones, and hit the top of the middle stump. Tom took his cap from the umpire and marched off to fine leg.

*'Well, John, you can say what you like about the run-out of Don Spiers, but that boy is a fearsome competitor. That was a googly from hell.'*

*'It certainly was. He's quite clearly angry – presumably about the response to the run-out. Perhaps a few words were said.'*

*'Well, they would have been. You just do not do that.'*

*'You know, it's quite possible Marlin simply didn't know that. He is very inexperienced.'*

Down on the boundary Tom was fighting back the tears. He was furious. Why was he playing this stupid, stupid game which had rules – or 'laws' – and then a whole set of things you weren't allowed to do but no one told you about? Spiers was out of his ground, trying to gain an advantage. Tom surely had the right to run him out. But no, apparently what he'd done was as bad as cheating at cards.

But everybody cheated all the time. Fielders appealed for catches that they knew weren't proper catches; batsmen stood their ground when they knew they'd nicked the ball to the keeper, hoping to fool the umpire. But run someone out while they're backing up halfway down the wicket and you turn into a leper.

It was the end of the over. Would Nick want him to go on? He walked in slowly, and Nick threw the ball to him.

'I want you to carry on. We can talk about the run-out later.'

Great, thought Tom. What if I want to talk about it now? Not that he did. But he was fed up with being treated like a kid, when he was the one, the *only* one, who had any chance of winning the match for them.

The first ball of his over hit the batsman hard in the stomach.

'Good wheels, Tom,' sang out Jasper from behind the stumps.

The next ball hit the batsman on the chest.

The third ball hit him on the helmet.

'*I don't believe this, John: he's roughing him up.*'

'*He's certainly working up some pace.*'

'*Jeepers, a 90-mile an hour googly. Thanks but no thanks.*'

'*Oh my goodness me, he's castled him. That was one of the most hostile overs I think I've ever seen.*'

'*He doesn't seem concerned about it, one way or the other. He's just taken his cap and walked off down to fine leg.*'

'*You know, Alan, what I think we're witnessing is a bit of a tantrum.*'

'*Yup, the toys are coming out of the pram, and it doesn't bode well for the Australians.*'

The crowd had really woken up now. As the Australian batsmen ducked and writhed under the assault the noise levels soared.

'That's your one for the over,' the umpire said after one short ball had screamed over the batsman's helmet, giving Jasper no chance of stopping it.

'My one what?' Tom asked, as the ball raced towards the boundary.

The umpire looked at him as though checking that he wasn't taking the mickey, and then said: 'Your one bouncer. You may be a spinner, but you're bowling faster than a lot of quicks.'

Tom turned with a shrug. Whatever. If they didn't want him to bowl the short stuff, he'd bowl the pitched-up stuff.

The next ball uprooted the off stump, and sent Nick at slip jumping out of the way.

Happy now?

'*You know, Alan, I have never seen anything like this. There's a kid out there, supposedly bowling spinners, intimidating grown men, and grown Australian men at that.*'

'*Has he ever done anything like this before?*'

'*Never. He turns it miles and no one, not even Don Spiers, can read him. But the 90-mile-an-hour stuff – that's completely new. Mind you, he's got a formidable throwing arm, so the power's there in that right shoulder, but – Oh, that's hurt him. Oh dear, oh dear, talking of not reading him. Ouch! You could feel that up here in the commentary box. Box perhaps being the operative word. He's down and I don't think he's going to get up again in a hurry.*'

'*And Marlin's just standing there, as though he's not interested. You know, he hasn't spoken to anyone in the last half an hour. It's as if he's in a zone of his own. That's some competitor you've unearthed there. Are you sure he hasn't got any Australian blood in his veins, John?*'

'*I don't wish to indulge in black humour, Alan, but if he keeps on*

*bowling like this he's going to have Australian blood on his hands.
Ah, there are some signs of recovery now. Siddons is on his feet, if
rather gingerly. Yes, I think we're ready now . . . Oh my goodness – middle stump! What a corker! You know the person I worry
about most is poor Jasper. He's been standing up to this stuff like
the trooper that he is, but it must have crossed his mind that his life
expectancy would be greatly improved if he stood back.'*

*'You worry about your wicket-keeper. The man I worry about is
the next fellah coming down those steps from the Australian dressing room. Because he's walking into a killing field out there. That
kid is lethal. There we all were resigned to another nice quiet afternoon of Test cricket, and he's blown that sky high. There's now
a smouldering black crater in the middle of the Oval. At this rate
Australia are looking at following on. It's unbelievable.'*

A black, sulphurous crater, that's certainly where Tom felt
he was. He had been angry before, he had felt he was the
victim of injustice before; but never had he had the means to
express that anger. He fired down an incredible spell which
one commentator would describe as 'a nightmare combination of S. F. Barnes and Jeff Thomson. Unplayable' – and yet
throughout out it all, he felt completely removed from his
normal self. It was as though he'd become a robot, a robot
with a very nasty personality.

He didn't mind making Goosey jump about a bit. He hit
him on the glove, and in an instant the tall fast bowler was
hopping about the crease, throwing his bat down and tearing
his glove off. The Australian physio, who had made several
trips to the middle already, sprinted on again, and Goosey
eventually stopped flapping his hand about enough for her
to administer the magic spray. Tom stayed at his end of the
wicket and looked into the sky. There was a plane, leaving
its vapour trail across the late-summer blue. It spoke to him
of freedom, of wide open spaces, of peace. Being confined
to this huge bear-pit where thousands were egging him on,

baying for blood, redoubled his anger, which by now was as much directed against himself as at anyone else.

His next ball hit Goosey on the toe. The stricken fast bowler went down like the proverbial sack of potatoes, just as the umpire's finger was raised to the South London skies. And Tom was OK with that; he was OK with Goosey hobbling off with his broken toe.

But when he cracked Brad Dawson on the elbow, he felt physically sick. He hadn't wanted to do that, but by now he was incapable of stopping himself. He had never experienced power like this. He heard people use the expression 'pumped up'. They didn't know what they were talking about. This was being pumped up. He felt he could bowl a ball through a plate-glass window. It was frightening and horrible, but also totally addictive. He hated it, even as he revelled in it. And he hated himself for revelling in it.

He knocked Dawson's leg stump out of the ground. If he'd walked down the pitch and kicked it, it wouldn't have gone further. The great Australian fast bowler stared down the wicket at him, a look of astonishment on his face. Tom couldn't look him in the eye. He wanted to disappear, evaporate, be anywhere but there, with the Oval crowd yelling and chanting deliriously.

Dawson and the not-out batsman walked towards the pavilion. Tom followed them. He knew the form by now. You take all the wickets, you walk in ahead of your team. So he did. The noise was deafening, but Tom didn't acknowledge the applause. He kept his head down, ran up the steps well ahead of his team mates, slipped down some other stairs, and dived into a Gents where he locked himself in a cubicle. He wanted to be sick, but all he could do was retch, over and over again. It was as though his body were being given electric shocks. A great fist thrust up through his chest and he would gag helplessly over the toilet bowl.

Tom had launched his last thunderbolt near enough to the interval for tea to be taken. The Australians had fallen far short of the follow-on target, and everyone assumed that Nick Appleton would invite them to bat again. But no announcement was made, and commentators and crowd were equally astonished when Don Spiers led his team out for the last session of the day, followed by the England captain and his fellow opener.

'*John, have we switched over to* Alice Through the Looking Glass? *Tell me I'm dreaming. What does Appleton think he's doing? His whizz kid gifts him a 240-run lead over the Aussies, and he opts to bat again. Explain that to me.*'

'*Alan, I can't. Like you, I'm all at sea, and there's a Cheshire Cat grinning from the mainmast. I guess all we can do is tell our listeners what is happening. Brad Dawson, who took a fearful crack on his elbow when he was batting, is going to open the bowling. Who will share the new ball with him remains to be seen.*'

'*And I think there may have been some collateral damage as well, John. Goosey's a proud man, and being blown out of the water by a kid is going to hurt a lot more than the smashed toe.*'

# CHAPTER 18

B Y the time that conversation was broadcast, Tom was out of the Oval, speeding away through the London traffic in a cab. Once he'd stopped retching, he put the lavatory seat down and sat on it. In all the excitement and frenzy of the last few weeks, one thing had been completely overlooked: it was the school holidays, and they were now coming to a close. He needed a break, and now was his chance. He'd put England back in the match. So now let them finish the job themselves. He was off. And with the money Mike Field put into his bank account every week, he could afford to go anywhere he pleased.

It wasn't until close of play that anyone noticed he was missing. He had made it so abundantly clear that he was not interested in team huddles and high-fives during his amazing spell after lunch that no one in the England dressing room thought to check where he was.

'Kid needs a bit of space,' was Charlie's take on it; and as Charlie was his County team-mate and buddy, the rest of the team were prepared to leave it at that. Nick Appleton was out in the middle, adding to England's substantial lead. He was planning to talk to Tom at the end of play, but in the mean-time had other things to think about.

It was in his press conference that he explained, the reason he hadn't enforced the follow-on was that he recognised that the Australians were unhappy at what he called 'an uninten-tional failure to observe the game's etiquette', and he didn't want it to seem that England were gaining any sort of un-

228

fair advantage. He then went on to praise 'one of the most extraordinary and devastating spells in the history of Test cricket', and to assure the press corps that, despite appearances, Tom Marlin was simply focused on the job in hand, and not behaving like a 'spoilt teenager'.

Mike Field was just going through the letter of apology he'd written for Tom with the Chairman of Selectors when the news reached them.

'Gone? Where?'

'No one knows.'

'We have absolutely got to keep this out of the papers,' the Chairman said.

Mike Field sighed his agreement.

Nick Appleton was called in and Operation Lock Down was hastily put together.

'Paul?'

'Yes, Dad.'

'Do you know where Tom is?'

'Some fancy hotel in London with the rest of the England team?'

'He hasn't been in touch?'

'No. I haven't heard a word. Do you want his autograph? I've still got some left.'

'Paul, this is serious. I've just had a call from Mike. Tom's gone.'

'Gone? Gone where?'

'I was hoping you might know.'

'Well, I don't. Sorry. He is old enough to go out on his own, Dad. I mean, all that money – he's probably gone shopping. I would.'

'You, I hope, would not run off without telling us what you were doing or where you were going. I know you've had a falling out – but Tom's still your friend. I thought you might have an idea where he might have gone.'

'Home?'

'They've looked in all the obvious places – obviously. But is there anywhere you can think of – anywhere he talked about wanting to go to? It's really important we find him before it gets out.'

'Why?'

'After what happened with Spiers –'

Little Paul groaned. 'I can't believe he did that. If we'd still been – if he'd run it past me, I'd have told him not to.'

'I know, son. It was all a horrible mistake. And it's bad enough that it's going to be all over the papers without them getting hold of the fact that he's done a runner as well. If the story comes out, it will cast doubt on Appleton's motives for not enforcing the follow-on – he'd just lost his main strike bowler. So we really do need to find him.'

'I'll go through his texts, Dad; see if there's any clues. But –' He shrugged.

'Good lad. Give me a shout if you come up with anything – anything at all.'

'Dad?'

'Yes, Paul. Have you got something?'

'Well, it's a really long shot. But –'

Little Paul showed his dad the photo on his mobile's screen.

'His texts sounded as though he really liked it there.'

'I'll go and talk to your mother.'

It seemed to Little Paul that his mother had done most of the talking, signing off with a heart-felt: 'You are completely mad, Charles.' But still, there they were, in the big Volvo, heading off into the night, with the sat-nav glowing above the dashboard.

Nick Appleton knew he wasn't going to be able to sleep. His mind was racing with the day's events. Should he have recalled Spiers? He might have, had the Australian captain not said what he said as he headed back to the pavilion. Should he have spoken to Tom then and there? But he could hardly have given him a dressing-down in front of a full house at the Oval. Once the red mist descended and Tom turned into the cricket equivalent of a killing machine, what could he have done? The exclusion zone Tom had thrown up was frightening in its intensity.

Frankly it had been a relief when Tom locked himself in the lavatory. The rest of the team had sat in the dressing room like witnesses to some terrifying act of God.

But now that Tom had simply vanished – into space, for all anyone knew – he felt dreadful. Angry and anxious at the same time. They'd done all the obvious things. He'd phoned the minute he got back to the dressing room and been told the news. It took just two rings for him to realise that Tom had left his phone. It had fallen down under the bench in Tom's mad scramble to throw some clothes on. All communication was broken. He could be anywhere.

'So where is he?'

'I don't know, boss. All I know is he's not where he's supposed to be. Surely that's enough.'

'It's a start. We can do SHAMED SPIN WHIZZ KID ON RUN. And we've got all your stuff about his bad sportsmanship, etc, at school. But it would be even better if we found him. You've checked the home and all that?'

'Sure – his parents came back a couple of hours ago. D'you get the pics?'

'Yep. No, they're good. AGONY OF RUNAWAY PRODIGY MUM. That's shaping up nicely. Seb's working on a little bit of mischief along the lines of RUNAWAY MUM OFF WITH AUSSIE QUICKIE, but we've got to clearance from upstairs on that one.'

'Can't wait.'

'Well, we haven't got all night. If we're going to find him, we got to do it pronto. Where does your source think he might be?'

'Hasn't got a clue. He has to be careful. His cover's going to be blown by the text. That's a dead cert. He wants more money.'

'Proper little Judas, isn't he? How much?'

'Three.'

'He can have five if he leads us to Marlin.'


'Are we nearly there yet? '

'No, Paul, we are not nearly there yet, and you are not six, so don't even think about starting on that one. Phone.'

'It's mine, Dad. Sherwin? Hi, man. No, it's fine. I'm – er – we're . . . I'm just doing something with my dad . . . Yes, yeah, we are. Just popped out in the car. Bit of late shopping. Some stuff for Mum. No, no, I don't. With the rest of the England team, I'd guess. Not returning calls? No idea. I haven't heard from him for a while. You know, the autographs thing. But if you talk to him tell him that I refunded the last of the money today. But what about his figures? You know that was the best spell at the Oval – OK, right. See you around. Bye.'

'Paul, whatever you do for a career, make sure it doesn't involve lying.'

'What? I didn't know Sherwin was going to ring.'

'No, but why am I somehow not surprised?'

'What do you mean, Dad?'

'Look, don't get me wrong. He's a nice kid, and he's obviously very fond of Tom. I accept all that. But – there have been leaks, breaches of security . . .'

'Sherwin wouldn't do a thing like that. I mean anyone could have found out where they were staying before Headingley. There are press people everywhere.'

'Yes, and some of them are pretty unscrupulous. They have budgets for this sort of thing. They pay people to betray their friends. How do you think Sherwin would react if someone waved a fistful of £20 notes under his nose?'

'He wouldn't do it. I mean look at the way he was the night we got chased. He was brilliant.'

'Yes, and look how that all ended up.'

'That wasn't his fault.'

'No, but it was someone's fault – someone who put a good picture above the safety of a boy's life.'

He drove on for a few more miles in silence, then he turned and said: 'Look, could you put a call through to Mike. On mine. Thanks. Ringing? OK, I've got it. Mike, hi, yes, we're – no, no we're not there yet. About another couple of hours. I don't know that we'll find him tonight, to be honest. Or even that he's going to be there. It's just a hunch. But listen, I've been thinking about things. They've got an in some-where. And someone almost certainly got to Tom today. You did say he'd left his phone, didn't you? Look, go through the messages –'

'Dad!'

'I know, Paul, but this is really important. Mike, yeah, sorry. Paul having his pennyworth. Just look through the texts that came in today. OK? As soon as I've got anything, I'll ring you.'

'I hope you never go through my texts.'

'You flip off the radar without a word about where you're going, and of course I'm going to read your texts. Especially if you walk out on England in the middle of a vital Test match.'

'Ha ha.'

He turned away and looked out of the window. There was nothing to see. The Welsh borders were very dark.

'Boss? It's me.'

'Location?'

'Haven't got it. But – there's something going on.'

'Yeah? Is that the sound of bears crashing through the undergrowth I hear? This is a newspaper. Give me some news, loosely defined as something I didn't know before you told me.'

'You know the little kid, Paul? The one that did the eBay stunt with the autographs?'

'Yes, I do know the little kid, Paul. It may surprise you to hear that I actually read the pages I edit. Go on.'

'He's going on a journey.'

'Oh no, please tell me you're not auditioning for Check Your Stars. We've already got someone who does that, and she wears bangles and has a dozen rings on her fingers.'

'Give me a chance. He's off with his dad in the car and they quite clearly are not going out for a bit of late shopping at Tesco.'

'FATHER AND SON DON'T GO LATE NIGHT SHOPPING AT TESCO. I'm not getting the angle on this one at the moment.'

'Well, they're obviously going somewhere else – very possibly to where Tom is.'

'Because?'

'Because they've been away for at least two hours. Plus, the kid was obviously trying to cover up what they were doing and where they were heading.'

'So where are they heading?'

'We don't know.'

There was a sigh down the phone.

'Boss, I'm sorry. There was no way I could have known, or I'd have tailed them. But even if we don't know where they are going, it means there's definitely something going down.'

'Yeah, no, I can see that. You're right. We can beef the story

234

up a bit. CONSPIRACY TO CONCEAL SHAMED PRODIGY. Stir things up a bit. Upstairs won't let us go with AUSSIE QUICKIE FOR RUNAWAY MUM, more's the pity. Lawyers. I'd drown 'em at birth, like kittens. OK. Keep your eyes to the ground and your ears peeled.'

'Anyway, Dad. Sherwin's a spender.' The voice came out of the dark. 'If he'd got loads of dosh, we'd know. New trainers, new tracksuit. He's known as Mr Bling at school.'

'You're a nice boy, Paul. You're very loyal, and I like that in you. But you've got a lot to learn about the world and the people you have to share it with.'

'Are we nearly there yet?'

# CHAPTER 19

Tom was on the brink of sleep. He snuggled down in his new super-lite duvet and and listened to the breeze blowing around the tent. It had been just as easy to put up as the man in the shop promised, and all in all he'd been very impressed with the kit he'd bought. The foam roll was surprisingly comfortable; ditto the little blow-up pillow.

He felt proud of himself. He'd only had a short time to make his plan, but he'd carried it out really effectively and, with his double change of wind-cheaters, was confident that he had foiled the CCTV cameras which seemed to watch over nearly every street in London. The cabbie had been surprisingly patient, dropping him off at the shop, waiting while he made his purchases, and then taking him to the station.

He'd had a bit of difficulty getting the name right, but the woman at the ticket counter was kind and, as she said, how could anyone be expected to pronounce all those double ls? He'd bought a cricket magazine in the bookshop, and had a scary moment when he opened a page and saw his own face smiling out at him. He put it away immediately, but after a while realised no one would recognise him because they wouldn't expect him to be there. He got the magazine out again and looked at the championship table. There were two matches to come, and with the returning Test trio they were well placed. If, that is, he wasn't dropped for disciplinary reasons. Too late to worry about that now.

It was a beautiful evening when he arrived. The air was still warm, and the sky was streaked with salmon-pink clouds. He got a taxi to the village he'd had in mind and enjoyed the fish and chips he'd been looking forward to for the last hour of the train journey.

Then he shouldered his camping gear, struck off up a little lane where he switched on his new torch.

He knew he was going to sleep far far better than he would have done in the team hotel with its boring bedrooms and the noise of the air conditioning droning all night. And in the morning . . . in the morning, he thought happily. . . red kites testing the thermals, and the distant sheep on the hillsides, hundreds and hundreds of sheep.

Little Paul's dad pulled over.

'What's happening? Aren't we going to look for him?'

'It's a mild night; he'll be fine. Look, if he's here – and it's a big if – he's here because he wants to be. He'll have thought it through. Even if he's asleep under a hedge, that'll be what he's chosen to do. He won't be expecting anyone to come and find him, and if we go crashing through the night yelling, he might very well hide and we'd never even see him. This is his adventure, Paul.'

'What about his parents? They wouldn't want him sleeping rough under a hedge.'

'No, but I'm sure they'd appreciate the reasoning. Anyway, they don't know, so they haven't got their hopes up. The morning will be soon enough.'

They woke at dawn. The car was all fuggy, and they were both stiff from sleeping in the car seats. But when they got out to stretch their legs, they were astonished.

'Look, that's the lake!'

'Reservoir more like – drinking water for Birmingham. Let's have a look at that photo again. Definitely the right place. But we need to be further round. Hop in.'

They drove along slowly, stopping frequently to get their bearings.

Suddenly Little Paul shouted, 'Look! A tent!'

'You're absolutely right. The question is, has it got Tom inside it? Go on. I'll stay here.'

'But he might be mad at me.'

'Son, you've driven halfway across England to do this. Think about it. Would he rather see you, or me? Which would you prefer if it was the other way round?'

'OK, Dad.'

'Off you go, and tell him we'll go back into town and have a full English breakfast before setting off.'

'If it's him, of course. Might not be.'

'My money says it will be. No car, for one thing. Anyway, the sooner you get over there, the sooner we'll know for sure.'

Little Paul set off across the rough grass, heavy with dew. His trainers were soaked through in no time, but he didn't bother about that. He was far more bothered about what he was going to say (a) to a total stranger, or even worse, to two total strangers; and (b) to Tom.

His dad watched from the car. Paul seemed particularly small in that huge landscape, small and somehow un-anchored. A gust of wind might catch him up and whirl him away over the hills. He yawned and rubbed the sleep out of his eyes. What was he thinking? Paul was just a kid stumbling about on a Welsh mountainside in unsuitable footwear. He slipped and lurched and nearly went down, but righted himself. Then he turned to the car to see whether he was being watched. His dad whizzed his window down and stuck out a hand. Paul raised his, and went on towards the tent.

When he got to it, he paused. It was zipped up. Once again, he turned to look back to the car. His dad leaned out of his window and nodded his head theatrically. Paul crouched down and very slowly unzipped the tent-flap.

238

Suddenly he disappeared, hoicked inside head-first. His dad assumed that was a good sign, but after a couple of minutes decided to drive a bit closer and investigate.

As he approached the tent there was a crash.

'Mind out, my lamp!'

'Ow! Get off my leg.'

'Get your elbow out of my eye.'

Paul's dad put his head inside the tent and found the boys engaged in a vigorous play-fight.

'Gently, guys,' he said. 'Hello, Tom. Be careful of your tent. It's nice.'

'It's wicked,' said Little Paul breathlessly. 'Where d'you get it?'

Flushed with the fight, Tom sat at the end of the tent, his face mottled a weird blue as the sun took the tint of the canvas. He told them the whole story. When he'd finished, he said, 'And how did you know I'd be here?'

'Just a hunch. Paul had that picture you sent him, and said you'd sounded really happy here.'

'I was,' said Tom. 'Is everybody mad at me?'

'There's a certain amount of anxiety in the camp, let's put it that way.'

'They'll kill me, won't they?'

'Who?'

'Everybody, my parents, Nick, the Chairman of the Selectors – not to mention the Australians.' He winced as the memory of the previous day stabbed back into the forefront of his mind.

'Was it bad? I mean, I know it was bad. But I didn't know.'

'I could have told you.'

'Well, we all know why that wasn't a possibility, don't we?'

'I'm sorry, Tom. I really am. I just thought – you know, for a bit of a laugh. And then people started bidding really high.'

Little Paul caught Tom's eye.

'Anyway, I tracked down the last one yesterday and repaid them, so that's done and dusted.'

Tom hit him quite hard in the chest. 'Muppet,' he said. And then sighed. 'Still, nothing compared to me. Why did I do it? I knew there was something wrong. But Sherwin –'

'Sherwin? What's he got to do with it?' Paul caught his dad's eye. His dad pursed his lips and raised an eyebrow just as he did when you landed on one of his properties with a hotel on it in Monopoly.

'He texted me. He suggested it. Well, he said his uncle suggested it. Said Spiers was taking advantage and I should do something about it. So I did.' He hugged his knees. 'Do I have to go back?'

'Tom, you know the answer to that. There's a Test match to be won. And the Ashes. Don't you want to be part of that?'

'Will they let me play?'

'Absolutely. You haven't missed anything.'

'What do you mean? Nick must have enforced the follow-on?'

'No, he didn't. But look, we can talk about all this at breakfast. I'm going to make a few calls. You are going to speak to your parents –' Tom's head sagged. 'OK, I'll ring them and break the news gently. But you're still going to have to speak to them. And then you get the tent down and packed and we'll be having the finest full English breakfast Wales can provide in less than half an hour.'

Talking to his parents wasn't as bad as he'd feared, and the breakfast was even better than he could have hoped. They sat at a corner table at the town's largest hotel surrounded by pictures of Tom in all the papers, and no one gave him a second glance.

Tom studied the scorecard.

Paul's dad said, 'So you see, Appleton will want to declare as

240

soon as he can and get the Aussies in. Which is why we need to get you back, pronto.'

'Here's your villain.' Mike Field came into the Ops Room where the Lock Down committee were feeling much better for hearing that Tom had been found.

'Sherwin Jones. Or rather, his uncle Winston.' Mike put Tom's mobile on the table. 'Shame. He's a nice kid. It was obviously a put-up job by that odious rag that's been on Tom's case. I guess the temptation was just too strong.'

The Chairman of Selectors looked at the text and sighed.

'He clearly had no idea,' said Nick. 'No idea at all. Which means that to him, the reaction was inexplicable. And horribly unfair. No wonder he lost it.'

'Thank the Lord he did, I'm tempted to say,' said the Chairman. 'He's handed us the Ashes on a plate. We just need him back to wrap it up. Any more news, Mike? Where are they now?'

'M4. Just passing Bristol.'

'Excellent. Get an ETA.'

'Wilco. And then we need to agree on our version of events.'

'And I think I'll give this so-called friend of Tom's a ring,' Nick said, reaching for the mobile. 'A call from the England captain – stand-in England captain – might shock the truth out of him.'

Both Mike and Nick raised phones to their ears.

'It's yours, Dad.'

'Well, answer it.'

'It's Mike Field. Do you want me to –'

'Give it here. Mike, hi. Yes, I'm driving but let's go for it. No, making fair progress. ETA . . . about, let me see. Oh-oh! Whoops. Ah, not good. Gotta go.'

The police motorcyclist strode back along the hard shoulder, stripping off one of his gauntlets. Paul's dad let his window down.

'Good morning, officer,' he said politely.

'Good morning, sir. Where shall we start – the speed, the lane-hopping, the lack of indicator lights – or the phone-call? Just who do you consider important enough to break the law to speak to while you're flying down the motorway at 89 miles an hour?'

'The Chairman of Selectors.'

'Oh, it's like that, is it? And I expect the captain of England was standing next to him waiting to talk to you as well?'

'Very probably.'

'We are feeling droll this morning, aren't we, sir? And what was the subject of this little natter with cricketing high-ups – the possible whereabouts of young Thomas Marlin?'

'No, there's no need to discuss that, officer. Tom Marlin's whereabouts are not a mystery.'

'I am relieved. Perhaps before I give you a ticket rather than the warning I might have let you off with, you might like to divulge the secret of the Runaway Spin Wizard, as my missus's paper calls him?'

'No secret at all, officer. He's in the back.'

Tom looked up and met the traffic cop's glance full on. He'd never seen a facial expression change so fast. The sneer of impatience was wiped off to be replaced by an open-mouthed wonder.

'It can't be – how on earth –?'

'It's a long story, officer, but as you'll be aware, there is a Test match to be won at the Oval, and it really would be good if we could get on.'

'Yes. Yes, of course. Can I just say' – here he leaned in through the window – 'that from what I saw on the highlights last night, you were speeding as well, son! I never saw anything like it. Brilliant!'

He withdrew his head and got something out of his tunic pocket. His face reappeared at the window.

'Just one little formality – if you could be so kind, Tom.'

Tom took the police notebook.

'To Frank, if you wouldn't mind,' said the policeman. And then, as Tom was rather self-consciously signing his autograph, he said to Paul's father, 'You wouldn't be wanting a police escort up to the Oval, would you, sir?'

'We were rather hoping to keep this under wraps actually. Hush, hush.'

The policeman winked knowingly and reached out for his notebook.

'Nice autograph,' he said with a smile.

'Autographs R Us,' said Little Paul, quickly followed by 'Ouch,' as Tom punched him.

Paul's dad said, 'Serve you right,' and pulled cautiously off the hard shoulder and onto the motorway.


'I've invited him to come in and see us,' Nick Appleton said.

'Who?'

'The Jones kid – and his uncle. They're both coming today anyway – Tom got them tickets.'

'What did he say?' asked Mike Field.

'He said he didn't send that text. And I believe him.'

'How come it came from his mobile then?'

'He said he couldn't explain that, but what he wanted me to believe was that he definitely didn't send it, and definitely didn't leak any of the other stuff that has come out over the last few weeks either. But he's pretty sure who it was. He was really upset. Practically crying. I've said he's to report to you, Mike. I think we'll get some useful stuff out of him.'

'OK,' said Mike. 'And now, just to remind ourselves of what

243

has been happening: Tom left London last night – with permission – to get away from the pressure-cooker atmosphere, etc, etc, and stayed with a close school friend, whose dad is kindly bringing him back today.'

'At – ?'

'Once Charles has shrugged off the traffic cop who pulled him over for taking my call, he should be here by start of play or shortly after.'

'Just time for you to get your well-deserved century, Nick,' said the Chairman.

'I hate delaying declarations just so someone can get a ton.'

'That's still a heck of a good track out there. Put the runs on the board. You can never have too many.'

'OK. But I want to know the minute he's back in the dressing room. And Mike, have we got his letter of apology to Don?'

'Yup. This is the draft we agreed yesterday. I'll get him to sign it the first thing he does. I'd also like to arrange a handshake to show there are no hard feelings. Any chance of Spiers playing ball?'

'I'll have a word as soon as he gets to the ground. He was still a bit frosty yesterday, but then having just seen his batting line-up mown down by Tom in tantrum mode, I'm not surprised.'

'What are you going to say to Tom?'

'I don't know. I've got to talk to him, I know that. But I'm not going to be too severe on him.'

'Quite right,' said the Chairman. 'Best thing that's happened to English cricket in generations. Absolutely brilliant. But we've got to learn to handle him a bit better. No reflection on you, Nick. I felt for you yesterday. I don't know you could have done anything different. I hope I never see him in that mood again, but I'll certainly never forget it!'

Twenty minutes before play was due to start, the Volvo drove up to the Oval's main entrance. Tom hopped out.

'Thank you. See you later,' he said, and hurried into the ground.

After a short interview with Mike and the Chairman of Selectors, he ran up the stairs to the dressing room, where Nick was waiting for him.

'Hello, Tom,' he said. 'Nice time?'

'Yes, thanks. Sorry.'

'Haven't time for that now. We need you to say sorry to Don. Has Mike given you the letter to sign?'

Tom nodded.

'OK, no time like the present.'

Nick led the way to the Australian dressing room. 'I've told Don about the text and tried to explain that you really didn't know.'

'I can't believe Sherwin would do a thing like that.'

'Well, maybe he didn't. But leave that for the moment.'

He knocked on the door and opened it.

The Australians were changed ready to go out onto the field.

'Morning, guys.'

There was a general mumble of greeting, but all eyes were on Tom.

'Jeepers, I thought he'd gone back to Planet X.'

'Can't trust the Limey press, mate. Shame though. We might have had a nice game of cricket.'

'Sorry, lads. Just had a sleepover with a chum. But back and fit for purpose. He's got something to say to you, Don.'

'Owzat, ump,' quipped one of the Australians. The others laughed.

'I'm sorry,' said Tom. 'It was wrong, and stupid and I apologise. I've got a letter –'

'I don't need a letter written by your PR team, thanks all the same. And I'm not standing on the balcony shaking hands for the cameras. But if you really mean it, I'll accept your apology and shake on it in here.'

Tom forced himself to meet the Australian's gaze. It was unwavering and seemed to bore into him, checking for any duplicity. When he was satisfied, Don Spiers put his hand out and Tom took it.

'Break his arm, Skip, now you've got the chance.' That was Brad Dawson, who showed Tom the bruise on his own arm. But then grinned and tousled his hair.

'Yeah,' said Spiers, 'if you could just not break any more of my team today, I'd appreciate it. We've got South Africa in a month's time.'

'How's –?'

'Goosey? He'll live, mate. Had it coming to him, some batsmen would say. The biter bit. He'll be along later – you can autograph his cast.'

The Australian captain's face split in a sharp grin. Then it was all over and they were back in the corridor.

'Well done, Tom. Now, put it behind you. We've got a job of work to do. This is the day we win the Ashes back.'

# CHAPTER 20

THE last day of the series went pretty much according to the script – right up until the very end. Nick Appleton batted for most of the morning, passing his century and building up England's lead. He declared leaving just enough time for his pace men to put the Australian openers off their lunch.

Tom was hungry for his – that breakfast in Wales seemed a long time ago. But he had a shock on his way down to the dining room. There, climbing the stairs with Mike Field, was Sherwin – and a tall, lithe man he assumed was Uncle Winston.

'Tom,' Sherwin said. 'I'm sorry, man, really sorry – but it wasn't me. I swear to God. I didn't send that text. Ask Nick Appleton. He believes me. Oh, and this is my Uncle Winston.'

Tom shook hands.

Mike Field said to Tom: 'I'll talk to Sherwin. You need to go and eat. You've got a busy afternoon ahead of you.'

'Go well, Tom. Knock 'em dead.' Sherwin grinned at him. And Tom gave him a smile back.

Charlie Cruze tore in after lunch. The crowd loved it as much as the Australian batsmen hated it. Tom said 'Well bowled' to him as they crossed between overs. 'Man,' he replied, 'I gotta do something special, or they going to give the new ball to *you*!'

They both laughed. Tom could see the big fast bowler was happy, enjoying this last fling in his first Test match. He felt happy himself, happy to have escaped the sulphurous crater.

The whole atmosphere was different. It was a full house but the crowd, he sensed, were not on the edge of their seats as they had been at Headingley. They had come to witness a great event, not take part in a white-knuckle ride.

Charlie finally got his reward with a late swinging yorker that demolished the stumps. As Tom joined the celebrations, Nick caught him by the arm.

'This over.'

Tom looked at him. There was a steely look in his eye as he called out: 'Thanks, Ahmed. Take a break. Great spell.'

'So, here we are again,' said the Australian captain taking his position at the non-striker's end where Nick was posting a field for Tom. 'Better keep behind the line.'

Tom grinned sheepishly and span the ball in his fingers. It felt good, hard, but with enough of the shine knocked off for him to get a really good grip. He ran in and bowled, and the ball was pushed out to midwicket. Spiers made an exaggerated play at pretending there might be a single, and then darted back. The crowd enjoyed the little pantomime. Tom was tempted to join in by pretending to take the bails off again, but decided that it was better left alone. A couple of balls later a leg-bye saw the batsmen cross.

Spiers took guard and relaxed into his easy stance. His bat tapped the crease. He chewed his gum and waited. Tom started with his stock leg-spinner. Spiers dropped his bat on it. Keith Jasper shouted encouragement, and Nick clapped at slip.

The next ball was the googly and it bowled the Australian captain all ends up.

'Perfect!' Nick said as he ran up. 'Just the perfect delivery.'

Charlie Cruze hit Tom so hard on the back his eyes watered. The decibel count around the ground went off the scale. At least half the crowd had shot out of their seats, and they remained standing as they clapped and yelled. The Ashes were coming home.

Spiers walked back to the pavilion with his head down. As he reached the picket gate, he turned to the crowd and clapped his bat with his glove, and then he was gone.

There was a lot of noise in the Australian dressing room for the next five minutes, but when the Australian captain finally emerged onto the visitors' balcony, he sat down and stretched his legs out.

'From now on,' he said, 'it's Don – *do* call me Bradman.'

'How d'you figure that out, skip?'

'Don't you guys know your history? On his last Test appearance – at the Oval in 1948 – the Don scored a duck, bowled, second ball – by a googly.'

'Yeah, I knew that. But you're not retiring, are you?'

'Not while that kid's out there bowling that sort of stuff. That's the ultimate challenge.' He gave a short, mirthless laugh. 'I was ready for it. I knew it was coming. But I couldn't get to it. It just wasn't there. Oh no, there goes another one. Come on fellers, let's at least try to see it out to tea.'

But the rout had started. With Charlie at one end and Tom at the other there was no comfort zone, no safe haven. Tom had done the psychological damage the day before, and now, although he wasn't bowling at that furious, venomous pace, he had them where he wanted them. The crowd cheered every dismissal, building up to the moment when the last Australian wicket would fall and the victory secured.

*'I don't know what you think, Alan, but this must surely be the greatest come-back of all time. England were out of it halfway through the Headingley test, absolutely out of the running. And now, within the next hour or two I'd say, they'll be claiming the Ashes back. And of course, we know who to thank for that.'*

*'You're right, John. It has been a remarkable turnaround. And that boy, Marlin – well, he's something else entirely.'*

*'Seems in a better temper today, doesn't he?'*

*'Yes, but he's still rolling our guys over. Look at that!'*

A sharp catch in the gully brought Brad Dawson to the crease. He swished his bat around, clearly not intent on trying to block out the remaining overs for a draw.

He swatted his first ball from Tom merrily back over his head for four. The crowd cheered, suddenly aware that at the fall of the next wicket the series would be over. Another ball was carted to the midwicket boundary. Nick stood impassively at slip, savouring the moment. To be the England captain – albeit only the stand-in – who won the Ashes. It didn't get any better.

'Come on, Tom. Keep it there.'

And Tom did keep it there – a beautifully directed leg-break just outside leg stump. Dawson took a dip at it but didn't connect properly. It was a thick edge that sent the ball back over Tom's head, but at such a trajectory that he judged he wouldn't have far to go to catch it. Yes! It was his catch. He turned and ran, craning his head up as he went.

The noise was unbelievable. Every mouth in each packed stand opened in a roar of sheer excitement. All eyes were fixed on the ball.

*'This could be it, Alan, the catch that clinches the Ashes. Marlin's going for it. What a fitting way to end this extraordinary – oh no, trouble. Charlie Cruze is steaming in from mid-on – oh, and Maitland's going for it too. They're all looking up at the ball. No one is calling for it. Marlin's leaping up for it now. But –'*

But so was Hector Maitland, and so was Charlie Cruze. Tom was completely unaware of his two team-mates until he was already committed to his leap. He felt the ball in his hand, but almost in the same moment he felt a terrible pain rip through his shoulder as Charlie crashed into him like an American footballer. Maitland came in at the same time and Tom was crunched between the two of them.

The pain in his shoulder was unbelievable. He fell to the ground writhing in agony, while the rest of the players, including the two Australian batsmen, ran towards him. Above the delirious noise of the crowd there was another noise, a kind of keening. He realised that he was making it. And then he blacked out.

Deep into the night, and seemingly after long and tortuous progress through endless dimly lit corridors, through flapping plastic doors and more and more endless corridors, Tom swam towards consciousness. He was speeding up, there was a breeze in his face. Although it was twilight he could make out something of his surroundings. Suddenly there was a spurt of gravel, he was flashing through strangely familiar gates. A car engine burst into life, headlights dazzled him, and he knew that a collision was impossible to avoid. His mouth opened to scream, as the bonnet shot out into his path and suddenly he was airborne. In the second of impact he looked straight ahead. A figure the other side of the windscreen put up a mask of fingers, but not quite fast enough.

'Devlin!' he yelled.

He found himself sitting bolt upright in a hospital bed, sweating and shaking. It had come back. The lost part of the jigsaw. It was Devlin in the car with the journalist. It all made sense. And it must have been Devlin who milked Sherwin for information, distracted him to get the use of his mobile and sent the lethal text. Tom fell back onto the pillows exhausted.

The door of his room burst open and a nurse came in, with his mum hard on her heels.

'Tom! Are you all right? Did you have a nightmare? Have some water. Take these, they'll help you get back to sleep.'

'Mum?'

'Yes, love?'

'Did I catch it?'

'Of course you caught it. Look, here it is. Nick insisted it went with you in the ambulance.'

She placed it carefully in his left hand.

'Go back to sleep now. Those pills will work very quickly.'

This time there were no long corridors and no car accident. Just a lift shaft, and he plunged down it into a deep, soft, cushiony blackness.

When Tom woke late next morning, it took him a moment to work out where he was, but at his first attempt to move he groaned. The memory came stabbing back. Not all that again. He couldn't bear it.

His mum was at his bedside almost immediately, helping him with his breakfast, opening the dozens of cards that had already started flooding in.

'Look, Tom – 10 Downing Street. It's from the Prime Minister!'

She put it in pride of place next to the ball.

'Dad'll be along soon of course, and everybody wants to see you. But they're not letting you have visitors yet. Except two rather special ones. That could be them now.'

The door swung open, and there stood Mr McCulloch and Dr Gupta.

'We'd come up to see the cricket,' Mr McCulloch explained.

'And of course, when fate struck, we were most concerned, most concerned indeed,' Dr Gupta added.

'Is it bad? Is it as bad as last time?' Tom asked.

'That we do not know. There will be X-rays and examinations, and then,' said Dr Gupta, 'we will hand you over to Mr McCulloch who will attempt to reconstruct your shoulder a second time.'

'But let's not worry about that now,' Mr McCulloch said. Smiling broadly, he went on: 'We must first congratulate you on winning the Ashes – almost single-handedly. The whole nation owes you a huge debt of gratitude.'

'There will be an open-bus celebration for the whole team winding up at Trafalgar Square,' said Dr Gupta. 'Obviously, everybody wants you to be there.'

'But he's far too weak for that now,' put in his mum.

'He is, Mrs Marlin. Of course he is,' said Mr McCulloch in his most reassuring tone. 'But it wouldn't be right to do it without him, so it has been provisionally scheduled for next Thursday. Don't worry, Mrs Marlin. We will consult with our colleagues here in London. No risks will be taken with Tom's health or long-term recovery, I assure you. And furthermore, we have decided that Dr Gupta will go with him –'

'Just in case there is a problem,' Dr Gupta finished the sentence. 'Not that there will be.'

'What do you think, Tom? Can you wave left-handed?' Mr McCulloch beamed down at him.

'I think so,' Tom said. 'And you really think you can mend my shoulder again?'

'Winning the Ashes is one thing – and a great thing. Defending them, especially Down Under, is quite another. We wouldn't stand a chance without you. I regard it as my duty to restore your shoulder fully.'

'Thank you,' said Tom, 'both of you.' He suddenly felt amazingly tired. He gripped the match ball tightly. His lips formed a smile and then his eyes slowly closed.

# TOM'S TEAM

You would not be holding this book in your hand without the generous help and support I have received from a great many people.

My thanks go firstly to Felix Dennis for the inestimable gift of a week's writing on Mustique. It gave me a flying start and I came home knowing the job could be done. Fellow guests, Arti Shah and Amit Gupta, took a real interest in Tom's progress over the dinner table, which spurred me on. Amit generously volunteered his family name for one of my favourite characters. I hope he doesn't disappoint. My companion on that holiday was Susan Hitch, who happily chomped through Agatha Christies while I pecked away at my laptop. Back in England, she was the book's first reader, and her enthusiastic endorsement, especially considering her relative lack of interest in cricket, was priceless. Other early readers were Henry Volans, Ian Smith, Becky Arnold, Michael Kynaston and his father, David Kynaston, Simon Fielder, Alex Martin, Tony Cox. Feedback from all of them was greatly valued.

Encouragement takes many different forms, and my thanks also go to Siân Hughes for lending me Stephen King's inspirational *On Writing* (and to Stephen King for writing it). I owe an enormous debt to Olivia Stanton for all sorts of things, not least persuading her husband, Nigel Stanton, to design the cover image. I am very grateful to the rest of the production team, led by Charles Boyle, who set the text; Hilary O'Shea, who copy-edited it, Shona Andrew, who designed the cover, and the proofreader Eugenie Woodhouse.

Alan Wilson designed the *Unplayable* website: www.unplayable. co.uk. And Richard Lackmann placed the first order.

I can't thank Frank Davis, commercial director of *Chance to shine*, enough. Frank met Tom late, but threw the considerable weight of the Cricket Foundation behind the project, to telling effect. The former Ashes-winning England captain Mike Gatting very generously agreed to write a Foreword to speed the book on its way.

Finally, and most importantly, thanks to you, my readers. If there are enough of you, I hope to write more adventures for Tom. His future is in your hands.

SIMON RAE

# Chance to shine
## EDUCATING THROUGH CRICKET

*Chance to shine* is the single biggest grass-roots sports development programme ever undertaken in Britain. The campaign aims to establish regular coaching and competitive cricket opportunities for at least two million boys and girls by 2015. To achieve this, £25 million needs to be raised through private donors, which the Government has pledged to match-fund. The Cricket Foundation, an independent charity, launched *Chance to shine* in May 2005, when fewer than 10 per cent of state schools provided competitive cricket programmes. In 2009 *Chance to shine* will be operating in 3,000 state schools.

www.chancetoshine.org